THE FIRST EXECUTIONER

THE FIRST EXECUTIONER

JUSTICE BEGINS™ BOOK ONE

MICHAEL ANDERLE

Copyright © 2021 by Michael Anderle
Cover Art by Jake @ J Caleb Design
http://jcalebdesign.com / jcalebdesign@gmail.com
Cover copyright © LMBPN Publishing
A Michael Anderle Production

LMBPN Publishing
PMB 196, 2540 South Maryland Pkwy
Las Vegas, NV 89109

Version 1.00, November 2021
ebook ISBN: 978-1-68500-575-7
Print ISBN: 978-1-68500-576-4

THE FIRST EXECUTIONER TEAM

Thanks to the Beta Readers
Larry Omans, Kelly O'Donnell, Rachel Beckford, Allen Collins,
Kit Mitchell

Thanks to the JIT Readers

Deb Mader
Daryl McDaniel
Diane L. Smith
Dave Hicks
Dorothy Lloyd

If I've missed anyone, please let me know!

Editor
The Skyhunter Editing Team

DEDICATION

To Family, Friends and
Those Who Love
to Read.
May We All Enjoy Grace
to Live the Life We Are
Called.

— Michael

CHAPTER ONE

A former U.S. Army truck rolled down the ragged expanse of the dirt road leading into the small valley. Within the vehicle were seven men, plus the driver. Everyone was armed.

Mick, the leader of the group, held an AR-10 rifle. It was the newest, most high-tech, and most expensive weapon in the vehicle. The men's employers had made one available to each of them, but he alone had been able to afford it. Barely. Once the dirty work was done, though, and the rest of their promised fee paid out, he would more than recover his losses.

He patted the rifle's barrel shroud. "This baby," he said to the others over the sounds of sucking mud and gravel crunching beneath the wheels, "was invented only nine years ago. This particular gun is less than a year old. The *design* is nine, though. State-of-the-art. They're distributing some version with a smaller cartridge back in America, so the pantywaist soldiers won't have to carry anything heavy for too long."

A couple of the other men laughed. They'd all been staring at the rifle with a mixture of curiosity and envy. Mick's dig about others needing a lighter weapon had alleviated some of the tension. Of the other men, one had an American M1 carbine, two held old German MP40 submachine guns, which worked splendidly enough when they worked at all, and the remaining three had to settle for surplus SKS rifles of Soviet or Chinese manufacture. The driver had only a Smith & Wesson Model 10 revolver, the .38 Special.

On Atlantica—or, as some people had nicknamed it, Atlantis —the Cold War was far away and of little relevance. Elements of West and East mingled freely. Global politics was a distant second to survival.

"Hey," the driver called. He was the sole man without a rifle or submachine gun, carrying only the .38 Special by his side. "We're almost there. I recognize this arch from last time.

"About three hundred meters ahead, there's a narrow choke point in the road before it opens up into the valley. I'll park there to block off the road. None of them will be able to get out the way we came in. They'll have to run off into the hills."

Mick nodded. "Good. They *better* run."

The Mongolian—no one could pronounce his name right, so they referred to him by nationality—piped up. "They have guards?" He checked the pocket of his jacket for his extra stripper clip of ammo.

A reedy-looking man named Kozlowski snorted. "Doubt it. Unless you count kneecap boys working for whoever runs the fuckin' local brothel and poker circle."

A few more chuckles went around.

The driver parked the truck at the mouth of the valley, as indicated. The men hopped down from the benches to stream out the back of the vehicle. Before them lay the dingy expanse of mud, grit, and spare parts that was their target.

It was a shantytown, a collection of sheds built on the spot by the cluster of workers or worker-wannabes who floated around through Atlantica's underclass. Such people were useful, at times, to those who owned most of the island.

At other times—like now—they were simply an obstruction.

Many had retired to their pitiful homes as afternoon was waning toward evening, but a crowd of perhaps two dozen bedraggled men, women, and children was already outside. Another dozen emerged into the pitted alleys that served as their streets.

Mick stepped forward, waving, as the village chatter died down and all eyes turned to him and his men.

"Right," he began, puffing up his chest and drawing himself up to his full height of six-foot-three, "none of you people are authorized to be here. You're all a bunch of squatters. I hereby order you to disperse immediately. Find someplace else. This land is *claimed.*"

Faint sounds of alarm and whispers of concern went around among the motley assembly of laborers.

A woman, perhaps in her late twenties or so, put her hands on her hips. "No, we will *not* disperse. Who are you to kick us out of the homes we've built?" Her accent was maybe Swedish. It was hard to be sure. "No one claimed this land. Except us. If someone back in the city did, they sure did not tell us about it."

Mick smiled. "We're telling you *now*. Get out of here."

His hand went to his waist, where he kept an old Colt single-action Army revolver in a new leather holster. In one smooth motion, he unfastened the strap and drew the gun, aiming it at the woman one-handed with his right thumb cocking back the hammer. She froze in place. Her mouth stayed open, but her protests had suddenly fallen silent.

The guy next to him on the right, holding his gun one-handed over his shoulder, snorted. "Jesus Christ, Mick, why you still carry one of those dusty ancient things? I knew a guy in Italy who got killed trying to reload one while the Germans was regrouping."

Mick ignored him, focusing instead on the woman. "You got five seconds," he informed her. "One...two...three..."

Another woman, older but similar-looking, appeared from

behind a long makeshift fence of scrap wood and sheet metal. "Ingrid!" she cried and yammered something in whatever her native language was.

Ingrid turned and ran toward her mother. Mick was only at the count of four, but he fired anyway. The gun *cracked* and blasted dust from the ground near the younger woman's feet. She screamed and dove through the air behind the fence.

"Smart lady," Mick quipped. "Let's see if everyone else has the same amount of...intelligence."

Then someone appeared from behind a shack on the other side of the road—two young men. One of them was more like a boy, perhaps sixteen or so.

"Bastards!" one of them screamed. Both began hurling chunks of rock at the newcomers.

Kozlowski was closest to them. He was too slow in dodging. One of the rocks struck him in the arm, causing him to flinch. "Ow. Goddamn trash." He raised his SKS and fired.

The air thundered with the gunshot's report. The younger of the two boys fell backward, shrieking and spitting blood with a red hole in his chest. His brother fell to his knees beside him, sobbing. The small crowd gathered farther back in the shanty broke apart as screaming men and women scattered in all directions, seeking cover.

Mick glared at Kozlowski but didn't bother to reprimand him. They'd all known there would probably be resistance and that they'd ultimately need to disperse the squatters with a little of the more forceful kind of persuasion.

"All right," he announced to his men, "they're going back in their homes like idiots instead of getting the hell out like we told them. Everyone open fire." He returned his Colt to its holster and raised his AR-10.

Seven guns roared in unison, drowning out the lingering howls of the terrified workers. Semiautomatic rifle rounds punched holes through the thin layers of wood, scrap metal, and cloth that constituted the squatters' homes. The two submachine guns, firing in full auto, sprayed rounds indiscriminately where children had played, and men and women had washed clothes and prepared meals not long ago.

The brother of the boy who'd taken a rifle slug through the chest twisted and bled, falling dead beside the younger boy under the barrage of an MP40. A woman in a hut not far from the fence where the first woman had ducked stumbled out of her house, holding hands to her bloodied stomach.

Screams penetrated the gaps in the noise, and a handful of the workers toward the rear of the village fled their shanties and clambered up the far hill. Since they were doing as instructed, the clearance crew ignored them.

The two men with submachine guns paused to reload, while those with rifles took slower, more carefully aimed potshots at anyone visible or randomly through the houses' walls or windows.

Mick spent half his magazine perforating two of the larger houses. He anticipated that more people would try to flee soon, although fear would probably paralyze some and his men would have to drag them out of their shacks. He shouldered his rifle on its strap and pulled his revolver.

He waved toward the village. "Advance," he ordered the others.

They moved in.

Then a gunshot rang out. Before anyone could ask who'd been in such a hurry to start shooting again, Mick's head exploded. He went straight back in the air, legs kicking and his right hand dropping the pistol as blood showered the ground around him.

Kozlowski bellowed, "Jesus Christ! Nobody said they were *armed!*" He raised his SKS again and fired three rounds in the general direction from which the deadly counterattack had come.

The others opened fire, trying to locate the opposing gunman, but they couldn't see anything. The Mongolian grabbed Mick's body and dragged him back to the truck before taking up position on the passenger's side within the vehicle itself. The driver frowned as though concerned that things might've taken a turn for the worse.

Halfway across town, hidden behind a fence with his old M1 Garand protruding between the slats, Tyler Katakura fired again.

His second shot took Kozlowski in the sternum, blowing half of his heart out the back along with a good-sized chunk of his spine. The man spun in place, gurgling and twitching, and collapsed into the dirt.

The man with the carbine waved his weapon toward the crude wooden fence in the middle of the settlement. "There!" he shouted. He was a tall man from somewhere in the Congo region who spoke little English but had good fighting instincts. "He is *there!*"

As the men opened fire on the fence, Ty had already sprung up, run behind a nearby hut, and advanced toward them from a different angle. He took another shot.

One of the men with an MP40 squawked as a .30-06 round ripped through his hip, sending him sprawling to the ground in agony. The Mongolian ducked out of the truck to pull him back, ignoring his screams of pain but putting pressure on the wound before lifting him into the back of the vehicle.

Anticipating counterfire, Ty bellowed, "Everyone, stay down! On the ground!" The last thing he wanted was for any of the people under his protection to get shot because *he* happened to be too close to them.

Then he bolted out into the street, firing once, hastily, at the clearance team before diving behind the engine block of an old pickup that someone had been trying to repair. He missed his shot, but the bullet struck the ground near the Congolese man's legs, sending him jumping backward and drawing the group's fire away from the houses.

One of the attackers grunted, "He's got a Garand. Holds eight. He's shot four so far. Keep track of—"

Ty popped up and fired again, taking the man who'd spoken in the throat before he could finish his warning. He died almost instantly, crumpling amidst his coworkers in a pool of blood.

The Congolese man waved his carbine again. "Cover! The truck!"

There were now only three gunmen remaining in the fight. The Congolese and a Russian guy covered their partial retreat with a barrage of gunfire toward Ty's new location. It kept him pinned down for the moment. The Mongolian leaned out of the truck's passenger side and responded with well-aimed shots toward the likeliest positions to which Tyler might flee.

Ty looked around, his nostrils flaring as he pressed himself against the engine block. He hadn't had time to grab an extra clip for his rifle. After his ammo ran out, he would have only his sidearm. Still, he'd already taken out half of their force. His black hair, damp with sweat, cushioned his head against the dirty steel.

Then he saw the older woman.

She had been trapped behind a barely functional fence of wood and sheet metal when the shooting started, too slow and scared to get away to better cover. Her position was partially in the clearance team's line of fire. Although she had sensibly ducked, it didn't look like her joints were in good enough shape for her to get back up if she needed to.

The fence was disintegrating. The attackers were spending all of their ammo reserves as quickly as possible, having diverted their attention from terrorizing the townsfolk into simply trying to kill their unexpected enemy through overwhelming force. Sooner or later, their shots would strike the tiny, cowering woman.

Ty drew a deep breath. Then, with a snarl of defiance, he

jumped up and sprinted across the mud-and-gravel expanse that had become a warzone, ignoring the *zing* of bullets past his head and heels.

He jumped and rolled, coming to a stop right behind the fence. Before the men could redirect their fire at him, he swiveled toward them and took a quick shot.

The Congolese man took the bullet through the gut and went down with a ragged cry, still clutching the carbine. The other man with the submachine gun was out of ammo. His hands shook as he ejected his magazine and fumbled for another.

Ty had a moment, then, before the barrage started anew. He turned to the woman and gave her a quick, curt bow.

"Excuse me, *oba-san*," he greeted her. "Please, allow me."

The woman stared blankly at the younger Japanese man. He slung his rifle back over his shoulder, knelt, and scooped her up in his arms. Then, trying to use his body as protection, he dashed back out into the street, bobbing and weaving as he made his way toward the engine block. It was the only reliable source of cover nearby.

The second MP40 wielder finished reloading his gun and squeezed off a short burst, but it struck to Ty's left. Carrying the woman slowed him slightly, but not by much. The Mongolian took another potshot. This time, the bullet grazed Ty's cheek and *whizzed* past his ear.

He gritted his teeth. He'd been out in the open too long, but his foes' nerves were fraying. In a way, he had the advantage.

Reaching the engine block, he squatted and deposited the woman safely behind it as she gawked in astonishment. He bowed to her again and returned to the fight.

The blond Russian guy was having trouble hitting anything with his submachine gun, so Ty focused instead on the Mongolian, who was lining up a careful shot. As Ty aimed back at him, the Mongolian heaved himself into the vehicle and was about to duck when the Garand fired again.

The windshield spiderwebbed, and blood sprayed across it and the seat. The driver, sitting dumbly behind the wheel, cried out in alarm.

Ty had one round left. The shack nearest him was next to a crate and had a low roof, so he hopped onto the container and jumped atop the building, hoping it would hold his weight. He was lean and wiry, but they hadn't built the shanties to last.

It held. There was only one man still able to fight. Seeing Ty get the drop on him, the Russian turned and ran. At first, he ran in a straight line, and Ty was about to shoot him through the spine and chest, but then he abruptly weaved to the left while half-ducking.

Cursing in his mind, Ty watched as the bullet took the man in the shoulder, causing him to scream and rendering his right arm useless, but probably not killing him. He hopped and hobbled toward the back of the truck, stumbling into the rear compartment and out of sight.

Tyler jumped down from the roof and ran straight toward the vehicle. Adrenaline and the confidence of experience had burned away his lingering fear.

The driver had taken a few shots with his revolver earlier but then dropped it at some point during the fray. At the same time the Russian got hit, the driver had leapt out to search for his weapon. Frazzled by the violence, chaos, and the suddenness with which the fight had turned against them, he couldn't remember when he'd lost hold of it.

Now, only one thing mattered to him. Seeing Ty bolt toward him, he grabbed the truck's frame near the driver's side front door and swung himself up to the seat, where Mick's dead body lay slumped. The Mongolian had deposited it there. He kicked it aside, and the man who'd briefly been their leader fell out and rolled on the ground.

The driver hopped in and stuffed the keys into the ignition. His free hand reached down for the gear shift and encountered the smooth surface of a leather jacket atop still bones and clammy flesh. He looked down. The Mongolian had collapsed across the console to die after the Japanese guy had shot him through the windshield.

"Shit," the driver gasped, shoving the dead man, then hoisting him up by the jacket. "Shit, shit, shit..."

Ty Katakura was charging across the now-empty expanse that separated the settlement from the choke point where the truck stalled. The driver couldn't remember seeing him reload. He must've been out of ammo. He was running toward the vehicle to get within arm's reach so he could finish the job.

The driver finally managed to throw the Mongolian aside so the dead man slumped awkwardly over the passenger's side of the front bench seat. Then his hand found the gear stick and clutched it, shifting into reverse.

Before he could back away, the Japanese guy tossed aside his empty rifle and took a running leap straight into the truck, crashing against the driver from the side and holding himself in place against the frame with one hand.

Ty's right hand, meanwhile, had fallen to his side and whipped back upward, now holding a Colt M1911 pistol. As the driver turned to face him, jaw hanging nearly to his chest, Ty shoved the gun's barrel into the man's mouth.

"Now, my friend," Ty said in a low, almost disturbingly soft voice while staring into the driver's eyes, "you're going to drive back to the people who hired you and show them what has happened. You will take all these bodies directly to them, which-ever rich bastards they might be, and explain exactly how they got the way they are.

"You'll explain that they do not have the right to drive these people from their homes. These are the same folks who have built this fucking island. *They* have no right to treat them like disposable garbage, just because they happen to be in the wrong place at the wrong time."

The driver tried to nod to the best of his ability. He barely moved his head for fear of jostling the pistol, whose slide and barrel were cold against his teeth. A bulbous droplet of sweat ran down his temple and cheek.

Ty added, "Tell them, the next time they try something like this, I won't send a driver back." He slowly retracted the Colt from the man's mouth but kept it aimed at his face. "Next time, I'll drive the truck back myself and deliver the message for the *last* time."

The driver swallowed. "Understood," he replied in a hoarse whisper. He looked away from Ty's dark, burning eyes. Then, as the settlement's guardian stepped off the truck and backed away, pistol still held ready, the man within the vehicle reversed, performed a three-point turn, and drove back the way he'd come.

He drove fast. Probably, Ty guessed, a lot faster than he'd come in.

CHAPTER TWO

Ty sat in a cheap wooden chair outside the shed that was his current home. It lay near the edge of the village, not far from the dirt road that the truck carrying the clearance team had rolled down before making its hasty retreat.

The community had been dead silent for a short while after the shooting stopped. Ty guessed perhaps ten minutes. Now things were beginning to rustle again with subdued activity. Eyes peeked out from behind makeshift curtains, and doors opened as the people tried to determine if it was safe.

Ty called, "They're gone. Everything's fine." He could've told them sooner but decided that he appreciated the few minutes of quiet.

After all, everything *wasn't* fine for the people of the community who'd died. At least three of them. Maybe more.

In his lap were all the .30-06 rifle cartridges he still had for his Garand. He'd finished counting them all for the third time to make sure he had the number right.

Fifteen. He had exactly fifteen rounds left. Enough to fill one *en bloc* clip to its maximum capacity of eight, and a second clip to mostly full. That was it.

"Yeah," he said in a low voice and loaded the cartridges into the clips. The full one he slipped into his pocket. The other one he took back into his shed, leaving it there beside the rifle itself.

While temporarily back indoors, he also grabbed his lone, battered box of .45 ACP ammunition along with his one spare pistol magazine. He took them out to the chair, sitting in the open air to try and relax—it also allowed him to keep an eye on the road. There was a slim chance that the clearance team had friends waiting around somewhere as backup.

Half a dozen residents had come out of their hovels in response to Ty's reassurances. Their movements were slow, careful, and tentative, but their eyes were wide, and they looked around with fast, darting head motions like birds.

Ty acknowledged their presence without reacting to it. He looked down at the items in his lap and drew his 1911 to check it.

The magazine in the pistol still held its full capacity of seven rounds plus the one in the chamber. He returned it to its holster. Within the old, weather-beaten ammo box, there were seventeen of the short, fat .45 rounds left. He loaded seven of them into his spare magazine. After that, he would still have enough for another reload and a half.

It wasn't much. It would do for now, but he would need more ammunition soon, or he might not survive his next gunfight. Later, he would check the ground closer to the road for anything the thugs in the truck might've dropped. It looked as though they'd managed to take most everything with them, even if the bulk of them would be in no condition to use their gear ever again.

A cluster of people approached him. Two were a thirtyish couple who, Ty was pretty sure, were the children of the older woman he'd rescued from the line of fire. Another five were random individuals from other parts of the settlement. Like most of the laborers, they were from all different parts of the world.

The male half of the thirty-something couple raised a callused hand. "Mr. Katakura," he shouted. "We can't thank you enough. You saved our Ma."

Ty didn't feel much up to socializing at the moment, but he made himself smile gently and nodded at them. "Yeah, you're welcome."

The other quintet approached him next, each coming up to clasp his hand in theirs or embrace him. Two of them were crying. The dark-skinned woman was from somewhere in the Caribbean and spoke a hodgepodge of English and some other language. The aging Polish man spoke no English and kept his mouth shut, and the Peruvian native couple thanked him profusely in Spanish.

More people came out, their joy and relief growing more apparent. Some wept while others laughed and cheered.

Some people were new to him, with origins he didn't recognize and whose languages were incomprehensible. Ty knew English, Japanese, and a little Spanish. That was all.

Here on Atlantica, representatives of nearly every nation on Earth had come in a teeming human mass. From the haughty to the lowly, all had arrived seeking wealth and opportunity, the opportunities afforded by a lawless but booming new society. Ty knew his history. The California Gold Rush, which had ended a hundred and ten years ago, had been similar.

Then, as now, a few people got filthy rich. Most weren't so lucky.

"A feast!" someone cheered. Ty found the owner of the voice, a portly man around his age. "We should get everyone together for a nice big dinner. Victory celebration! Mr. Katakura earned it, didn't he?"

Most of the crowd cheered. There were no objections. Still, Tyler knew the parents of the two boys gunned down in the street, and the family of the woman who'd been shot in her house didn't have nearly as much to celebrate.

Ty gave a short bow. "Thank you, but you don't have to do that."

"Nonsense!" countered the portly man. Ty couldn't remember his name. "We could use a big feast, anyway. We're all wasting away here. Well, aside from me."

Ty watched in silence as some of the laborers suggested who would do what to prepare their humble banquet. Their exuberance was strangely admirable.

Most of these people, he reflected, were good and useful workers. Many were skilled tradesmen or artisans, and all were willing to do what it took to survive. The super-rich of Atlantica needed them to continue building their new civilization.

Yet they'd been willing to sweep them aside like trash as soon as someone wanted to construct a new vacation home next to the desolate little valley. Ty's hand clenched into a fist, the knuckles turning white.

As the crowd began to disperse, Ty noticed an older woman who stayed behind. She was looking at him. Her name, if he recalled right, was Mrs. Bertollini. She lived in the far corner of the settlement. From what he knew of her, she was a kind woman and well-respected by the community.

Bizarrely, it took him a moment to realize that she was the same woman he'd saved from behind the disintegrating fence. Combat played strange tricks on the memory.

She came up to his side, speaking in a soft voice meant for his ears only, her Italian accent making her a bit hard to understand. Ty managed, though. He had a good ear for quirks of language.

"Tyler-a," she began. She tended to add a vowel to the end of almost every word whether it belonged there or not, although her English was otherwise excellent. "What is bothering you so much?"

He thought about lying to her. It would've been easier to simply say that he was tired and that otherwise, everything was fine.

Still, she was offering her confidence. Her counsel. He couldn't bring himself to deceive someone like her.

He sighed. "I've been protecting this little workers' town for months now. Around three, maybe four. The days and weeks have begun to blur together. I feel like...like it's the right thing to do. But it doesn't pay much. I had no money to my name to begin with, and I still have next to nothing. And..."

He hesitated, not wanting to start a pond-ripple of alarm or anxiety that might spread throughout the settlement. However, they deserved the truth. Mrs. Bertollini's brown eyes were full of empathy.

"Getting access to hardware—gear, weapons, ammunition, I mean—is becoming harder and harder. The rich folks, the ruler types, keep tightening their control over the market here. The price of everything keeps going up. I have enough ammo for one or two more serious gunfights. That's it. After that, all I'll have is, I don't know, a knife or a sharpened shovel like they used back in World War I or something."

He'd also used one during his service in Korea but chose not to mention that. The details were a little too gruesome for most people.

"Then," he concluded, "it will be all over. They'll keep sending more hired thugs. I might take another one or two of them down with me, but they'll always have what *they* need to kill or terrorize people, and they'll shoot me down like a dog. You'll all be left defenseless. There won't be anything more I can do."

Mrs. Bertollini took another two steps forward. She clasped his right hand between both of hers.

"Tyler-a," she began. "We came here from Development Sector Twelve. Do you remember? When the rich and powerful came to claim the land, there was no one there to protect us. They drove us out, as they tried to do again today. We got to this place and thought we might find peace. But it has not lasted, has it?"

She shook her head and muttered something in Italian.

They both sat in silence, a silence that seemed to encompass the two of them while the sounds of gaiety and activity resounded from the rest of the makeshift village. Tyler could think of nothing useful to say.

Mrs. Bertollini was the first to speak again. "Will you leave? Since you know it's hopeless. You are right, of course. It's understandable."

Tyler Katakura couldn't answer that immediately. It required reflection. The older woman was giving him *permission* to leave, in a way. He'd done all that he could, all that was possible. After today, no one would blame him for moving on.

But...

"No. I'm not running. I've been doing too much of that over the years. Atlantica was my last shot." He exhaled, and to his distaste, there was a hint of weakness in the sound of it. "But it looks like even that isn't going to turn out."

Mrs. Bertollini's gnarled hand reached for his face. With the knuckle of her index finger, she gingerly touched the red line running across his cheek, the bullet slash he'd earned in the process of saving her life.

"So, you will keep fighting anyway, Tyler-a? Until you cannot anymore?"

He thought back on the thirty-two years of his life and the lives of those who'd come before him. The generations stretched back through Japan's warlike history long before his family came to America, and even longer before he'd drifted out to the island where the world's newest civilization was going through its birthing pains.

He shrugged. "Fighting is all I know how to do at this point."

CHAPTER THREE

There were two boys and one girl who tended to follow Tyler around, or loiter in his general vicinity, whenever they could get away with it. They were maybe seventeen or eighteen, he guessed, which made them among the youngest people in the settlement, and the youngest on Atlantica altogether. No one was a native inhabitant of the island. Few children had been born since people began to settle it.

"Hey," piped up one of the boys, a gangly redhead whom Ty was pretty sure was of Scotch Irish descent and hailed from somewhere in the northeastern United States. "How did you do all that? They said you hit guys with a rifle while you were running. My pa always said to stop and line up a shot with a rifle if you're going to shoot at all."

Night had fallen, but the fires lit near the center of the town to cook their big communal dinner kept the place surprisingly cheery.

Ty smiled again, but there was an edge to it with an undercurrent of regret. He was sitting on a crate near the wall of one of the larger shanties, toward the far end of the circle of humanity around the fires.

"Well," he began, "what your pa taught you is solid, for most circumstances. If you're shooting long-range, say, if you're hunting. In that type of situation, you have time to take careful aim. Yes, the deer, hog, jackrabbit, or whatever might get away if you wait too long, but you don't necessarily have to make a *split second* decision."

The redhead and the others listened, rapt, and Ty pantomimed holding a rifle while he spoke. He'd left his Garand back in his makeshift home—he knew no one would try to steal it—but he still had his pistol holstered by his side. Just in case.

He went on, "In combat, at relatively close ranges of say a hundred yards or so, you might not have that kind of time. You can't think faster than a bullet can move. You have to know your weapon, be totally aware of its capabilities and limitations. You must trust yourself. Your reflexes. Without bothering to really *think* about what you're doing."

The other boy frowned and wiped his hands on his denim overalls, which were at least one size too big for him. "That don't make no sense, though. How can you stop yourself from thinking?"

He was a black American from somewhere deep in the South. Back in the States, he and the redhead youth might not have gotten along at all, thanks to old wounds that were slow to heal. On Atlantica, people left the past behind. The frontier mentality prevailed. Anyone who was useful to the business of survival—or the business of *business itself*—was, on some level, accepted.

Ty's eyes went distant. He noticed that the girl's attention was wavering slightly. Though all three were friends, she tended to be marginally less interested in the finer points of combat. He supposed she would wander off if she wanted to. The food was almost ready, and there were plenty of people to talk to.

Ty raised his hands. "Let me try to explain. Back in my family's home country, Japan, we have a long tradition of martial arts, practiced and developed by the ancient warrior caste, the samurai."

Redhead asked, "Are you a samurai? I heard about them."

Ty shook his head. "No, my family comes from peasant stock, although my great-grandfather served in the Imperial Army. That was before the war with America in the Pacific, by the way, and my father came to the U.S. before that ugliness began." He left out the fact that his father had fought for the United States in the European theater of the same war, at the same time that...

"Nonetheless, we learned some of the old ways of battle, as many Japanese did."

The southern boy said, "I thought it was mostly fighting with swords. Or sticks and that sort of thing."

Ty couldn't help laughing. "That's part of the tradition, but there's more to it than that. The martial curriculum also includes mindset training. How to discipline one's thoughts, and let the body act according to...what the spirit knows to be right, without conscious thought getting in the way."

He closed his eyes. It was difficult to explain, especially to kids, and especially in English. "We had words, *zanshin* and *mushin*, for this state of no-mind that takes over in battle. A good warrior must be able to shift into that state instantly when the need arises. It affects how well you can use a rifle, as well as a sword or your bare hands. It does not matter the weapon, really."

To his surprise, the girl was the first to respond. "Yes. I can see that. Some people are good with different tools because they know how most machines work. Something like that?"

If Ty wasn't mistaken, she was of mixed British and Chinese descent, and her father had taken her mother back home to England after serving in Shanghai for a time.

"Yes," Ty agreed, "that's a good way of putting it."

The redhead suddenly grinned. "You should teach us! We need someone to teach us how to fight since those bastards will be back sooner or later. A man is supposed to know fighting. I know some, but only from fistfights with my friends back home and hunting deer. Nothing fancy."

Before Ty could decide how to react to the boy's request—whether with a gentle excuse or a vague promise to show him a few basic things—a woman appeared. Her hair was as red as the boy's.

"Martin, stop bothering Mr. Katakura all the time. He did all that to save us, and he's probably tired now."

As the boy groaned in protest, Ty smiled and held up a hand. "It's all right, ma'am. They're curious about things, and I don't mind talking to them."

"Well," the woman added, "supper's about ready. You're the guest of honor so you can have first pick of the food. Everyone agreed as much."

He went through the motions of pretending to refuse out of politeness, but of course, he would have to accept in the end, or they would be offended. Growing up Japanese in America, the vagaries of etiquette had always been doubly apparent to him.

She led him deeper into the crowd, where people congratulated him, shook his hand, or patted him on the back. A couple of older American men called him a "stand-up guy." Others, from different countries and speaking different tongues, said things whose exact meanings he didn't know. But he got the gist of it.

It was...nice, if a little embarrassing. These people loved and respected him.

Still, there was the unspoken fact that he hadn't returned to the town quickly enough. At the elders' request, he'd been out on a brief scouting jaunt when the decommissioned Army truck had rolled in. The two boys who had thrown the rocks...the woman who had staggered out of her house...

There was nothing he could do about it now. Everyone else was happy and safe and alive.

The community had set up crude tables, chairs, and benches near the cooking area. Much of the meal was already being portioned out onto rough ceramic plates or into wooden bowls. People were distributing old, rusty utensils.

Some of the food, which required a less intensive degree of cooking, was merely being heated up on crude portable hotplates plugged into the pair of generators. The big, noisy devices were the community's only source of electricity and among its most prized possessions.

Ty had known about what to expect in terms of the fare on display. There had been no new shipments, no sudden glorious hauls of luxury cuisine of which he'd personally been aware. Therefore, the night's feast was simply a larger helping than usual of what they ate all the time, and with more of an emphasis on the richer, fattier, and more expensive—relatively speaking—ingredients.

Someone had butchered a goat a day or two ago, and it looked as though most of the animal's meat had gone into the stews or set to roast over one of the fires. Additionally, one household raised chickens, mostly for their eggs, but they'd agreed to allow a handful of the birds themselves to be killed and added to the banquet.

Aside from that, most of their repast would consist of simple plant-based foods. Specifically, homegrown vegetables from the gardens that around half of all residents kept. Not all crops grew well on Atlantica, but basic things like onions, potatoes, and cucumbers flourished in the warmer months.

Additionally, those of the locals who could find work tended to pool their earnings to buy bulk sources of carbohydrates. Last Ty had checked, they possessed a giant sack of brown rice and a smaller but still substantial bag of coarse, unbleached wheat flour. Both were more than half empty.

Some of the more talented cooks had put them to good use for the night's purposes. The smells were intoxicating.

The same portly gentleman who'd initially called for the feast appeared from somewhere within the depths of the crowd and clapped Ty on the shoulder. "There he is! You get first dibs on everything, good sir. Eat as much as you like. As much as you can! Ha. You're on the scrawny side so maybe that isn't much, but don't let it be for lack of trying, dammit."

Ty laughed. "I'll do my best to eat as much as possible." He was famished, and overeating sounded appealing right about now.

Then again, a man with a stomach bulging to capacity was slower—both physically and mentally. And a warrior should never handicap himself if he didn't know when the next battle might arrive.

With that in mind, Ty resolved to eat his fill but slowly, paying attention to his body's signals to avoid gluttony and satiation. If more hired thugs came back later that night, or in the wee hours of the morning, the community would thank him more for being able to spring back into action than they would be offended by his slight restraint.

As he sat and ate, someone began passing around a couple of jugs of hooch. Ty recalled at least one family of moonshiners from Appalachia among the workers, and they hadn't been idle in pursuing their special discipline.

A big, hairy man passed a jug Ty's way. "Ha, ha. That'll put hair on your chest, boy. Do you people *have* hairy chests? Not that it matters. You've got balls the size of boulders to make up for it."

Ty smiled, nodded, and accepted the jug. He poured himself a half-cup of moonshine. A single drink wouldn't hurt. He could use one after everything that had happened earlier.

People talked and laughed as they ate and drank. As they cleared plates and the fires died down, some rowdier sorts called for a dance.

Ty watched with a calm smile as the alcohol worked its subtle magic. A man from Louisiana pulled out a banged-up blues guitar, and a pair of coal miners from somewhere in Canada produced peeling violins. A family from Egypt had a pair of *mizmar* horns and joined in, and someone had created makeshift drums by stretching old patches of leather over buckets and pots.

As the music began, everyone took to their feet. Some danced, but most stood or browsed around, conversing. Everyone seemingly wanted to talk to Tyler Katakura.

"Oh!" A young woman bumped into him. "I was trying to get close to you earlier, but people always surrounded you!" It looked like she was blushing.

He nodded. "It's all right. Admittedly, I'm not as sociable as I should sometimes be."

They talked about trivialities. She tried to lead him away from the crowd, but others came to speak to him as well, passing him around from group to group. He was the hero of the hour. The men congratulated him, and women of all ages grew flirtatious, especially with the booze flowing freely.

Ty wasn't sure how to react. He did get lonely sometimes, but he'd always been a bit shy. For years, he'd rarely stayed in one place for more than a few months at a time. Somehow he always found himself shuffled from place to place, from battle to battle.

Like many soldiers, he didn't necessarily expect to be around for a long time. Anyone who ended up involved with him romantically might be left behind, heartbroken, and reduced to leaving flowers in his memory. Probably sooner rather than later.

It was hard to dwell on such thoughts. The music swelled and swept more of the community into the riotous, impromptu revelry that now encompassed the whole center of town.

Someone seized Ty by the forearm and pulled him into a line dance. He found his energy again, swayed in time with the music, and lost himself amid the people who'd adopted him and accepted him regardless of his background or appearance, who loved him for what he'd done for them.

For a short time, perhaps twenty minutes, he stayed lost in the celebration. For a blissful third of an hour, he forgot who and where he was. He didn't need to think of himself as merely a wandering gunman, who might be only one more firefight away from a shallow, ditch side grave.

CHAPTER FOUR

Tyler awoke to the unmistakable sound of commotion. As he sprang up from his bed, forcing his thoughts into order and awareness as rapidly as nature would allow, he couldn't yet identify what *sort* of commotion.

As the saying went, it was best to prepare for the worst while hoping for the best.

"God*dammit*," he grumbled, snatching his rifle as he swung his legs out and stuck his feet into his boots. Long years of preparedness had allowed him to awaken quickly, but his heavy meal had put him into a deep sleep. It might be another full minute or more before his mind and body were back up to one hundred percent functionality.

He steeled himself, nostrils flaring, and stomped toward the curtain that served him as a door. "I can't ever catch a break, can I? Who and what did they send this time? A real army? A fleet of Panzers?"

There weren't any gunshots yet, which was a good sign that he had an extra moment or two to prepare himself.

He grabbed his jacket, shrugged into it, and patted one of the pockets to make sure he still had a spare rifle clip therein. He did.

Then he strapped on his pistol holster, with his loaded 1911 still there, and snatched his old Army helmet for good measure.

Yesterday, he'd been off scouting for any new development vehicles moving in on their location when the truck filled with mercenaries had come. There hadn't been time to prep as much as he would have liked. If the bastards hadn't shown up at the worst possible time—one of the few instances when Ty wasn't there—he might've been able to save *everyone*. The delay had cost the lives of three innocent people.

The grim thoughts swirling in his head faded away as he pushed aside the curtain and stepped out into the muddy lane. The commotion had begun to identify itself. The noises were those of the community's excitement, curiosity, and even joy.

"Strange," he muttered, lurching out. "Good news isn't supposed to happen these days, is it?"

The two boys he'd spoken to last night ran past. The southern kid looked back. "C'mon, Ty!" He waved for the older man to follow.

Ty fell behind them and marched toward the road, where another truck had arrived in a waiting throng of people. This time, the vehicle's purpose was *completely* different from that of the previous one.

Although there was too big a crowd surrounding the truck to see what was going on, Ty put two and two together easily enough by observing the people who were already on their way back to their homes. They held baskets and crates filled with brightly colored objects that, to them, would've been more valuable than gems. Perhaps even more valuable than Atlanticore crystals.

Today's haul was fresh fruits and vegetables of premium quality and exotic breeds, the kind of stuff that the poor of Atlantica rarely if ever saw. The verdant farmlands near the coast yielded all manner of produce, but the rich generally hoarded the best of it.

The townsfolk heading back chattered happily among themselves. Most of them either hadn't noticed Ty in his combat gear or were simply ignoring him since there was no real threat.

He caught a snippet of conversation from a pair of older women passing.

"...such a nice lady. Of course, you got to wonder if there's more to it all, but I'd like to think there's still decent, God-fearing, generous souls here who understand..."

Ty nodded and continued toward the spectacle at the mouth of the valley. The pieces were falling into place. Their settlement had been the lucky recipient of a "relief mission" by a church or charitable organization that wanted to help out.

Probably. Ty hitched up the strap holding his rifle behind his shoulder. He was pretty sure there was an old saying about "free lunches." On Atlantica, even more so than in most other places, everything had its price.

As he approached the truck, the crowd started to thin out. The visitors had already bestowed most of the gifts. Ty saw only about three crates left of the fresh produce. The truck was a large stake-body style used for carrying big loads, so it must have had a lot to begin with.

He scanned the scene before him for clues as to who their mysterious benefactors might be. Off to the side of the truck, a group of the community's unofficial "council" of elders, including Mrs. Bertollini, stood chatting with a woman.

Ty leaned forward and squinted. The lady in question was striking, with wavy black hair and tan or olive skin, attired in the type of dress one usually saw at things like university speaking events. He guessed her age at around twenty-five to thirty, and the expression on her face bespoke oddly serene confidence.

He moved toward them. The elders looked around, sighted him, and pointed toward him, motioning with their hands. Nodding, the woman turned and walked in his direction, intending to meet him halfway.

"Well," he mumbled under his breath, "this ought to be interesting."

The young woman's face moved gradually into a smile as she came within speaking distance. She was even more attractive up close. Given her fancy dress and excellent grooming, her presence in the dirty little settlement was beyond incongruous. Tyler nearly felt as though he were moving through a dream.

He stopped, allowing her to close the rest of the distance, and waited.

She took a few more steps and paused perhaps ten feet away from him. "Good day," she began in a slight Latin accent. He couldn't identify her exact nationality yet. "I'm Eleanor Cervantes."

"Hi." He gave her a short bow of his head. "Tyler Katakura." Again, he waited for her to explain herself rather than bothering to ask questions.

The woman wasted no time. "I've heard of you, Mr. Katakura. It would seem that I'm not the only one. You're locally famous. And not only in this village."

He allowed a grim smirk to tug at the corner of his mouth. "I believe *infamous* would be a better term."

Ms. Cervantes didn't react to his little remark but only pressed on with her pitch. "I'm reaching out to you on behalf of...certain business interests...who have come to realize something of great importance. Something that involves you directly."

Ty maintained a poker face, which he'd always been good at, but his brain kicked into overdrive as he tried to stay one mental step ahead of her. His immediate suspicion was that she worked for more or less the same people who'd sent the clearance team yesterday, and that after failing to seize the land by brute force, they were now willing to attempt diplomacy. Which would presumably lead to an offer to buy them out.

"Oh?" was all he said.

"Yes." Eleanor nodded. She took two steps closer, ignoring the mud. She was wearing leather boots, which though still of abnormally fine quality by the neighborhood standards, were at least better suited to the environment than her dress was.

She continued, spreading her slim hands as she spoke. "You, Mr. Katakura, have carved out something of value here. What you have enabled in this humble labor town is unique on Atlantica. Like many unique things, it might be of great benefit if properly used and understood. The entire island might benefit from your example."

That wasn't quite what he'd expected to hear. He narrowed his eyes.

"I will assume," he stated, "that you expect something in return from me for the gift of all this nice fresh food." He inclined his head toward the few remaining crates of fruit and vegetable.

She was unfazed by the implications of his words. Her serene confidence was clearly of the highest caliber of resilience.

"Not necessarily. You may consider the food delivery a token of our goodwill, of course. We had heard that this was a poor community and thought you might benefit from a gift of some of our surplus provisions. As we admire what you are doing, however, nothing is necessarily *expected*. Oh, that reminds me."

She looked down and reached into her rather voluminous leather purse, producing two objects that again highlighted how out-of-place she looked. Ty couldn't be bothered analyzing the contrast between her and what she held. His eyes bulged and fixated on the things in her hand.

A full *en bloc* clip of .30-06 rifle ammunition, as well as a 1911 magazine loaded to capacity with .45 ACP rounds. Purchasing that much ammo these days would've cost Tyler the wages of a month's labor—and that was if he could get access to it to begin with.

"For you," Ms. Cervantes declared. "Another token of our appreciation."

Ty looked her in the eye. "Nothing is ever free."

Eleanor cleared her throat, and the first crack appeared in her unflappable self-assurance, though it was barely noticeable. "We do have an offer for you as you've seemingly guessed. Even if you flatly refuse, these aren't 'advance payment,' but gifts from the Executives. They come attached to no price tag. My instructions are to give them to you regardless of your answer to us. We appreciate your...vision, Mr. Katakura."

Ty glanced around, waiting for the other shoe to drop. Mrs. Bertollini and two of the other elders continued to watch them from afar. Otherwise, nothing was amiss. He reached out and accepted the ammunition. "Thank you."

"You're very welcome." Her smile grew.

Tyler added, "I'm confused what you mean by 'vision,' though. Vision is for scientists, business people, and artists. I used to be a soldier. These days, I barely qualify as a security guard."

The woman laughed, and the sound of it was more tinkling and girlish than he would've expected from someone so elegant-looking. "We don't necessarily see it that way. Would you be willing to come along and talk with my partners and employers?"

Again his mind tried to tease out the worst-case scenarios that might await him. If her employers were indeed the same people who wanted the valley for themselves, getting him away from familiar territory and making him overly comfortable might be an excellent way to set him up for assassination.

Somehow he doubted it. There were simpler ways of having a single man killed by deception that didn't involve giving his friends a week's worth of expensive food for free.

He recalled his conversation with Mrs. Bertollini last night, his confession that he feared the end of his supplies might mean the end of his ability to protect them. Whoever Ms. Cervantes worked for, they were the generous type.

He could always turn down their offer. While allowing them to try and persuade him, he might also humbly be able to accept a few more "gifts."

Slipping the new clip and magazine into his jacket, Ty said, "Very well. I'll come along and hear your proposition, but if you can't tell me what it is beforehand, I can't promise I'll accept, either."

"Of course." She walked back toward the truck, glancing over her shoulder to see if he followed her. He did. "There's no obligation. The Executives would rather inform you of the full details themselves."

Ty nodded. "Where are we going?"

"A private plot of land," Eleanor explained. "It's not far. You'll be back home in time for supper." She climbed up into the truck's bed, where someone had made a makeshift seat from a pair of cushions, and he realized that she'd ridden back there the whole way into the valley like a farm kid.

Ty hopped up beside her. "Well, it's nice to know that you intend to bring me home afterward. Still, I'm coming armed. The guns go where I go."

Eleanor ran a pair of fingers through her wavy dark hair as the truck's driver started the engine. "I wouldn't have it any other way."

CHAPTER FIVE

Tyler stared at his new host, not long enough to make it too obvious that he was staring at her, but long enough to take in all that there was to see.

She was beautiful, for one thing. He enjoyed looking at her. Still, that wasn't his only reason for examining her.

What both baffled and impressed him was how imperturbable she was regardless of circumstances. Sitting on her cushion in the back of a truck meant to transport bulk cargo, she might as well have been seated behind a fine mahogany desk or at a silk-clothed table at some high-society formal dinner event.

Finally, she noticed. "Mr. Katakura," she began, her demeanor not changing in the slightest, "is there something you would like to know?"

He tried not to let his face flush. "You almost seem like you're *accustomed* to riding in the back of a truck. It's odd since you look more like the limousine type."

She responded with another brief peal of her tinkling laugh. "Yes, when I worked for my family on our estates in Jalisco, I would sometimes ride in trucks while inspecting the farms and construction projects. It's much the same here, aside from the winter weather."

Ty shrugged. "I see. Pardon me, but where is Jalisco?"

"In western Mexico. The city of Guadalajara is there if you've heard of it. My family is based there, but we own property all across the state."

Ty felt slightly foolish. His grasp of geography was good enough for his day-to-day purposes, but he knew he wasn't as worldly as some. "Ahh. I've heard of Guadalajara."

"It's better known than the state of Jalisco, for whatever reason." Eleanor waved it off. "But, no matter. Atlantica is my place now."

Ty didn't press her further. He imagined that it was easier to call Atlantica "her place" while working for the wealthy class of the island than it might be for those who weren't so fortunate. It sounded like she came from a wealthy background, besides.

Still, she'd brought food to his neighbors and ammo to him. He resolved to give her the benefit of the doubt.

From the valley where the workers' shantytown lay, the truck had rumbled up the dirt road through the surrounding hills and was now moving down toward the coastal plain region. The land grew gentler and more fertile. The greens of the season brightened in their intensity.

Once they came to flatter ground, where the truck made less noise, Eleanor turned to her guest. "As I informed you before, the Executives wish to tell you the details of their offer themselves, in person. But I'm permitted to fill you in on more of the situation until then. I can tell that you're curious."

"I am that," he said.

She stroked her hair, brushing part of it behind her left ear. "The Executives have noticed that over these last few months, an interesting thing has occurred with regard to your little labor town. Or, to be more precise, a thing has *not* occurred."

The truck rolled past a stand of trees that a lumber crew was felling with a mixture of old-fashioned crosscut saws and modern equipment. There was too much noise for Ty to bother replying verbally, so he raised his eyebrows.

"Since the settlement's establishment and its population of workers and transients arrived," Eleanor continued, "the town's boundaries haven't changed in any meaningful way. Almost none of the people there have forcibly relocated. Except for internal community reasons. Personal disputes that arose from within, not things imposed from the outside."

Ty nodded. He thought back to a couple of times last month and the month before when the locals had called him out in the middle of the night to deal with domestic fights that had broken out. One was a lover's quarrel. The other, a drunken brawl between friends who'd had a stupid misunderstanding.

Both instances had resolved without anyone getting hurt seriously. Still, he knew well why they'd asked for his help. He was the local expert on violence. They required someone who could, if necessary, *hurt* those who might otherwise hurt others.

It demonstrated their need for him. He'd wondered if he was up to the task—he was a gunman, a de facto mercenary, not a bouncer or cop or counselor. Nonetheless, he'd talked the aggressors out of doing anything stupid and imposed judgments that had banished one man from the village for the sake of everyone else's safety.

The truck bumped and rattled along the road. Past the thicket where the workers were clearing trees was another labor town for the lumberjacks. Ty wondered if it was a better or worse place to live than the one he'd adopted. Probably about the same.

As though she'd sensed his thoughts, Ms. Cervantes added, "Most settlements aren't so lucky. They spring up in a week, and at a whim of those with the power to do such things, they vanish in a day. Your town is unusual. The people under your jurisdiction are fortunate."

Tyler laughed. "Jurisdiction! You make it sound like I'm some kind of authority figure. I'm a hired gun. They feed me, let me live there, and give me a few spare coins in exchange for driving off anyone who wants to ruin their lives. That's it."

Eleanor spread her hands. "Your role is much like that of a sheriff in a town on your American frontier a hundred years ago, is it not? But, as you say, your gun is for hire."

Ty watched the lumber camp dwindle behind them as the truck left the forest. "Yeah. So, you're wondering what it will cost you to get me out of the way. To convince me to leave them all behind and let you plow them aside so some local warlord can turn that valley into his hunting ground or something. Or perhaps you would even think to pay me to turn against them and clear them out myself. Is that it?"

He didn't bother trying to keep the edge out of his voice. His fingers compulsively ran along the fabric of his rifle sling.

A barely perceptible tightening of her jaw muscles betrayed Eleanor's slight unease. Aloof and self-confident though she was, she'd at least noticed that something had struck a nerve...and that Tyler Katakura was potentially a dangerous man.

"No," she replied. "Just the opposite."

Her jaw muscles relaxed as Ty's hand dropped away from the sling.

Ms. Cervantes elaborated as her guest leaned forward to hear her better. "The Executives realize that having workers ported in and out constantly, based on temporary contracts, isn't a viable long-term solution to our island's growth problems. A stable community is needed to provide both the workforce and the infrastructure necessary to help Atlantica reach its full potential."

"What," Ty inquired, "is that potential?"

They'd crested a low rise in the ground before coming to the bustling heart of Atlantica. The broad coastal plain that extended from the ocean partway into the island's interior was where much of its population—and wealth—was centered.

Eleanor waved toward the fledgling city, where the lowly residents of the labor camps, including many of those in Ty's settlement, went to work every day.

"Look out there," she proclaimed. "Although the island was effectively unknown to the world until only five years ago, Atlantica is well on its way to housing a wealthy and modern metropolis like nothing ever seen before on this planet."

Ty's gaze followed her hand. He hadn't been far from the valley in over a month, and much had changed in Atlantica Central. The contrast with his rather peripheral backwater of a settlement was stark.

Here were no makeshift lanes of unpaved mud and gravel. No rickety slapdash housing, thrown up as quickly as possible to provide the bare minimum of amenities needed to keep people safe from the elements until one day they might attain something better. Already, many of the sloppy and hastily constructed buildings in the labor camp were beginning to sag and crumble. The elders had been discussing who should begin work on the repairs.

Instead, the central plain, soon to be a city, was strewn with vast resource processing facilities of various types and huge machine shops that were impressive enough by themselves.

The foundations and scaffolding surrounding the half-completed skyscrapers, the broad office buildings and housing complexes nearing completion, and the entertainment complexes that would soon cater to the ever-burgeoning population dwarfed them. A sports stadium was taking shape. Movie theaters would be along soon, and gymnasia, and shopping malls. A city to rival New York might quickly cover an area that was nothing but a wilderness a mere half a decade ago.

The industrial facilities, of course, had been the first to go up. Those were the key. They were utterly necessary to convert Atlantica's unique resources into wealth. Those who'd paid to construct them had done so fully expecting to reap their fat rewards from everything dug out of Atlantica's hills and caves.

Other, more mundane resources were there for the taking. Still, the boom would never have been as big as it was without Atlanticore, the mysterious crystal that was found nowhere else on Earth.

The truck slowed as it entered the fringes of the fledgling city, despite the roads now being paved with asphalt on the main thoroughfares. Other cars and trucks clogged the streets, many of them transporting workers and materials or overseers and investors from place to place. Construction crews labored close to passing traffic.

"Yes," Eleanor stated, "it will be a great city, all made possible by the incredible wealth of the land itself. But as you certainly know, money in such quantities as this, and the power that goes with it, can often end up in the hands of...*less thoughtful* individuals."

Ty let out a brief, snorting laugh. "I can't argue with you on that. I've seen more action as the cockamamie town marshal of that little valley than I did the whole time I was in Korea with the Fifth." He shook his head.

Ms. Cervantes peered into his eyes. "Oh, really? We know more about your career here than you might think. We don't know everything, of course."

Her guest frowned. He didn't like the thought of people knowing too much about him, especially when he had no idea who they were or how long they'd been watching him. He imagined they'd reveal most of that soon, once he had the opportunity to speak to the so-called Executives.

"The law in Atlantica," Ty expounded, "is whatever you can enforce. The people in that settlement look to me to enforce peace and safety against all comers. There aren't many formal rules. Mostly, those folks all get along. Still, I've had to break up fights.

"I've had to kick people out—one man from within, who refused to get along with the rest. A few visitors we had from other camps, who came in looking for trouble. They were probably sent by the local bosses in some of the other labor towns, trying to scare our people away from taking the jobs they wanted."

Eleanor said nothing but listened with composed interest.

Ty's nostrils flared again. "The most serious shit has always been the clearance teams. Those sons of bitches—pardon my language—whom the rich hire to kick everyone out. They *need* workers to keep getting rich, and the workers have to live *somewhere*. So they settle on unclaimed land. Then along come these idiots to claim it. That's when things get bloody."

His hands clenched into bony fists.

"Mm," Eleanor replied, and her attitude became more grave. "We've noticed. Things here don't go as smoothly as they should. That's part of what my employers wish to discuss. We're almost there."

After traversing the corner of the city, the truck passed into a less developed, more private area farther inland, climbing a slight incline before reaching flat land again. They drove through a gate beyond a loose circle of trees and onto the grounds of a small villa. It was, beyond any doubt, the home of someone who had tremendous vested interests in Atlantica's future profitability.

Outside and inside the gate were pairs of armed guards. Ty's gut tensed and he examined their gear. Helmets, armored vests. Black rifles, probably AR-10's. The men looked imposing.

The house was set about two hundred yards past the gate, and Ty estimated that the whole property was around twelve acres—not an enormous plot, but incredibly roomy and palatial compared to the crowded and squalid conditions he was used to. The ground had a raw look to it that spoke of recent landscaping. Patio furniture was arranged on a broad concrete porch, next to a small marble fountain and below the villa proper.

The patio setup allowed anyone sitting there to look out over the new and growing city. Observing and overseeing.

The truck slowed as it neared the paved area before grinding to a stop. Eleanor sprang to her feet with surprising speed and agility, then hopped down to the ground. Ty did likewise.

He waited beside her as she spoke to the driver, who seemed to be a fellow Mexican. Ty's Spanish was rusty, but it sounded like she was telling him to go back to the city to help with something and return to the villa in about an hour.

The truck rumbled off. Ty glanced around and noticed that more security personnel, at least half a dozen, were patrolling the inner grounds of the estate, and there might well be others in the house. His neck and face flushed with envy. The owner's private muscle were well-fed, well-dressed, and outfitted with state-of-the-art equipment. It was impossible not to contrast their gear with his battered old war-surplus jacket and outdated rifle.

That made him wonder why they thought him so valuable. All things considered, he was a nobody.

Eleanor walked toward the patio, with Tyler following close.

"So," he remarked, "you want stability and predictability so you can build some great and glorious super-city here. Well, you've clearly got the money to buy it. Why are you talking to a bum like me when you can load up a bunch of your thugs with big shiny guns and have them keep things quiet? You can buy people's obedience, as long as you can also buy other people to enforce it."

It came out sounding more bitter and confrontational than he'd intended. Eleanor had attained the patio but stopped and turned to look at him with an open expression of faint curiosity.

Then someone else answered his question.

"Because we both know that it will not work that way, Mr. Katakura." The voice was deep and smooth, tinged with an accent that Ty didn't immediately recognize. Probably European.

Eleanor stood aside as Tyler advanced toward the marble fountain. At last, he could see a man reclining on a broad chair lined with soft cushions. The back of the furniture had hidden him from sight at their angle of approach.

The voice went on. "If we try to set ourselves over this land so arrogantly as that, like feudal lords in centuries past, we'll all end up at each other's throats, exactly like the petty kinds of old. That would wash our profits away in a river of blood."

Ty took a couple of hesitant steps closer to the enormous chair. The man rose in a slow, fluid motion and extended his right hand. "Lucas Montrosse."

His hand was huge, far larger than Tyler's. It was noticeably soft, however. Mr. Montrosse wasn't well acquainted with a hard day's work. A similar pattern emerged as Ty examined the rest of him, a curious impression of pampered softness and expansive power.

He was at least six-foot-two and must've weighed two hundred pounds or more, with a mane of black hair and a short beard of the same color. His eyes were a light brown, almost orange. His skin was copper-tan.

Ty was beginning to place his accent as vaguely French, but now he wondered if the man might have been a French Algerian or French Tunisian. His teeth were perfectly white, and so was his expensive suit.

"Tyler Katakura." He shook the massive hand. "Ms. Cervantes has led me to understand that you want to talk to me."

Montrosse released his grip, then folded his hands behind his back. "Indeed. You seem like a man who grasps that the current state of affairs in Atlantica is...unsustainable."

Ty kept his poker face on. He had to. The man had earned his instant dislike. He thought about thanking him for the gifts but decided to wait.

Instead, he queried, "So, if we both understand, as you say, that everyone is going to end up killing each other unless something changes, then how, exactly, do I fit in?"

Lucas responded by smiling, his lips pulling away from the vast mouthful of white teeth in a way that reminded Ty of a shark. The man looked happy. But nothing about his smile was exactly encouraging.

CHAPTER SIX

The interior of Lucas Montrosse's villa was staggeringly opulent, at least by Ty's humble standards, although he found it curiously tasteless. Japan had long prided itself on the subtle aesthetics of minimalism, and he recalled well how his mother had decorated their home accordingly when he was a boy.

America, for all its flaws and hypocrisies and brutalities, was a land that had, in its way, achieved something similar in the way its common folk valued simplicity. At least, when they weren't gallivanting into cities to allow themselves to be mesmerized by brightly lit streets, obnoxious advertisements, and musical pageantry on the silver screen.

The Montrosse estate, by contrast, was overfull with things intended to look sophisticated and impressive. It was the house of someone imitating the refined and Baroque styles of Europe but not quite succeeding. Quantity seemed to rule over quality.

Lucas spread his hands as he walked. "Be careful. That statuette is a licensed reproduction by the best man in the business. I should've known that I needn't ask you to remove your boots before you step indoors, of course." He chuckled.

Ty nodded. His parents had tried to assimilate the broader

strokes of Western culture, but certain distinctively Japanese quirks had never left them behind. Even in the rough surroundings of the labor town, he always took his boots off before setting foot inside his dirty little shed.

"Right this way," Lucas went on. "My office is on the second floor, at the end of the hall."

Montrosse led the way, followed by Tyler, with Ms. Cervantes in the rear. An armed guard had let them into the house, and another had stood watch in the hallway with the reproduction statuette.

A third man, armored and toting an AR-10, patrolled the second-story corridor. When he saw Montrosse approaching, he opened the office door and held it until all three had gone in, then closed it behind them.

Ty looked around. The office's decor was somewhat more down-to-earth than the garish tone that prevailed in the rest of the house. Here, he suspected, was where Montrosse wanted to convince his guests that he was a shrewd and serious businessman. The first-floor lobby, halls, and dining areas were for convincing other types of guests that he was as rich as possible.

Lucas headed immediately for the tall, velvet-backed chair behind the enormous mahogany desk that dominated the center of the room. Behind it was a broad window half-covered with red curtains, and off to the sides were well-stocked bookshelves and cabinets.

The large man flourished his hand toward the corner. "There is a small bar if you'd like to have a drink. Help yourself."

Ty glanced at the bar. About half a dozen liquor bottles were there, along with tumblers, an ice cooler, and straws. Part of him wouldn't have minded a nip of whiskey or vodka, but he decided it would be best to keep his wits as sharp as he could.

"Thank you, but I'll abstain. I don't drink during the day."

Lucas shrugged. "Suit yourself. Please, have a seat. You too, Ms. Cervantes."

Two chairs, smaller than Montrosse's but equally plush, were arranged near the front corners of the desk. Ty took the one to the left, and Eleanor settled into the other.

Lucas spread his arms and leaned back in his seat, adopting the same relaxed, almost slouching posture he'd languished in when Ty had first seen him on the patio. "Now, then, let us begin with a review. This will also serve to demonstrate that before you agree to any suggestions of ours, you should consider our substantial bank of knowledge."

Tyler gave a gentle nod. He wasn't sure he liked the sound of that, but Eleanor had already divulged that "the Executives" knew a great deal about things most people would've regarded as private or obscure.

Lucas reached into a drawer and pulled out a thick dossier. He tossed it onto the surface of his desk, so it made a loud slapping sound on impact, and let it sit a moment before opening it. On the cover was printed *Katakura, Tyler*.

Ty chuckled drily. "In Japan, the family names always come first."

"Of course," Lucas said. "In the West, family names come first when things need to be alphabetized. Let us examine the contents."

Ty said nothing.

Eleanor chimed in, "Lucas, I informed him earlier that we were familiar with his career on Atlantica. It is unnecessary to repeat the basic facts of his activities in the labor town."

"Oh," Montrosse snapped, holding up a hand, "but there's much more than that. Let's go back to the beginning, first of all."

He pulled out a sheaf of papers and examined them.

"Benkei Katakura, born 1900, in Honolulu, Hawaii. Moved to California in 1910 along with his family. In 1928, married Hatsumi Ueto, born 1902 in Fukuoka, Japan. Your mother was a first-generation immigrant, then—*Issei*—whereas your father was born second-generation American. *Nisei* seems to be the term."

Tyler didn't like discussing his parents with strangers. "Yes," he stated. His poker face held firm. "That is what 'generation' means."

"January twenty-seventh, 1933, the couple finally had a son. I think we can safely assume who that was." Lucas paused to smooth the edges of his beard.

"Can we?" Ty asked. "Neither of you bothered to ask if I had a brother."

Eleanor sighed. "We know you were an only child, Mr. Katakura. Lucas, I think we can focus on the important things without unnecessary detours."

Lucas glared at her. "It is *all* necessary to make our point." He turned his gaze back toward Ty. "It seems you grew up quite happily, leading a thoroughly normal existence. Until, of course, the outbreak of the Second World War."

"I'm flattered that you think I'm the only one whose 'normal' existence that particular event disrupted. I had no idea I was so important."

Lucas chuckled. "Your family's fate during the war is most interesting. Yes, we know all the details. Perhaps you haven't thought about them in some time. Revisiting them might be instructive."

Ty bit his tongue. Montrosse wanted to rattle him, to upset him in some way. Why? To intentionally drag a man through a field of bad memories, there had to be a purpose—a reason for softening him up or riling up his anger.

There was nothing to do except wait for his host to play out his little game and come to the point.

Lucas went on. "Following the day of infamy at Pearl Harbor, President Roosevelt issued an Executive Order on February nineteenth, 1942, that led to the forcible relocation and intern-ment of all Japanese Americans. It sent your family to the camp at Manzanar. You were ten years old and would remain there until the program ended in early 1946."

Ty brushed his nose. "I vaguely seem to recall something of that nature, yes."

"Meanwhile," Montrosse continued, "your father volunteered for the 442nd Infantry Regiment of the United States Army. Despite his relatively advanced age, by military standards, he was accepted and served with distinction in the war in Europe. It seems that he was an avid correspondent with you and your mother, averaging one letter per week. We briefly reviewed most of the letters in question."

Ty's nostrils widened, and he could feel his knuckles turning white. "Oh."

Eleanor cleared her throat. "Lucas, please. Tyler, you don't have to pretend that this doesn't bother you. We only review it to demonstrate the depth of our research and help us reach an understanding. Don't take it personally."

"Indeed," Lucas agreed. "Your father survived the war, fortunately, and you all were reunited afterward. Although it seems you had to start over from scratch, as the Americans say, having lost most of what your parents built before their internment. Alas. But you got by.

"In a truly stunning display of patriotism, another generation of your family volunteered to fight for the United States in the next war. You, Tyler, joined the 5th Infantry Regiment and participated in the Korean War. It appears that you barely missed out on the Battle of Pusan Perimeter but still saw your share of action."

Ty coughed. "*Action* is one way of putting it. You've done a truly outstanding job of reviewing public records accessible to almost anyone in America, as well as citing basic historical facts. When do we get to the part that's supposed to impress me?"

For a split second, Lucas's eyes narrowed, and his broad body tensed, but then his usual mixture of confidence and unctuous charm returned. "Coming by this information required a bit more work than that, particularly as we aren't Americans. Just wait. We haven't finished yet."

"Well, that's comforting," Ty shot back. "I was afraid you might ask me to do something besides sit here and listen."

Eleanor rubbed her eyes. Ty wondered if she was about to get up and make herself a drink.

Lucas chortled and continued to flip through the pages of the dossier. "After you returned from the Korean Peninsula, now a decorated young war hero, it seems you had some difficulty adjusting to civilian life. Your efforts to hold down a job were largely unsuccessful. You had several unpleasant brushes with the law, including a pair of brief stints in jail, and you increasingly found yourself associating with people who weren't well-liked by mainstream society. May I ask why?"

Tyler stared directly into the man's orangish-brown eyes. "You have, in a fashion, already answered that question. I came back from Korea and ran directly into people who thought I was a Chinese or North Korean Communist—the exact people I had been fighting. I encountered individuals who somehow blamed me for the actions of Imperial Japan during the previous war, despite my father fighting for America at the same time. Do you think I took it *well?*"

"No," said Lucas, "it would appear you did not. You were involved with a couple of student groups who began to clamor for redress to the Japanese American community over the ravages of the internment camps. You got involved with a few labor unions who had branched out into illegal activity.

"As I understand it," he leaned back and allowed his eyes to drift upward, gazing vacantly, "you came to Atlantica because you might, *possibly*, be wanted for certain felonious crimes in the United States."

Tyler cracked his neck. "Possibly. You've finally arrived at the present day. So, what does my life's story have to do with what the hell you want from me?"

Montrosse refocused his eyes on his guest and folded his massive hands in front of him on the desk. "Mr. Katakura, your personal history, as well as your, shall we say, defiant and self-possessed demeanor are what make you perfect for the job we have in mind.

"Part of the reason we forced you to sit through all of that—which we assume was unpleasant for you—was to gauge your reaction. You have remarkable self-control, but at the same time, you aren't the type of man to buckle in the face of adversity or pretend to be something he is not."

"Thanks. Now, if you would be so kind, please tell me what this job is so I can decide whether it's worth the annoyance of being put through your test or if it's simply hired thuggery. If you plan to hire me to do the same shit as the guys I killed yesterday...you might find yourself disappointed."

Eleanor stood and shook her head, wandering toward one of the bookcases. "I already informed you, Mr. Katakura, that we didn't have such a role in mind for you. Something better."

Lucas sat up straight. "Much better. Much more *lucrative* for everyone involved."

Ty clenched his jaw. "Yeah, I need money like anyone else, but I have standards. I'm not purely a hired gun. Clearly, whatever you plan to do, it's because you only want to profit off the—"

Eleanor rushed back to his side. "Tyler, please calm yourself." His tone had alarmed her, although Lucas seemed unworried.

"Mr. Montrosse and I, and the rest of the Executives, do intend to profit from Atlantica's development, it's true. But we wish to do so in a way that is less...difficult for everyone, including the workers. Your aims are noble. It's admirable that you stand by your principles. But you must acknowledge reality. You cannot singlehandedly protect your friends from all the rapacious and powerful people wishing to carve up this island for themselves."

His head snapped toward her. His black eyes were bright.

MICHAEL ANDERLE

"At least," she added, "not without more resources and connections than you currently possess. When we arrived at this villa, I saw you looking at the armor and rifles of Mr. Montrosse's security forces. They're among the best that money can buy. With the support of the Executives, you, too, will have access to top-of-the-line equipment. All the weapons, ammunition, and armor you could need are only the beginning of what we can provide."

Ty hesitated. "That...would be useful. Of course, it would also be useful to know that I can trust you to fulfill a bargain like that."

Lucas laughed again, and his massive pearly grin was suddenly back. "A wise man. You might make a fine poker player, Mr. Katakura, if you aren't one already."

Before Ty could respond to the remark, Montrosse rose from his seat and bellowed, "Guard! Come in here, please."

Ty tensed. They hadn't bothered to disarm him, so if by some chance Montrosse was about to order the guard to attack him, at least he would be able to fight back. Although in that case, fighting his way off the villa and getting the hell out of the city might prove to be...difficult.

He doubted it would be an issue. Lucas probably had another "point" that he wanted to make.

The door burst open and the man who'd been patrolling the hall burst in, his gun at the ready. "Is everything all right, sir?"

"Yes," said Montrosse. "I want you to give your rifle and all of your spare magazines to Mr. Katakura here."

The guard blinked. "Ah, are you sure about that, sir?" Ty couldn't tell if the man was more worried about giving the weapons to him or the prospect of being unarmed.

Lucas nodded. "Quite sure. It will be fine. I'll provide you with replacements. For now, we need to make Mr. Katakura understand how serious we are about helping those who can also help us."

"Yes, sir." The man advanced into the room and handed his AR-10 to Ty, butt-first and with the barrel aimed toward the corner of the floor.

Tyler smiled. "Thanks." The guard then handed over three twenty-round box magazines. Ty couldn't begin to calculate how much it all would've cost him. For someone on Atlantica, in his dire straits—a small fortune.

Lucas dismissed the guard, telling him to go see the armorer and not worry about guarding the house's second floor until he finished re-outfitting himself. The man awkwardly saluted and marched out the door.

Ty stood, examining the gun. "Well, Mr. Montrosse, it seems you have good taste. I've wanted one of these. Shorter and lighter than the Garand while being chambered for the new 7.62 NATO round if I'm not mistaken. Which is ever so slightly weaker than the good old .30-06, but more accurate. And twenty rounds certainly beats eight. Of course, the Garand has served me well. But a man has to keep up with the times."

"Indeed," Lucas agreed. "Keep it. Another token of our goodwill."

Examining the rifle further, Ty noticed something. "The sights are a little strange, aren't they? Might take some getting used to. I ought to start zeroing it as soon as possible."

He turned toward Montrosse, holding the rifle to his shoulder in a ready-to-fire position, with the barrel aimed straight at his host's face. He wondered if Montrosse would think it was an "accident."

He wondered if Montross still believed he was the only person capable of "testing" people to gauge their reactions.

Eleanor's eyes widened. For the first time since they'd met, she looked alarmed. "Mr. Katakura, please..."

Lucas stared back at Ty up the sight radius. He was perfectly still and said nothing, but he didn't cringe or flinch. His oddly-colored eyes held Ty's gaze with a steady glower, and his mouth lay in its default position of a half-amused smirk.

Ty had to admit, he was impressed. He couldn't be sure, however, if Montrosse was truly fearless or if he was simply too arrogant to admit to fear. Possibly a bit of both, combined with sheer disbelief that someone like Tyler Katakura could or would kill him in his office.

Eleanor took a hesitant step closer to Ty. "Mr. Katakura. We needed to make our point, and now you've made yours, too. We appreciate that you're a man to take seriously. Don't let your prejudices and insecurities distract you from seeing what a good opportunity this is. Please put the gun down, and listen to the rest of what we have to say."

Ty blinked as though suddenly realizing he was aiming a loaded rifle at a man and brought it down to a low ready position. "Oops. Yes. I figured there would be more to this meeting yet."

He sat, putting the AR-10 across his lap. "Especially since I still don't know what you want me to do. You haven't gotten to that particular detail yet."

Lucas and Eleanor exchanged a glance and smiled in unison. For the first time, Lucas's grin looked borderline pleasant.

"As you might have guessed," he explained, "I'm one of the people we simply call the Executives. With all the feuds and violence that have consumed this island, we've all come to recognize the need for a long-term solution. A neutral keeper of the peace. Someone we'd collectively fund while operating independently of any individual Executive—to give no one of us an unfair advantage, of course. Someone we could trust to apply a rather broad code of law and order across Atlantica, which needs law and order so badly."

Ty was unsure how to respond yet. He was intrigued but still skeptical. "Go on."

Lucas folded his hands once more and leaned forward. "This

person, or group of persons, would possess great power in terms of the resources they could access and the authority they would come to wield, once established in their role. So part of the task of selecting a candidate is choosing one who wouldn't allow such power to go to their head."

Eleanor had remained standing. Now she closed the rest of the distance with Ty and placed a hand gently on his shoulder. "That's why we've come to you, Tyler. We believe you're the person most qualified to start this new peacekeeping force."

Silence reigned for half a dozen heartbeats. "So," Ty inquired, running his tongue along his teeth, "My job would be to execute the will of the Executives?"

"No," Eleanor clarified, "not quite. You're here to execute justice for all of Atlantica. So it can grow."

"Oh," Lucas interjected, raising a single finger and grinning unpleasantly again, "but I like this talk of 'executing.' Ha, ha. How would you like to be Atlantica's first Executioner, Mr. Katakura?"

Ty's head buzzed with questions. They'd allayed some of his fears and suspicions. Others had only grown stronger. "May I have that drink now?"

"Certainly," said Lucas.

His hosts waited, silent and patient, as Ty stood and walked over to the bar. His Garand still hung over his shoulder, and he set the AR-10 down beside the bar, leaning it against the wooden surface after double-checking the selector.

He selected a nice crystal tumbler, added a single cube of ice, and poured in two fingers' worth of top-shelf Scotch whiskey. Then he returned to his seat, swished the beverage around, and took a long, slow sip.

"I'm intrigued by the idea," he stated. "I haven't accepted as of yet. I'm considering it. Before I agree to anything, I have several concerns you need to address."

Eleanor returned to her chair. "Yes, by all means, ask us what you wish to know."

Tyler began asking questions. He asked them quickly and often rephrased the same question repeatedly, forcing Lucas and Eleanor to answer it three times from three marginally different angles, using other word choices each time. They grew mildly irritated as they grasped what he was doing but played along for the sake of humoring him.

"So," Ty sipped his drink while he glanced out the window. "To summarize and confirm once more. I will be operating under my determination. My jurisdiction is all of Atlantica; no part of the island lies outside it. The Executives will abide by my judgments, provided I don't go off the rails and start acting like a madman—even if it means that I have to put down some of their hired goons or enforce edicts that are inconvenient to their business interests."

He turned his eyes back toward his hosts. "Is that correct?"

Lucas puffed out his substantial chest. "It is. You are most thorough, which is a useful trait for law enforcement."

Eleanor elaborated further. "Along with that, you'll be able to establish 'protected zones' where Executive security forces will protect from incursion but won't function as an active police force. In this way, while you're busy pursuing some other case, an opportunistic clearance team won't rush into a labor town while you're away."

Ty nodded. It all sounded better and better by the minute. Still, as Montrosse had observed, he would make a good poker player, and he wasn't about to change that anytime soon. "Mm. Interesting. That *could* be a good idea if implemented right."

Lucas laughed. "We can see that we're swaying you, Mr. Katakura. Once you're satisfied with the terms, you can begin your duties within a day or so. There will be no pointless bureaucratic delays. That's one of the advantages of a lawless society." He guffawed again.

Eleanor remained calm, but her usual confidence was nearly starting to resemble smugness.

After a long, deep breath, Tyler said, "I accept. With things the way they are, it would be better for me to...try to do what I can to improve them, than to allow things to go the way of 'petty kings,' as you put it." He finished his Scotch and set the glass back down on the bar.

Lucas clapped. "Marvelous! I knew you would love the idea. We picked the right man. Now, let us toast. Yes, you had a drink, and you don't strike me as the type to get badly sloshed, haha. But we must. It is tradition. Champagne!"

Ty shrugged. "Very well. I'll have another small drink."

Montrosse used an in-house telephone hidden within a drawer of his desk to call his servants, who brought up a tray with a bottle of champagne and three glasses. They opened it and served the foaming beverage, filling two glasses nearly to the rim and leaving one only half-full for Tyler.

Eleanor raised her glass. "To our success—and to peace and order across Atlantica."

"To peace and order," Ty repeated. They all drank.

Lucas wiped his mouth. "Good stuff, is it not? But, anyway. We'll see to it that you get outfitted with whatever you need. Anything on the island is yours. If you need something more esoteric, we can have it brought out by ship or plane, if necessary. Ms. Cervantes will be your prime point of contact. She'll help you determine where you're most needed."

Ty drained the last drops of champagne from his glass before returning it to the tray. His head buzzed pleasantly, but he wasn't truly drunk. He trusted himself to maintain good self-control until total sobriety returned.

"So," he offered, "does that mean you've already got problems lined up, things that need sorting out?"

Lucas took Ty's glass in hand and arched his eyebrows, but Ty shook his head, so he refilled his and Eleanor's glasses instead. "Oh, I very much doubt that we'll ever *run out* of problems. Like I said, Mr. Katakura—we need you."

CHAPTER SEVEN

Tyler stood in the muddy street outside his home. The duffel bag filled with new toys and new tools was heavy, but he could afford to hold it for a moment longer. The redhead boy—his name was Danny—had kindly offered to take the smaller bag and find a good place for it within the little shed, provided he handled it gently and didn't look inside.

"Well," Danny had protested, "*that's* no fun, but okay."

As the younger man pushed through the curtain, Ty called after him, "Later on I'll tell you more about it, if I can. Have patience."

He examined his surroundings as the boy dropped off his luggage. His apartment, such as it was, was little more than an add-on shack that they'd hastily attached to the labor town's communal hostel. There, the settlement's more temporary or short-term workers stayed apart from those who were on Atlantica for the long haul. The community had allowed Ty to use the shack free of charge after the first time he'd stepped up as their protector.

The curtain parted, and Danny emerged, sans bag. "Okay, Ty. I put it over in the back corner on top of your bed. Is that okay?"

"That's fine." Ty walked past him and patted his shoulder. "Tell your friends I might not be around as much. But I'm not leaving yet. Even if I'm not here in person, I'll still be watching over you. All of you."

He left the young man behind and half-stumbled into his apartment, groaning and exhaling as he dropped the duffel bag on the floor. It had taken tremendous effort not to reveal how much his arms hurt from carrying the fucking thing. New gear *packed* it.

Although the finest, most expensive accouterment of them all was in the smaller bag. Hence, letting Danny choose a place to set it down carefully.

Ty sat on his bed. He was used to the place, a bit attached to it, in a way. It wasn't much. A narrow room with a crude bed that was little more than a cot, a small, cheaply constructed desk and chair, and a basic toilet-sink combination at the far end. And the curtain. That was all.

"Moving up in the world," he said in a low voice. "Soon. I hope they don't think I'm abandoning them. I'll still be around. But..."

Would he still really be one of them if he became a servant of the Executives? The question bothered him to contemplate. Still, by accepting the Executives' offer, his ability to protect these people would increase by tenfold at least. A hundredfold, even.

He pushed the lingering doubts from his mind and opened the bags to examine his new haul.

Resting at the top of the mass within the larger bag was his new AR-10 rifle. He had broken it down for easier carrying but not completely field-stripped it. His best guess was that it had had two or three hundred rounds put through it. Enough for one man—presumably the guard whom Montrosse had ordered to hand it over—to attain a fair degree of proficiency with it, but not enough for there to be any meaningful degree of wear and tear. It had also been cleaned and oiled since the last time someone had fired it.

Ty pulled the pieces out and put them back together, pausing to admire the weapon's sleek, modern appearance. Though still a full-sized rifle and hardly insignificant in its overall mass, it was about two inches shorter and probably two pounds lighter than his old Garand.

The 7.62 NATO cartridge its manufacturer had chambered it for was of similar power while also having a shorter casing, making it easier to carry more rounds.

"Good," he murmured.

Beneath the rifle was a collection of accessories to go with it. There was a nice leather bandolier harness that would allow him to carry up to six spare magazines for the AR-10, also included, and another two mags for his 1911 pistol. Additionally, he could rig other belts or pouches to it for other stuff he might need.

They had given him a radio set, new and shiny and state-of-the-art. They'd already tuned it to a frequency broadcast by a tower they'd erected on top of one of the new skyscrapers in the city—the building wasn't fully operational yet, but the tower was. The Executives had their priorities straight. Ty would supposedly be able to get reception across the entire island, barring underground, of course.

He switched it on. Static emerged, followed by silence, followed by members of a security team reporting to one another that everything was clear and all was well. Ty nodded and turned it off.

Finally, beneath the radio set and filling out the bottom of the duffel bag was a set of body armor like what the guards at the villa had worn. He would need to examine it more carefully to get a better feel for it. He would've preferred to test some of it against his guns, but that hadn't been an option.

According to Montrosse, Cervantes, and their people, it was a fresh Atlantican improvement on the cumbersome flak jackets Ty had used. He picked it up, looked it over, and poked the reinforced sections. Unless it was an ultra-tough material unknown to him, he doubted it would provide complete protection against multiple full-powered rifle rounds. It might stop one or two and would almost certainly offer him acceptable defense against pistol rounds, shrapnel, and the like.

He nodded. "Good, good. This will work."

Setting the larger bag aside, Tyler went over to the smaller one. He paused before it and lowered himself to his knees, falling into a traditional sitting position as a sign of respect.

As a way of testing Montrosse and the others—to determine if they would truly do as they had promised and provide him with whatever he asked for—Ty had requested something a little more esoteric, at least by their standards. They'd come through.

Ty unzipped the bag slowly. The movements of his hands were steady and cautious. Within was a vaguely oblong shape. It was, he knew, four separate objects held in place with a small amount of packing foam.

First, he pulled out most of the foam. Then he found the wooden stand, which was carved of oak and quite beautiful in a simple and functional way. He placed it on his desk.

Then, the swords.

He'd demanded from the Executives a set of *daisho*, the traditional full complement of blades in the culture of his forefathers. The katana, or long sword, the wakizashi short sword, and the tanto dagger, each with black silk wrapped over rayskin on the hilt, and a finely wrought brass *tsuka* handguard. If his benefactors hadn't lied to him, each blade was high-carbon steel forged more or less according to classical procedures. Although with one or two modern tweaks to improve the blades' reliability.

The cost would have been enormous. He and his family would never have been able to afford such a thing on their own before.

Ty turned the swords, still in their *saya* scabbards of lacquered wood, over in his hands. It was difficult not to regard them with something approaching outright reverence. A lump had formed in his throat, and he tried to ignore it.

His branch of the Katakura family—unrelated to the kin of Katakura Kojuro, who had served as noble retainers to the Date Clan—were of peasant stock, though after the Meiji Restoration they'd served honorably in the Army. Long ago, before the Tokugawa Shogunate had unified the country, it was not unheard of for peasants to rise to samurai status based on military service.

"We've come a long way," he whispered and arranged the three weapons on the oaken stand. The katana went on top and the tanto on the bottom, blades facing up in each case. "So have I. All the way to goddamn Atlantica. The only way to go now is up."

The total gear he'd requested possessed a dollar value that probably exceeded the worth of everything he'd ever owned in his life so far, as well as all the money he'd ever earned from odd jobs or his service in the U.S. military. In sixteen years he'd never had anything as expensive as the stuff he'd examined over the last ten minutes.

He reflected on his conversation with Eleanor over the specifics of how the Executive would fund his office. They'd gone over the details after leaving Lucas's office.

"Now," she'd begun, speaking in a soft voice while they'd traversed the second-floor hallway and descended the stairs, "the Executives will keep two further accounts open for your various needs, which you can draw funds from at any time."

He had tried not to scoff. "Two accounts, eh?"

"Yes. One for any tools, gear, equipment, and so forth you might require for the long-term success of your operation. Another to take care of typical daily needs. Food, fuel, admittance fees, ammunition, and so forth."

It was staggering to contemplate, given how long he'd lived in poverty. "How much is in each account, and when do they get refilled?"

Eleanor had laughed. "Don't worry about it. I *dare* you to try and deplete what's already in the accounts. You would probably fail."

Ty blinked, shoving aside the memories and returning to the present. His head spun with slight dizziness as he looked at his hands and thought about the responsibilities that would soon rest on him.

"I need," he breathed, turning his focus inward, "to earn this. To prove that I deserve it and am worthy of it. Not only to the Executives. They might have good enough reasons, but they're not the most important ones. I need to prove it to the common folk of Atlantica. They're the people who matter most. They're who I signed up to protect."

He turned, not looking at anything in particular. His gaze fell upon the vest of body armor. There was an insignia on the right shoulder. He hadn't noticed it before since he'd focused on inspecting it for its practical value.

Ty picked up the vest and looked at the emblem. Presumably, it depicted the official symbol and motto of the new office of the Executioners. A front profile skull stared outwards, and driven through it, point down, was a European-style cruciform sword. Beneath the skull's jaw, a curling banner framed the words "Justice Before Mercy."

Ty nodded. A harsh motto, but not necessarily an evil one.

He closed his eyes. "I promise, to myself and the memory of my family, that people will see this symbol as one of *honor*. Not of corruption and not of tyranny. For the sake of Atlantica's people, I will live up to the highest ideals that my office is capable of. I will *earn* the right to wear it, as I must deserve the right to wear those swords."

Memories, unbidden and unwanted, flashed in the dark space behind his eyes.

Acid pooled in his stomach as he saw again, for the hundredth time, the uniformed and grim-faced men who came for him and his family almost a quarter-century ago. Then the trucks that shuttled them away from their home to dump them off at the camp at Manzanar, where they'd waste years of their lives.

Then his brain moved ahead to early 1946, after they'd all been released, and returned to their family home. It wasn't theirs any longer. Now, some family called Adams owned the cozy house and tidy little property, people who were...*polite*...to them when they asked what had happened, but who weren't about to give up their new home. As Mr. Adams had explained, they'd gotten a good deal on it. All thanks to the government's generosity.

Then the Katakura family had searched for a new home and new ways to support themselves, traveling the length and breadth of California and not having much success. Ty's father, a decorated combat veteran of the American armed forces, had struggled to find work.

They made do. Somehow, they'd survived.

"Never again," Tyler said to himself. "I won't let it happen—to me, or, if it's within my power, to anyone else."

He picked up his gear, strapping himself in to prepare for his first assignment.

It came as no great surprise that Danny was waiting for him.

"Mr. Katakura," he opined, whistling and shaking his head, "you look all different in that getup. Holy..." he stopped and swallowed, probably as a way to control his language in case one of his parents was within earshot. "Is that a real samurai sword?"

Ty glanced down. He'd left the katana behind. Owing to its length, it might be cumbersome. But he had fastened the shorter wakizashi to his left hip, opposite his pistol. It never hurt to have an extra sidearm. Additionally, he'd strapped the tanto knife to his right calf.

He looked at the boy. "Yes, it is. Gifts from my new employers. It was sure nice of them, but it's only because I might need it. Later, when I'm not as busy, you can have a closer look. Please, though, do me a favor and don't go into my place until I get back. If you want to guard it, I can't think of a better man for the job."

Ty doubted that anyone in the community would try to rob him, but it was impossible to be entirely certain. They were poor people, and the poor sometimes did foolish things out of desperation. Still, given how well-respected he was, anyone who tried to steal from him would be denounced and thrown out of the town.

Danny blinked. "You want me to be your watchman? Okay, sure."

Ty smiled, nodded at the young man, and strode off toward the edge of town, near the mouth of the road between the hills. Seeing him go, a few of the townspeople waved and called their well-wishes. He waved back.

"I wish," he muttered, "that I could remember all of their names. I know pretty much all of their faces. Names are harder. They all know *me*. I ought to return the favor."

What he was about to do, ultimately, would be for their benefit.

Two trucks had stopped about fifty yards beyond the mouth of the road leading out of the valley. Both were military surplus, big, bulky, and dark grey rather than olive drab, but otherwise easy to identify. Canvas covered the blocky rear sections, but the entirety of both vehicles appeared to be armored. They would be relatively slow to accelerate and horribly inefficient on fuel, but it would take anti-tank weapons or a well-planted bomb to disable them.

Ty smiled grimly and advanced.

Eleanor Cervantes was there, dressed once again in a dress that looked too nice for the occasion, albeit this time in royal blue. As before, she wore incongruously rugged and pragmatic boots.

"Hello, Mr. Katakura," she greeted him. "I see that you're

63

making good use of your new equipment. It suits you." She nodded politely with a subdued smile.

Ty returned the gesture. "Thanks. So far, I have to say that I'm impressed with the Executives' generosity. I don't intend to abuse it. Especially since I consider it merely a sign that they're committed to giving me the tools I need to get the job done. I don't consider it a bribe."

Eleanor tittered. "Of course not." She held up her right hand, and a keyring dangled from her index finger. "One of these vehicles is for you. Can you drive a truck?"

"Yes," he told her. "It's been a long time, but I sometimes drove a similar class of vehicle back in Korea, and I drove a produce truck for a few months before I left the States. If there are any new bells and whistles on these things, someone will need to introduce me to them. I should be fine, otherwise."

She handed over the keys, and he slipped them into his pocket. Before he could ask if they were ready to leave yet, a tall, gangly white man appeared from around the side of the truck. He was wearing fatigues that were much the same ashy color as the trucks themselves along with a plain cap. A 1911 pistol much like Ty's hung holstered at his side. He waited with his hands folded behind his back.

Ty inclined his head toward the man. "Who's that?"

Without looking, Ms. Cervantes stated, "Senior Officer MacLeod. I'll introduce you to him momentarily, but first, we'll allow you to examine the truck."

Ty would have preferred to know who the individual was, but he went along with Eleanor's preferred order of business for the time being. He scanned the vehicle again.

"This thing is going to guzzle gas like a drunk during happy hour," he grunted. "Even by the standards of your Executives, bringing in that much fuel could get difficult."

Now, Eleanor's smile broadened. "That's one of the features I wanted to show you. Come this way, please." She beckoned and stepped toward the front of the truck. As Tyler followed, she popped the hood and braced it. "Observe."

Ty peered into the front end's interior and was momentarily speechless. His jaw fell open until he realized how stupid he probably looked and closed it.

A cluster of blue stones, jagged and crystalline, lay near the center of the engine block. Or, rather, it had *replaced* the engine block. A complex harness of cables was plugged into the sky-blue surface, running out to every part of the machine that might require power.

Eleanor waved over the bizarre contraption. "Atlanticore crystals," she explained. "Already, the best minds in Atlantica have begun putting them to good use. Don't worry if you're uncertain; we've tested them, and this vehicle has been running well for over a month."

"Well," Ty responded in a low voice and rubbed the side of his nose. "I imagine it was only a matter of time until I got to see the things in action. I've heard of them. They're the most valuable thing we have here, aren't they? Supposed to be some kind of miracle energy source. No wonder the common folks don't get to see or handle them. Unless they're mining them out of the ground."

Clearing her throat, Eleanor added, "Yes, they're supremely valuable. You might not have seen, but I opened the hood with a small key, like the one on your ring. That's to protect what's inside. Please do not *advertise* that Atlanticore powers the truck. There's no reason for the general public to know that a crystal of this size lies within it.

"Accessing it without the proper keys is difficult. Still, it's worth enough to warrant caution on your part. No vehicle, safety box, building, or anything else is completely impregnable."

"Understood," Ty acknowledged.

Eleanor closed the hood and motioned for the military-looking gentleman to come over, which he did.

"Mr. Katakura," she began, "this is Senior Officer MacLeod. Mac, this is Tyler Katakura."

The tall man extended a broad, bony hand, and Ty shook it. "Pleased to meet you," MacLeod rasped. His voice was so age-roughened, perhaps also by whiskey and cigarettes, that it was difficult to tell if he was Scottish American or simply Scottish. His mustache had once been red but had lost most of its color, giving it the appearance of a strip of rusty iron across his face. "Sounds like the Executives were impressed with your abilities. I've heard a lot about you."

Ty nodded. So far, nothing about the man specifically indicated that he should either trust or mistrust him. He kept his demeanor neutral. A bit of cautious probing should reveal whatever was necessary to know.

"So," Ty inquired, "what is it you're here for?"

"Security," the man stated. His mixture of gruffness and relaxation was, oddly enough, reassuring. Still...

Eleanor stepped in closer and added, "Officer MacLeod will be supervising the town's protection while you're in pursuit of other points of concern. We understand that you've grown attached to these people and want to ensure that they're not defenseless while you're engaged elsewhere."

Ty raised an eyebrow. "Well, that's good." He turned back toward the Scot.

"I know everyone who lives here, and they know me. Their protection has been my business for some time now. As far as I'm concerned, it's *still* my business. In agreeing to my new position, I specified that they would stay protected from outside aggression but otherwise be left alone. I'd like it to stay that way. Any infractions against them are something I would be willing to deal with personally."

MacLeod bobbed his head and laughed a little, the sound like crunching gravel. "We understand. We're here to keep things peaceful. Oh, and you can call me Mac."

"Mac," Ty repeated. "I'll trust you. Don't betray that trust."

The older officer didn't seem cowed or offended. He took everything in stride, preferring to save his energy and his feelings for more serious matters than mere verbal threats. Ty decided that he liked the man. Provided he was telling the truth, he was probably up to the job and wouldn't tolerate any bullshit.

Ty suspected that by drawing a line in the sand regarding how others should treat his people, he'd earned the starchy fellow's respect.

Mac nodded and turned away. Five other men, outfitted and armed like him, had leapt down from the truck. They conferred among themselves on how best to keep watch over the little settlement. One of them would also bring Eleanor back to the city, then scout the outer edges of the town on his return.

Ty listened for a moment, then turned to Eleanor. "Let me introduce Mac and the others to the community. Then you can tell me what you have for me to do. My people are understandably wary about armed newcomers. I'd like things to start off on the right foot."

"Of course." She motioned for him to take care of the matter.

A few minutes later, Ty had introduced Mac, explained what he and his men were there to do, and had left his people's safety in their hands after receiving Mrs. Bertollini's barely imperceptible nod. He returned to Eleanor at a brisk walk. "All right then, Ms. Cervantes. Where am I going?"

"The coast." She put a hand on his arm and drew him closer to his new vehicle, lowering her voice. "A small community of fishermen has been claiming of late that smugglers have appeared on the scene. They're under pressure to collaborate with these individuals and pay them 'protection money' or offer them services for free.

"At one point, the smugglers commandeered a fishing boat for their permanent usage. When problems developed with the vessel, the smugglers assumed that the fishermen had sabotaged it and they've been threatening to retaliate with deadly force."

Ty snorted. "Sounds like a great bunch of people. Steal things from hardworking types, then complain that it isn't good enough for them. Yeah...I can deal with them. One way or another."

He climbed into the driver's seat. It was exciting, being behind the wheel of such a large and powerful vehicle after how long he'd been relegated to walking anywhere he needed to go. Or sailing.

Eleanor approached and stood beside his leg at the opened door. "We knew you could handle it. But don't you want directions to the part of the coast where this happened?"

"Sure. I can probably guess based on where the heaviest fishing activity is or figure it out myself by trial and error. For the money you're paying me, it might be in *your* best interest to save time by giving me the specifics."

Eleanor laughed. "Exactly."

CHAPTER EIGHT

Ty could no longer ignore the grin creeping across his face. Driving the big, Atlanticore-powered truck was so much damn *fun*.

It rattled down the winding road, sometimes seeming at first to be on the verge of spinning out of control, but as long as he corrected its course every time it lurched a bit, its sheer mass kept it holding steady. It was probably the largest vehicle he'd ever piloted. Getting used to it had taken a minute, and the brief climb into the hills immediately surrounding the labor town had been awkward and laborious.

Then he got the hang of the surprisingly responsive wheel, the heavy but well-calibrated brakes, and lengthy stopping distance. He soon adjusted to how the huge vehicle handled going around turns and the quirks of its groans, sighs, and rumbles.

"God," he muttered, "I missed driving."

He shook his head and refocused on the task at hand. According to the directions Eleanor had given him, which he'd hastily jotted down on a slip of paper, he was almost there.

Not that the directions were all that necessary. The fishing community she'd mentioned was exactly the one he'd expected it to be—another squatter town, about half again as large as his in the valley, which had grown up along the northwest coast of the island. He'd been through there once or twice shortly after he'd first arrived on Atlantica.

Then again, since he had come, so had others. The settlement might have grown enough in the meantime to have subdivided.

Ty reached over and switched on his radio, pulling out the microphone to hold it near his mouth once he'd found the appropriate frequency. After the static cleared, Eleanor's voice came in. "Mr. Katakura? Hello. What do you need? Over."

"Just wanted to ask," he began, "is that fishing settlement still a single village? I haven't been there in a while, so I'm wondering if there are currently two, three, four villages side-by-side and if only one might've been having the issues with the smugglers. Over."

Eleanor paused a moment before she answered him. "As far as I know, it's still a single community. Even if that weren't the case, the smugglers would likely have tried to extort all the villages equally. Proceed as planned. Over."

"Roger. Out." He hung up the mic and switched off the radio.

Fortunately, a crude road led around the northwestern periphery of the city and out to the coast where the fishermen dwelled. Based on what Ty had seen of the road quality and traffic situation in the burgeoning metropolis, trying to direct his truck through its center would have been a severe hassle. He shuddered at the thought.

"No escaping it forever, though." He shrugged. "They'll need me in town soon. At least I'm getting some practice time behind the wheel beforehand."

He had passed beyond the broad, flat plain. The terrain grew more unforgiving as the road began to hug closer to the sea.

Strangely or ironically, the most productive fishing waters off Atlantica's coast were adjacent to some of the island's most rugged, mysterious, and unsettled tracts of land. The dirt track that led away from the central area skirted the edge of a hilly, densely forested badland whose strange temperate jungles stayed perpetually swathed in mist.

Rumors spread, of course. People chatted drunkenly or whispered to one another late at night about what might be lurking in those mysterious woods. Human habitation on the isle was restricted to the coasts and the central plain so far—or, in the case of Ty's recently adopted home and a handful of other villages, the foothills close to the plain. Other parts of Atlantica were still a shadowy wilderness.

He wondered how long it would take. People were afraid, for the time being. The fact that Atlantica had remained hidden from humans for so long, its strange and sometimes paradoxical weather and foliage, its unique mineral wealth... All of those factors had revived a certain primitive and superstitious dread when discussing what might lie in the unexplored regions.

In the end, greed and necessity were stronger forces than fear. Sooner or later people would move into the fog-shrouded jungle and begin to cut it down to make room for new developments. That would be a good thing in some ways. Less so in others. It would tame one of the world's last true frontiers.

Then Ty turned a corner, and the village appeared. He blinked, stiffened, and shook his head, clearing it of random speculation and refocusing on his mission. He did occasionally tend to drift off into rumination and even daydreaming. Still, his years of combat experience had taught him the skill of instantly getting back on the clock when necessary.

Based on what he could see, it was even *more* necessary than he'd anticipated.

A small convoy of vehicles—three, unless there were others somewhere out of sight—had arrived in the settlement, seemingly not long before Ty. There was one big closed-bed truck and two long sedans. Around ten men had occupied them. Ty counted six near the center of town, with at least three others stomping and shoving through the gathering crowd.

It looked like they were herding the fisherfolk away from their homes or boats and toward the beach, in between two docks. A crowd of at least fifty people already huddled there, silent and terrified.

Ty breathed in deep through his nose and let it out slowly through his mouth. Whatever he was about to get into, he could not, under any circumstances, assume that things would work out *nicely*. It behooved a man to expect the worst.

As much as he liked his truck, its size and noisiness meant that he would be spotted momentarily. There was no sneaking into the village undetected.

He cleared his mind of all cluttering thoughts. It was time to be ready for anything.

The fishing town had been haphazardly thrown together along the shoreline according to similar principles as his home up in the valley. Most buildings were scarcely more than sheds or shacks, aside from a smattering of larger, communal structures, which were more like barns. They were all far enough back from the water to avoid flooding at high tide. There wasn't much room available before the rocky crags of the jungled hills began. Thus, the community formed a long strip, rarely more than one or two buildings deep.

Again, there were two major docks, and the bulk of the available boats were tethered to one of these, though a few other, smaller craft were simply moored on the beach at the far ends of the town and secured crudely with ropes tied around boulders or stakes driven deeply into the mud.

The place smelled of fish and sea salt. Ty couldn't see any fish though, at least for the time being. He wondered where it all had gone.

Coming closer, he squinted. The strange men would get a

look at him shortly. He wanted an idea of how well-armed they were before anything else.

Only one of them had a rifle. It was difficult to tell what type it was from a distance, but an old bolt-action, full-length battle rifle, beyond any doubt. Probably a Lee Enfield or a Karabiner 98k. He didn't think it was a Mosin-Nagant. The others either held submachine guns, pistols, or nothing at all, but the ones in the last category likely had weapons of their own concealed somewhere on their person.

"Well," Ty muttered, his tone dark, "I hope the rifle guy knows he has a target painted on his back. He goes first." He patted his armor. The manufacturer rated it against all known pistol-caliber rounds.

Then the crowd noticed him. One of the gunmen was first to look up. Less than a second after, his face turned toward the rambling approach of the truck. Others did likewise among his thuggish-looking buddies and the locals. There were still a few seconds to spare. How they all reacted in the space of the next half a dozen heartbeats would determine what came next.

Ty slung his rifle over his shoulder as he watched them, his brain preparing itself for any of four or five possible courses of action. *If* he could resolve the situation without firing a shot, he would.

If not...

The armed men began to regroup. Another one, whom Ty hadn't seen, emerged from the line of buildings along with two fishers who'd been hiding. A line of four men massed out in Ty's direction, aiming their weapons at the truck.

Two others grabbed locals roughly by the arms and forced them to their knees. A woman and an older man shuddered and clasped their hands as pistols were pressed to the sides of their heads.

Ty's lips drew back from his teeth. He had only two options.

The first of those involved immediately braking, looking at

the thugs for directions, and trying to negotiate with them from a position of weakness, assuming that they were too heavily armed, well organized, and ruthless to confront directly.

"No. If there are any negotiations, they're going to be on *my* terms. Fuck these pricks."

Ty stomped on the gas pedal.

People amid the gaggle of fisherfolk screamed in horror as the truck barreled toward the center of town. The smugglers shouted and barked orders. Two men out in front opened fire with their submachine guns, and Ty ducked. The bullets ricocheted harmlessly off the truck's armored hood, sides, and grille. None hit the windshield.

"Shit!" someone cried. The four men who'd tried to form a human roadblock all ran and dove aside for cover.

The truck rushed past them, directly into the cluster of cars and trucks. Ty picked up speed as he came downhill. A surge of savage glee sprang up from the bottom of his heart and filled him with energy and drive. His lips split into a grin.

Metal screamed as the armored truck ripped the entire back end off one of the sedans. The nicer one, probably the ride of whoever their leader was. The front half of the car spun aside, wobbling and skidding across the muddy ground, while the rear half crumpled into a mass of sparking detritus against the grille of Ty's hoss.

He glanced to the side. Two or three of the gunmen stared at him with open mouths, too stunned to open fire. The others cursed and hollered at one another, advancing toward him and shoving civilians out of their way.

The locals either screamed and ducked or stood frozen in fear. None tried to flee. Their backs were against the ocean, and the thugs had them penned in.

"Okay," Ty said, "time to get a little more up close and personal." He stomped on the brake.

The truck squealed and swung around, trying to fishtail but prevented from moving much by the mud and wet sand as it got closer to the sea. Water splashed as the wheels entered the shallows. Ty took firm hold of his rifle, did a quick calculation as to how and when the truck would come to a complete stop, and opened the door, bursting out of it while the vehicle was still in motion.

The truck lurched, and his stomach did likewise. There was a brief sickening sensation as he thought he might crash into the hood, but then the vehicle kept rolling forward as its rear swung gradually around in a circle.

He sailed through the air for a second or two, hit the ground hard, and rolled, tucking his rifle beneath himself to protect it. Then he sprang to his feet.

The voice of the men who had occupied the village rang out, echoing across the beach. "Get over there! Surround him!"

Ty moved closer to the armored truck, which was rolling at last to a stop. Out of habit, he positioned himself beside the hood, putting the engine block between himself and the thugs. It was probably unnecessary since the whole truck was armored. But the hood was also barely low enough that he could rest the barrel of his rifle across it, aiming it while remaining mostly behind cover.

All ten of the men from the cars came into his line of sight. None of them were trying too hard to flank him—probably because they didn't want to move too far away from the civilians and risk any of them escaping or attacking from behind.

Since Ty hadn't opened fire yet, the men were hesitating. He wasn't about to grant them the initiative to begin their friendly discussion.

"Attention," he pronounced, liking the way his voice boomed across the shoreline. "I am the first Executioner of Atlantica, empowered by the people of this island to enforce justice on those who earn its wrath. I know who you are. I know why you're here. Now is your chance to peaceably disperse. Get out while you still can, and leave these people alone."

A couple of the smugglers scoffed or muttered things to their friends in foreign languages. Ty guessed French, which would mean that at least some of them were probably Quebecois from the mainland. The others were a motley band. Like everyone else on Atlantica, they'd come from all corners of the world to try their hand and make their fortune.

Someone pushed to the front. A squat man, brawny and tough-looking despite being short, wore a fine cap tilted to the side on his head and carried a polished Russian submachine gun with a drum magazine. Ty could never remember the name of the firearm despite having faced the damn things in Korea.

"You," the man called, waving a thick hand, "you have no right to be here. Executor, you say? We don't know what that is. Get out! This is none of your business." The accent was possibly Greek. Ty couldn't be sure. He also wasn't sure whether the man had deliberately used "Executor" instead, but he dismissed it from mind.

Tyler's vision focused on them. The guy with the rifle—which was indeed a Lee Enfield—had come up alongside the group's boss and was taking a bead on the intruder.

"No," said Ty. "It *is* my business."

The leader raised his submachine gun and fired, the familiar sound of it like a buzzsaw, though the rounds all sparked and shattered uselessly against the truck's armored shell. The others raised their guns.

Ty's mind shifted gears as easily as the truck had while driving, adjusting and adapting to the situation. *Zanshin*, the state of remaining mind, the paradoxically relaxed alertness. *Mushin*, the state of no-mind, the purely intuitive and reflexive version of the human consciousness that could deal with any problem and confront and overcome any obstacle.

In one fast, fluid motion, he stepped out from behind the corner of the truck, lowered and aimed his rifle, and fired twice.

The man out in front, involuntarily blasting his old British rifle into the sky, took the first of the two 7.62mm rounds through the eye. He jerked backward, twitching, as red mist appeared in the air behind his head. Then he fell to the ground like a sandbag someone had thoughtlessly dropped.

The second bullet struck the ground between the feet of another guy next to the first. "Shit!" he exclaimed, stumbling backward and losing the sight picture he'd been lining up with his revolver.

More gunshots rang out as the other smugglers opened fire. While the squat leader retreated to the back of the group, Ty put his head down and ducked farther along the side of the truck, toward the front end where pieces of the sedan were still half-attached from the earlier impact.

Two bullets struck home. One hit Ty above the right nipple. The other found its mark against his helmet. His heart leapt into his throat, but he knew he was well-protected. The first round vanished within the heavy material of his body armor. The second deflected, although his skull rattled from the impact and he had to blink and shake his head to reset his vision.

When he regained clear sight, his eyes bulged in terror and anger. Two civilians pounced upon the nearest smuggler and bashed his head with rocks, and now three men were turning toward them to retaliate. The others kept shooting at Ty.

"No," he whispered. Ty raised his rifle and squeezed off four shots. One struck the water near the crowd of locals, kicking up a tall column of spray. One each struck two of the guys preparing to shoot at the civilians. They screamed and crumpled into the shallows. The fourth hit a stand of barrels where the other men had grouped, causing two of them to flinch.

Then Ty charged. His foes had spent most of their magazines

blasting away at the truck, and half of them were frantically attempting to reload.

Despite their superior numbers, they'd already lost four men, and the ferocity of the assault had broken their morale. The time to crush and overwhelm them was now.

Ty aimed down the sights of his AR-10 and dumped the entire rest of the magazine at the half-dozen remaining thugs. He took another two bullets to the torso, but with their rifleman out of the fight, none of their remaining weapons could overcome his armor. Two of them fell bleeding and shuddering under his barrage while the remainder of them dove for cover.

Then someone scored a lucky hit, striking Ty's rifle in the magazine. The mag was torn halfway out of its well, and the weapon spun from his hands. Not bothering to reconsider, thinking of nothing but pressing his advantage to victory, he drew his 1911 and ran toward them.

Amid the confusion, he saw one of the smugglers standing perhaps three or four yards away, his right side toward Ty, frozen in an instant's hesitation between the option of turning toward his enemy or running away. The man clenched a Carl Gustaf m/45 submachine gun in white-knuckled hands.

Ty raised his pistol and squeezed the trigger twice. He wasn't sure about the second bullet. It might've hit the guy in the upper scalp area, or it might've gone clear of his head altogether after the muzzle rise pulled the gun off-target.

However, the first round went right through his ear. Blood poured from the other side of his head, and he spun, went limp, and crashed into the empty fish barrels behind him, dropping his weapon.

Two other men opened fire with handguns. Gritting his teeth, Ty ran and jumped and rolled. He would have to trust that their aim was less than expert—or if it were true, that it would strike him where armor protected his body. If the fight went on much longer, they might start thinking rationally enough to shoot him in the legs, arms, face, or throat.

A bullet glanced off the side of his vest. It felt like someone kicking him, but without as much force as he might've feared. Then he sprang out of his roll as his hands found the fallen submachine gun. It came up into a firing position at the same time he did.

Ty blasted away at the trio of men on the other side of the square. The Gustaf roared to life, spitting 9mm slugs at a relatively slow rate but fast enough to disperse the smugglers. All of them dropped or flew aside. Ty doubted he'd hit more than one of them, perhaps none at all, but laying down suppressive fire would be good enough for the moment. It would buy him space to get his goddamn rifle back.

He sprayed lead until the gun ran dry, moving sidelong toward the cluster of barrels, and tossed it aside after it *clicked* empty. By the time the smugglers noticed, he'd already ducked behind cover.

He couldn't find his AR-10. It had fallen somewhere out of sight and nowhere close to his current position. He strangled and dismissed any thought of panic or surrender. There was no time for that.

He raised his pistol and fired a single shot to make the men jumpy, then did a visual scan. Only two remained. He might've taken out more than he'd thought with his volley from the Gustaf. One appeared to be the leader. The other was a scrawny hayseed who looked about as twitchy and nervous as an oversized pumpkin the week before Halloween.

Somewhere in the background, the civilians were sobbing and gibbering in terror. Ty had no idea if any of them had been wounded or killed yet.

He released the magazine from his pistol, so the distinctive sound echoed in the momentary silence, but caught it and slapped it back as soon as the ruse took effect. The Greekaccented leader barked, "No!" but the skinny guy took the bait, bounding up from cover to try and finish Ty off.

Ty brought the pistol up in a flash and put two .45 caliber slugs in the center of the man's chest. He staggered back, face taut with confused disbelief, and slumped to the ground.

Then the leader charged, roaring in fury.

"Fuck," Ty spat, re-aiming his pistol. He still had three rounds left. Enough to finish the—

The stout man opened fire with his Russian submachine gun, dumping dozens of the small rounds at an incredible, buzzsaw-like rate of fire, and Ty's heart skipped a beat. He'd forgotten how much ammo those drum mags held.

He ducked and tried to protect himself, firing one more shot from his 1911 before the onslaught of lead took its toll. The pistol fell from his grip, and the sheer number of bullets drove him back. If he'd taken any to the limbs, he was unaware of it. The adrenaline was flowing too strongly for him to register pain.

When he looked up, though, the shooting had stopped, and the leader was bolting across the beach. "Out of the way!" he barked, shouldering aside frozen fishermen and still carrying his finally empty gun. He hopped behind the wheel of the undamaged sedan, which still had the keys in the ignition.

Ty sprang forward. There was no time to look for his guns, so he half-ducked and swiped up a fallen .357 Magnum revolver mid-stride. The car's engine started, and the leader began his escape, trying to drive in the opposite direction from which Ty had come.

"No," Ty stated. In a second or two, the car would be out of range, but for the moment it was only about fifteen or twenty yards away. He aimed, hoping the gun was still loaded, and fired. Two shots rang out before the cylinder *clicked* dry.

One of the rear tires exploded. The vehicle swayed and veered toward a shallow ditch that the villagers had dug at the far end of the town, designed to direct rainwater downhill toward their waiting buckets and troughs. The car crashed and lay still.

Ty sprinted, crossing the ground in seconds. It occurred to him as he reached the side of the sedan that all he had on him was an empty handgun and his sword and knife. But the leader was probably dead or unconscious.

He looked in through the windows. No one was inside.

A strangled cry sounded from the rear of the vehicle as the stout Greek pounced. He'd slipped out the other side either right before or right after the crash, though his clothes were bloody.

Ty reflexively sidestepped the attack, and the man's thick arms missed him by an inch. In the same motion, his right hand went to his leg, sliding the tanto out of its hiding place.

The leader spun with surprising speed and lunged at him again, but Ty had the blade up. In a single fluid stroke, he stepped past and outside the man's grasping strike while drawing the tanto's edge across his throat.

The leader squawked and gurgled, his hands clutching his neck, but it was too late. He collapsed to his knees, knowing he'd lost.

Then it was over. Ty moved to the side and slowly stood straight, allowing the corpse to slump over. The man's blood flowed out in a torrent, staining the mud and sinking into the ground. Ty dodged most of it. Bright red coated his tanto's blade. He wiped it off on the smuggler's pant leg, then inverted it in his grip and slid it back into its sheath along his calf.

Silence reigned along the shoreline, aside from the calls of a pair of gulls.

CHAPTER NINE

A shudder went through him, the delayed shakes of a hard-fought battle combined with a suppressed sigh of faint revulsion at the necessity of spilling so much blood. Not that he regretted it. The people he had killed were trying to kill *him* and threatening to do the same to the villagers.

He turned toward the fisherfolk. They'd barely moved from their huddled position on the beach between the docks. They stared and cowered as the tide came in around their ankles. Only the two young men who'd brained one of the thugs with rocks had done anything at all.

Ty walked closer to them. It was time for a friendly chat.

Near the front of the crowd was a man of sixty or so, with a bent back but otherwise powerful-looking for his age. His long bushy beard was mostly a salty white but with remaining flecks of darker colors. His thick arms folded inward near his waist and his hands grasped an old wooden cane whose point dug into the ground before his booted feet.

Ty looked at the man. He would've been surprised if the bearded fellow turned out *not* to be the settlement's unofficial leader. "I've come to help you, where these men came to steal from you and threaten you. They won't any longer. And you, sir," he called, "what do you have to say about all this?"

The elder glanced at Ty, then back at the dead smugglers. "I already said all that need be said. To them, and now to you. We're simple fishers, that's all. We don't want trouble from nobody."

Ty couldn't help snorting. "That's strange. Looks to me like you already got it."

A girl amid the group, who had been placid till now, covered her face with her hands and groaned.

The older man with the salt-colored beard looked down at the bodies of the thugs before returning his gaze to the battle-armored young Japanese man moving toward him.

"They had friends," he pointed out. "There were more of them than this. Killing these men might scare them off, or it might make them want revenge. Reprisals against us. They could send more to burn down our whole town. What do we do *then?*"

Ty frowned, stopping about four yards in front of the man. For a moment it had looked as though the crowd might cheer. Their fear and uncertainty were wavering, and seeing Ty prevail over their tormentors had sent a ripple of energy and inspiration through them. The younger folks' eyes were wide and shining, and the older ones held their shoulders back and heads up higher.

Now, the exchange between Ty and their elder had ruined everything. The older man was right. That didn't mean Tyler had to like it.

"If they come back," he declared, "they will suffer the same fate as their comrades, or worse. As I said when I first arrived, I am the Executioner. *They* should fear *me* more than you should fear them."

Murmurs and whispers went through the crowd. Bodies shifted.

Someone asked, "The Exec—what? Like one o' them guys in

Middle Age times with the hood who chopped people's heads off?"

Ty grimaced, but the expression might as well have been a wolfish smile if he'd opened his mouth. "Close enough. My position on Atlantica is new. Someone has to keep the peace and enforce justice. Those who hired me have given me total authority to deal with people like this." He gestured toward the dead. "They wouldn't obey my command to disperse. They made an even worse mistake in trying to kill me."

Old Saltbeard, as Ty had mentally nicknamed him, clasped his hands atop his cane. "Do you plan to deal with us the same way as them? We've had dealings with smugglers before. Is that against this new law? Because there ain't been no law on Atlantica. None except what people agree to. Or what they're strong enough to make happen themselves."

The geezer had a point. "You people," he announced, sweeping his arm in front of him to encompass them all, "are mostly honest, hardworking sorts, aren't you? I came here because I heard they stole a boat of yours and threatened to murder some of you after they had problems with it. If there are to be laws, then the law should stop things like *that* from happening. Your minor infractions from before aren't my concern."

The older man, and the rest of them, relaxed a little.

A stringy-haired woman stepped forth. "Aye, it's true, we've worked with some of the boatmen who smuggled things off the island. You can't ship things out, otherwise. Nothing is supposed to leave this place. All thanks to TINA. How much longer they goin' to keep up that charade?"

For an instant, Ty thought she might be referring to an actual human being, but the mention of a "charade" clarified things instantly. The woman was referring, of course, to the acronym for the various world governments' collaborative policy regarding the isle—"There Is No Atlantica."

Officially, this place didn't exist. Officially, no one lived here at all.

Tyler glanced around, taking a quick account of the weapons left by the dead men. The fisherfolk would undoubtedly confiscate them for their protection, which was probably for the best, so there was no point in Ty intervening in the situation one way or another.

He looked back at the lady with stringy hair. "I don't know. The Executives have plans for this place. Atlantica in general, I mean. They want peace and stability. People like you are the lifeblood of the economy here. It's not in their best interests to let these kinds of thugs abuse you. As for whether they'll tell the rest of the world to acknowledge that this island is real...I can't say."

More rumblings and gossip.

"*But*," Ty added, in a louder and sharper tone, and he locked eyes with the whole group at once, "it won't matter as far as your protection is concerned. Defend yourselves as you must, but there will be more like me. No one will prey upon you as long as I, and anyone under my command, has anything to say about it. You saw what I did alone. Imagine if there were others like me. Soon."

A hush fell over the crowd. Perhaps they were frightened of *him*. In a way, that might be a good thing. Still, he was their defender, their champion. They would have to learn to trust him.

Though his long face frowned, Old Saltbeard nodded. "All right, very well, yes. You damn well put a stop to whatever they were planning to do to us today. But the rest of them will be back. Or others like them. It's not like they came out of nowhere. We had a business arrangement that went sour, you see."

Tyler had begun dragging a couple of the bodies toward an open stretch of ground away from the water, wooden shacks, and docks so the fisherfolk could safely cremate them *en masse*. Dropping off the body of the stocky leader, he turned back to the fishermen.

"Tell me all about it, then." His left hand came to rest upon the hilt of his wakizashi.

The stringy-haired woman was the first to start filling in the details. "Well, sir, like I said, we always worked with some of the boat smugglers. People need things from the mainland or have things they need to sell off the island so they can afford to support their families, and the smuggling types can make that happen."

Ty nodded. "Yes, I understand. Go on."

Old Saltbeard picked up where the woman left off. "About a month or so ago, we got this new crew. Rougher sort of people. The men you see there were among them, of course. They had heavier backers. Rich people, dangerous people, I'd guess. They wanted more secrecy for whatever it was they were moving. They were into something serious. Very concerned with keeping prying eyes away."

By now, some of the crowd had begun to disperse. Ty saw a young couple looking toward him as though for his approval. He nodded. Their faces relaxed with blatant relief, and they quietly slipped away. Others did likewise, leaving the more senior and important folks among the community to speak to the Executioner.

They explained the situation further. Ty listened, patient and intent. The new crop of smugglers didn't only wish to work with the fisherfolk but insisted on "renting" their boats for a small fee while making drop-offs with their contacts.

Ty asked, "You accepted the deal?"

"We got no choice in the matter," Saltbeard protested. "They was pretty clear. People would get hurt if we didn't do what they wanted. And don't go asking what they wanted to transport that was so secret. They never told us, and we didn't think it was smart to snoop around."

It was starting to make sense. Prodding them further, Ty found that the community was becoming comfortable with the arrangement after a couple of weeks, but the real trouble began when one of the boats didn't come back. For that, the smugglers blamed *them*, accusing them of sabotaging it and claiming they would pay dearly if it happened again.

Then, two days ago, a second vessel failed to return as well. The smugglers looked around and found their people dead in the water, surrounded by wreckage, as though a bomb had destroyed the boat. This, the men asserted, was all the proof they needed that they needed to teach the fishing community a lesson.

The wild-haired woman added, "But we had nothing to do with it! Why would we go out of our way to make enemies of people like them?"

Ty nodded. "I believe you. There's more going on here than any of us know about. So far."

He cleared his throat and raised his voice for an announcement. "I'm going to try and figure out who these bastards were working with. Anyone want to volunteer to help me? I could use a couple of assistants. Mainly to comb through their cars and see if they have anything in there that could shed some light on this stuff."

Only a third or so of the original crowd remained, most of the fisherfolk having slipped off to their houses, to the docks, or their boats. Of the ones who'd lingered to hear Ty speak, a handful brightened with interest at the prospect of aiding him.

Three men, two quite young and another middle-aged, as well as a thirtyish woman, offered their services.

"Okay," said Ty. "You three, start by searching the back half of that nice Ford. You," he pointed at one of the younger guys, "help me check the truck. Not mine; the other one."

They did their best, combing through the two vehicles nearer the center and the crashed car in the far ditch where the smugglers' leader had almost escaped. Little of interest turned up. Extra ammo. A bit of cash. Cigarettes, soda bottles, a flask of whiskey. A map of the western coastal region near the village. That was all.

Ty sighed and scratched his head as his helpers massed around him.

"Well," he began, "I'm a soldier by trade, more so than a detective. If there's some big, fat, important clue here, I don't see it."

The middle-aged man admitted, "Us neither. Don't think they were stupid enough to bring anything that would give away their whole game. But, you know..."

Everyone's eyes turned to him as his voice grew quieter.

"...you could try talking to a woman in the city. A lady who spends her time at Absentees—a club for people who don't want to be bothered much, you see. Her name is Daria Barruk."

Ty glanced at the faces of the others for any hints as to who this woman was, but they only looked curious. He got no sense of dread from them. "Who is she?"

The young woman among the group stated, "Oh, she's a smuggler. One of the good ones, though. Always dealt with us fairly, never used threats or violence to get what she wanted, unless the other people in her profession tried to get rough with her."

Ty shrugged. It sounded like as good a prospect as any, although he didn't relish the thought of walking into some den of vipers on unfamiliar turf.

"I'll see if I can find her or arrange a meeting. Thank you folks for your help. Soon, you'll have a way to get in touch with me if you need anything. If the friends of the men I killed come back, tell them exactly who's responsible. Their quarrel is with *me*, not you."

The fisherfolk agreed, and Tyler went to his truck, driving it back toward the edge of the village before he fired up his radio and contacted Eleanor Cervantes. He wanted her input before he made his next move.

The radio crackled. "Yes, Mr. Katakura? Over."

"Hi, Eleanor. Rough workday so far..." He explained what had happened, giving her chances to respond, but she patiently waited to hear everything until at length he reached the part about the suggestion that he meet a known smuggler in the city. Eleanor seemed totally unfazed by everything she heard.

She made a low sound in her throat. "Yes, thank you for the update. May I call you back soon? I can, perhaps, acquire some information about this Ms. Barruk, as the name sounds familiar. Is there anything else?"

"Yeah," Ty added. He was mildly disturbed that Cervantes didn't express much concern over all the violence, but such was the way of things on Atlantica. "Some of my budget is going toward helping these people repair damage to their huts, docks, and freshwater ditch system. Damage done by the smugglers, and also by me. This is non-negotiable. They're not bearing the cost of the recovery by themselves. Over."

Eleanor paused. "Yes, that's fine. Your accounts contain ample funds. Out."

He hung up, sighed, and ran a hand through his black hair, moist with sea spray and sweat, and possibly blood.

"Already," he mumbled, thinking of what lay ahead, and hoping his donations would be enough to make up for the village's troubles, "this job is more complicated than the bastards made it sound."

CHAPTER TEN

Ty had been on the road for about twenty minutes when Eleanor called him back.

The drive away from the coastal fishing village had been peaceful. His visit there had, at first, erupted into sudden violence right from the get-go, only to then trail off into reconciliation, discussion, and uncertainty. It had put him into a thoughtful mood. His progress along the dirt track hadn't been interrupted by any other vehicles.

When Eleanor came through on the radio was right when the rural sticks were beginning to fade away, and the telltale signs of his proximity to the city were returning.

Ty picked up the microphone. "It's Tyler. Ms. Cervantes, is that you? Over." He doubted it could be anyone else, but it had occurred to him that she might have assistants or be only one of several people of equal rank who performed similar functions for the Executives.

Her familiar voice responded. "Yes, Mr. Katakura, hello. You were fortunate. You caught me when I didn't have anything else pressing to do, so I could investigate your query immediately. I've already turned up some information that might be useful to you."

He mused on how good, and how extensive, her contacts must have been to have had such rapid success. Although granted, human settlements on Atlantica were small enough that there was only limited territory to cover. Not to mention she worked for people who pretty much owned the whole island.

"This place you mentioned, Absentees," Cervantes went on, "is an entertainment establishment, a club. But it's not an ordinary one. I was able to ask several people who had been there or who knew individuals who had, and it seems that the consensus in the underground is clear. Absentees is a refuge."

She paused, and though she hadn't said "over," Ty felt it appropriate to interrupt.

"Pardon me, but a refuge for what? Or *from* what? I'm guessing it has something to do with smuggling. Over."

Eleanor laughed. "Of course. You're observant, as always. Smugglers and other sorts of criminals all attend this club. Even by the standards of Atlantica, it's an establishment that attracts a rough crowd. No one I spoke to seemed to know who owns it or protects it.

"The agreement is that underworld types can go there with the expectation of peace and safety...from one another, mostly. It's a neutral territory, a place where feuds and gang wars aren't allowed. Anyone can go there and have time for themselves. Without fear of robbery, assault, or assassination, as would be the case in open territory in the world of criminals. Over."

"Yeah," Ty muttered, in a low, dry tone, "that sounds about like what I'd guessed. Good thing I'm not a criminal."

He'd come to the outskirts of the city. Here, the road that led to the western coast ran through an area undergoing expansion and development. Much of the ground had been torn up, bull-dozed, and flattened, except where ditches were dug to lay pipes.

Men worked laying the foundations of buildings to come. To Tyler's eyes, it looked like they were beginning work on a California-style suburban neighborhood, but it might also be a commercial district full of rental space for small shops.

Eleanor said, "Of course you're not, Mr. Katakura. Since there is no law—officially, yet—no person can be stigmatized as a lawbreaker. But you *are* an Executioner, which makes you a law unto yourself.

"However, the standards of etiquette go beyond any law. Allow me to suggest that you *not* barge into the place with guns blazing and hostile intent. They might react badly to a heavily armed man in body armor demanding information from them at the point of a weapon. There's no need to alarm anyone, especially since we have no idea what sort of response you can expect from this Daria woman."

Ty slammed on the brakes as a construction tractor appeared without warning from behind a half-completed wall. The vehicle screeched and slowed. The tractor driver didn't appear to notice the armored truck at all and mechanically puttered about on his business while Ty waited for him to get out of the way.

"Yeah," Ty said into the microphone, "I hadn't planned on killing everyone in the club if that's what you're thinking. It's always better to try talking to people *first* and shooting second if you have to. So I'm not going to disarm. But I'll give them the chance to cooperate before I do anything hasty. Over."

Despite having the chance to satiate his anger earlier, the rigors of driving a big truck in the city were already starting to grind his gears. His hand itched for the grip of his pistol, his sword. Fighting was in his blood.

Eleanor made a low humming sound. "Yes, that's sensible. Perhaps you might leave the rifle behind? People such as the Absentees' clientele would be the sort to carry knives and pistols, but an AR-10 would be bad form. Over."

Tyler sighed. "Fine, the rifle will stay behind, but that's it. If they have a problem with anything else, as far as I'm concerned, that's *their* problem, not mine. Plus, people tend to be more honest, not to mention cautious, when they know someone can put holes in them if they step out of line. Over."

The girlish laugh sounded over the radio as Ty turned onto a busier street, the skeletons of half-completed offices and skyscrapers now growing out of the ground around him. "Your tenaciousness should serve you well in this position, Mr. Katakura. Please recall that English expression, the one about hammers and nails. 'Everything is like a nail to a hammer,' I believe?"

Ty cleared his throat. "It goes, 'when all you have is a hammer, everything looks like a nail.' So, you were close. Over."

"Thank you. So, consider my advice, though otherwise, I won't tell you how to do your job on the first day. Now, I have other things I must attend to. Good luck. Out."

The radio fell silent.

Past the nascent subdivision and the outer streets, and having come to the city proper, traffic increased by a massive and exponential factor. More construction vehicles and supply trucks *clanked* around and more sleek, flashy cars that belonged to new residents or shady foreign speculators.

It had been only two days since the last time Ty had been into the capital. Somehow it seemed to have grown busier in only that short time. Or it might've been the fact that last time, someone *else* had been driving while he was a passenger.

"*Hey!*" bellowed a man in sunglasses and a colorful, well-pressed shirt driving a convertible sedan with the top open. He slammed his hand down on the horn. "Get that fucking thing off the road. Who do you think you are?" He pulled up alongside the truck's left flank.

Ty had been driving along the right side of the street at what he considered a reasonable speed. The armored truck's bulk made it difficult to weave around other vehicles or navigate sharp curves and turns, but he was managing so far. Nevertheless, not all the other motorists appreciated his efforts.

He glared at the rich man, saying nothing but only looking down at him from his elevated seat in the much larger truck.

The guy in the convertible frowned, shut his mouth, and abruptly passed Ty's truck, stomping on the gas and veering around the side before changing lanes in front of him and rocketing ahead. He narrowly missed two other cars coming from the opposite direction.

Ty shook his head. Whoever had built the streets to begin with had installed speed limit signs. With no police to enforce the restrictions, the city's people seemed to ignore the signs altogether, driving as fast as they could without crashing into buildings or running over pedestrians.

He slowed down. Other motorists began to pile up behind him, some of them honking their horns. Many tried to pass him at the first opportunity, and he wondered if he might be endangering people by motivating the drivers to speed around him with reckless abandon.

"No," he grunted, and his hands tightened around the wheel. "If they drive that badly, it's their doing, not mine." Still, he did have to think about the general welfare.

But, he wondered, what if there were an ambush waiting for him somewhere in town? The city was a place he'd avoided since his first arrival. He was in unfamiliar territory, controlled by unknown adversaries.

Per his directions, he turned left. Here again, the city was in the grips of repairs, construction, and expansion. Anywhere he went there was disorder. The metropolis birthing on the island was never stable or consistent. All things were in flux.

He was almost there. The club lay on the next block.

Ty failed to see the place at first. He passed a mass of interconnected low buildings, faceless and unobtrusive, which occupied the space where Absentees should be. Seeing no sign, though, he let the truck rumble to the next intersection.

"Dammit," he cursed. "I should've stopped somewhere *ahead*

of the place and searched for it on foot. I guess driving again for the first time in two or three years is a double-edged sword, isn't it?"

Five minutes later, he'd managed to find parking in an empty lot and walk back to the block where the club ought to be. With the truck locked up, it would probably be safe. Still, he'd made enemies. If the smugglers from the fishing town or anyone associated with the clearance teams he'd fought off discovered his whereabouts, getting his tires slashed might be the *best* thing he could hope for.

People had stared at the massive, military-grade vehicle as it ground past and shuddered to a halt, and now they stared at him. Per Eleanor's suggestions, he'd left his rifle hidden within the truck and had put his old Army jacket on to hide his fancy new body armor partially.

There was only so much he could do to blend in. Everything about him suggested he was someone who existed outside the usual informal hierarchy of society. Someone who was on a mission of a serious, grim, and dirty nature. There weren't many Asians here, besides. Half of the pedestrians he encountered crossed the street to avoid him.

He reached the appropriate block. Beneath his boots, the pavement was wet with the leftover residues of mist and rain, and dirty from the muddy feet of others treading over it day and night. The day was on the cooler side of mild, as was nearly always the case. Atlantica's climate didn't vary much from season to season.

The mass of buildings contained four shops, all of which were marked. Vendors, haberdasheries, pipe makers, and private security. There was a fifth door as well. It bore no name or logo.

Ty smirked. That would be the one.

The bar was in the basement, which didn't surprise Ty much. What he hadn't expected, though, was how fancy the place ended up being. Or at least, it tried. Perhaps it had delusions of grandeur.

Curtains hung along all the walls, although usually tied back since they served no real purpose but decoration. Most of them were deep wine-red velvet. The lamps housed dim bulbs that kept most of the place illuminated with soft, yellow light. Reproductions of popular paintings, mostly from the 1940s, completed the ensemble. The place resembled a moderately swanky nightclub in New York or Chicago circa fifteen or twenty years ago.

Ty shrugged. He'd expected a classic "bucket of blood" tavern. Then again, with all the money on Atlantica, it made sense that even the unsavory elements would try to live it up. Only the common laborers lived in squalor.

He advanced toward a front desk positioned next to a partial wall that blocked guests from the main seating area. Accessing the rest of the club would require going past it.

Two men stood near the desk, one on either side, and both of them advanced toward the newcomer. Their role as bouncers—*or maybe they called themselves "security,"* Ty thought—was obvious despite their fine quality, freshly pressed pinstripe suits. Both were over six feet tall and wore dark glasses despite being indoors.

The bulkier of the two stood directly in front of Ty to block him from coming any farther. The other circled to Ty's flank.

"Weapons," he said in a tone mixed with equal parts boredom and subdued aggression, "have to get checked at the front desk. You leave them there, or *you* leave. Those are the rules, pal."

Ty scanned everything before him. The two bruisers undoubtedly had pistols under their suit jackets, for one thing. Better still, as he looked past them at the patrons who'd gathered at the bar or the various tables, he noticed some interesting things.

A young woman with a bob haircut in a knee-length dress sat across a small table from a guy who looked like he was trying to reincarnate John F. Kennedy within himself. The woman had a noticeable lump on her thigh under the hem of the dress, a lump about the size of a Colt Detective .38.

As for the JFK wannabe, something with a sharp corner protruded against his jacket from the back of his waistband. Possibly a "something" of real quality like Ty's 1911 or a Browning Hi-Power; maybe a cheap Saturday Night Special, perhaps a European-made .32 pistol of dubious reliability.

Better still, there was a haggard man in what looked like an old Soviet greatcoat with the insignia removed who had openly slung a submachine gun over his shoulder, keeping it within easy reach of his right hand while he guzzled vodka with his left.

Ty looked at the guard who'd spoken. "Well, that's odd," he mused aloud. "I see at least three people you missed. The rules must not apply to them."

"*The rules,*" the bruiser repeated, tightening his jaw muscles and cracking his knuckles, "are that you leave your weapons at the desk, or we leave *you* in the street. Got it?"

For a second or two, Ty hesitated as the bigger man closed in on him. He wasn't here to fight. His only purpose was to find Barruk and have a friendly chat with her. Complying with the bouncers' demands, galling though it was, would make things simpler.

But it *wasn't* that simple. He now had authority over the whole of the island, and he needed to enforce it. To build a reputation. In a country where the strong flourished and the weak struggled, it wouldn't be good to be known as someone who could be intimidated into compliance by a couple of low-rent thugs.

He smiled and tapped the insignia on his shoulder. "I am an Executioner of Atlantica," he stated, "and we don't disarm. Ever."

The less massive of the bouncers snorted. "Get a load of this guy. Yeah, buddy, we'll see about that."

His partner, now only two feet or so from Ty's side, extended his hand.

Two things happened at once. Both happened because Ty *made* them happen, although his conscious mind was scarcely involved.

With his right hand, he quick-drew his 1911, holding a bead on the more distant guard's torso before the man's gun had fully cleared its holster. The guard had to sweep away his suit coat and draw from concealment, which slowed him down, but Ty suspected he would've beaten him to the draw even if they'd both been carrying openly.

With his left hand, Ty swept his wakizashi out from its holster, flicking it through the air in front of him so the dim, soft lamplight momentarily reflected off the blade's polished steel surface. The man reaching for him stopped. As Ty swiveled the sword back toward its saya, the light caught the steel again. Bright red spotted it.

The guard's eyes bulged as he realized what had happened. Retracting his hand, he saw the entire end joint of his middle finger was missing, along with a good quarter-inch chunk off the tip of his index finger. He screamed, his gaze focusing on the hand as blood ran down what remained of his fingers and into his palm. He clutched the wrist in his opposite hand.

"Oh, Jesus. Fuck! Holy shit. Oh, God..."

Ty stood and waited. What happened next was up to them.

The other guard, farther away, slid his pistol back into its holster and rushed to his partner's side. "Get some pressure on it. Pressure, man!" He took the corner of his friend's expensive-looking suit jacket and pressed it against the injured fingers, then had the other man keep his hand jammed against his hip. "Where's the finger joint? Did anyone see where it went? We got to save it."

Ty saw that the severed finger had rolled toward the wall opposite the desk, under a lamp. He nodded toward it, and the guard rushed to pick it up.

"Ever," Ty repeated. Ignoring the security goons for now, he turned to the front desk.

The man there was sweating and trying not to shake too obviously, and he watched Ty so intently that his eyes might as well have been fastened to him by nails. His hands were out of sight, under the desk.

Ty had resheathed his short sword, but he still had his pistol out. He kept it in sight of the clerk but without aiming it directly at him. "Don't reach for a weapon," he suggested, with a hint of a friendly smile. "It would be a bad idea. All I want to do is talk to someone. I never wanted trouble."

The clerk relaxed. Slightly. Ty kept one eye on him but scanned the rest of the bar. Most of the patrons were staring at him in the newfound silence. The only exceptions were a couple who were shamelessly trying to avoid looking at him and hoping he wouldn't notice their presence at all.

Of the ones who'd taken an interest in him, about half looked scared or concerned. The others were probably annoyed more than anything. Some strange Asian man, in their view, had barged in and made a nuisance of himself while they were trying to relax.

Ty had every intention of allowing them to get back to their drinks and conversations.

"I'm here to speak to Daria Barruk. Only to talk to her since someone said she might be able to help me. I have no quarrel with anyone else. If Ms. Barruk is here, I would appreciate it if she'd identify herself." He pitched his voice at the appropriate volume for an announcement, though the club was quiet aside from the faint moaning of the guard who'd lost the ability to flip someone the bird.

He hadn't expected an answer. He had no idea if Daria was

personally present, and at best, he'd hoped that someone might know her and be able to pass on a message, perhaps setting up a meeting later at a set location.

Life was full of surprises. Sometimes even pleasant ones.

"All right, then, *ronin*." It was a woman's voice, high and clear, with a noticeable trace of East Polish inflection. Ty had known a family from Warsaw back in California, and he recognized the accent at once.

He glanced around, trying to find the source as the club's acoustics bounced the sound around in misleading ways. A slim hand had extended into the air above the seat of a booth in the far corner, and it waved, motioning him over. "Come have a chat," she continued, "before you make a mess of the place. I don't wish to come back here next week and find it closed for repairs."

Ty nodded. He looked over his shoulder at the guards. The wounded man appeared to have staunched the bleeding and was now trying to regain his dignity, while the other man watched Ty with a baleful grimace.

Leaving them to their thoughts and the other patrons to their beverages, Ty strode toward the booth. He didn't holster his pistol until he stood beside it, though.

CHAPTER ELEVEN

Ty kept his ears open after the gun was no longer in his hand. It sounded as though, behind him, the other patrons were happy to ignore him and return to their business.

The woman in front of him, meanwhile, wasn't quite what he'd expected. He reserved judgment until he could get a better look.

"Hello," she began. "I'm Daria Barruk. May I ask who you are?" She lifted her right eyebrow, though both eyes stayed on him. She was alert and focused without being too blatant about it.

He inclined his head and shoulders toward her. "Tyler Katakura. Executioner of Atlantica."

"Oh." She had been smoking a black clove cigarette, and she tamped it out in the ashtray before her, which occupied the center of the table. "I haven't heard of any 'executioners' so far. You haven't come to execute me, have you?"

He managed a wry smile. "No. If I had, I wouldn't have said that I only wanted to talk. Someone recommended you to me as someone who might be helpful. May I sit?"

She waved assent. Her left hand, the same one she had used to put out the cigarette. Her right hand remained in darkness under the table, near her lap.

Ty had little doubt that she was armed. He would have to risk it. If she'd meant to kill him, she probably could've struck already.

He slid into the seat across from her in the booth, which gave him a decent view across much of the club. One or two patrons stole glances his way, but otherwise, they seemed to take little interest in his presence.

He looked again at Daria. His first impression had been correct—she was *definitely* not what he'd expected.

In its idle moments since the mission of finding her had been thrust upon him, his mind had begun composing a picture of what Ms. Barruk might look like and the airs she would give off. Somehow he'd anticipated a rough sailorwoman, someone scarcely distinguishable from a man. Alternately, he'd envisaged a rakish young woman playacting at being some kind of pirate queen, with leather pants, a bandanna, and a cutlass.

Instead, the woman seated across from him resembled a schoolteacher or a librarian. She was pretty, though the passage of time was beginning to catch up with her. He guessed her age at around thirty-eight. Grey streaks ran through her wavy dark brown hair at the temples. Something about the stern set of her chin combined with her steely, all-seeing eyes put Ty in mind of every woman he'd ever known who'd spent years bossing around children.

Yet he could see her as a smuggler. She would escape notice, getting the job done.

He grew more certain than ever that she was aiming a pistol at his groin or belly under the table, waiting for him to make a wrong move.

He noticed another interesting detail. At first, it had seemed odd that Daria would sit with her back to the rest of the club, leaving him the seat that afforded a good view of the floor. From where *she* sat, there was a straighter, faster course to the rear stairwell door—and she would instantly be able to tell if someone approached by *that* route. She'd carefully chosen her setup based on the ease of making a quick exit.

As a sign of trust, Ty placed both his hands on the table in front of them.

Daria glanced at them, noting the gesture. "So you say that I might be helpful to you. I should like to know what you want help with, of course."

Ty glanced around the club once more. Still peaceful.

"There was recently some trouble between the fisherfolk on the coast, about an hour's drive northwest of here, and a new ring of smugglers. I hear you're in the same business, so I thought you might have insights into the matter.

"Don't worry about your business. I'm not here about that. There's no law against smuggling in Atlantica. Hell, the only reason people even *call* it smuggling is because the governments of the other nations don't want anything coming off this island to be too obvious."

Daria ran the tip of her finger around the rim of her glass, which contained about half a sip's worth of vodka and tonic. "I had heard something, whispers and gossip, about a police force coming to Atlantica at last. It was inevitable, to be sure. Always, the big people demand law so they can run their operations more smoothly, and the little people demand law so they don't get killed on a whim. What I didn't expect was that our first cop would be a blade-swinging *ronin*."

Her pronunciation of the term was impeccable. The sound in Japanese, which in English was semi-correctly registered with the letter "R," was often difficult for Westerners to get right. Then again, she seemed to be Polish, though Ty didn't know enough about her native language to say whether that was truly a help in grasping Japanese.

His smile came from a place of indignities and old wounds that were finally beginning to heal.

"I'm not a ronin," he pointed out, "at least, not anymore. My family didn't come from samurai stock. I suppose that if they had, the term might've applied to me for some years.

"It means 'wave men,' you know. Like people cast out to sea, who drift in and wash up on forlorn beaches; men without a true place in the world. The tide no longer casts me about. I think I've found my place, and I intend to fight to keep it."

Daria stared. At this point, both her eyebrows had raised as she took him in and processed everything she'd learned about him. Something in her demeanor changed.

It took Ty a moment to comprehend what had happened. She was impressed by him and his words, if only slightly. He got a distinct impression that she wasn't a person easily impressed.

"Well, then, Mr. Katakura," she responded, "what can I do to help you with your problem? Information, yes. Tell me more about what happened that drove you to seek me out."

He drew a deep breath and related all that had occurred during his visit to the fishing village. He left out most of the details with his battle against the smugglers, as there was a chance she wouldn't believe that he'd defeated a group that size more or less singlehanded. Glossing over the violence, he explained next what the fisherfolk had told him about everything that led up to the events of a few hours past.

Daria listened with careful attention. Ty suspected that she was evaluating him the whole time, trying to determine if he was lying by reading between the lines. She also kept a part of her attention on her surroundings. It was a skill he knew well, borne of many years of living in hostile or uncertain circumstances.

When Ty reached the villagers' anecdote about the sunken ships, their insistence on their innocence, and the smugglers' determination to retaliate against them anyway, Daria's eyes narrowed, and something within her turned to steel. The tips of her left hand dug into the table.

Briefly, Ty considered that she might be angry at him. He doubted it. Perhaps she blamed him for not handling the situation as well as he could have. He would have to wait and see what she said. It appeared to him that she understood who was truly the guilty party.

"So," he wrapped up, "finally, someone mentioned you and told me that I might find you here. As it happens, they said that you'd always dealt fairly with them. I'd like to know what you know. About who these people are, what they were doing, why they were so secretive about everything and so willing to kill over it."

Daria studied his eyes again and brushed a lock of fading brown hair away from her striking face. Then, to his surprise, she laughed. It was a soft laugh but with an undercurrent of cynical harshness.

"You ask me so bluntly," she observed. "You don't hold anything back. You don't imply that you know more than you truly do or that you have something you're waiting to...*unleash* upon me if I don't simply give you what you want at once. In everything, you're honest and earnest but short-tempered and impatient. These things together, for one in your position, cannot be mistaken. They're the mark of an amateur."

Ty blinked. He hadn't expected her to say anything of the sort and it threw him off too much to be offended. Yet.

Daria went on. "I can tell that you don't have experience as a policeman or investigator. Or, for that matter, as a confidence artist or even a law-abiding salesman. You lack skill in, as we say, 'working people.' But don't think that means I'm dismissing you, exactly. Oh, no."

Ty put on his poker face. If she were analyzing him to *that* extent, he would aim to reveal as little as possible.

"But," she added, "I can tell that you are most determined. And apparently dangerous enough to keep pursuing these matters as far as it takes. Yes, you might not be an expert, but you would keep pushing, I think. You would continue to make a nuisance of yourself and injure or kill anyone who tries to stop you or quiet you. That can count for as much as subtlety and experience, even if it has its drawbacks."

Sniffing and leaning back, Ty bit down on his tongue to keep himself from speaking out too hastily. He wanted to tell her to shut up, that she didn't know anything about him, and not to characterize him as someone who was a loose cannon or a bully. He hated bullies.

Yet, he doubted that her assessment had come out of nowhere. She was a shrewd woman. Perhaps she was testing him with exaggerated accusations to see how he reacted, or maybe her mind was made up, in which case he would never convince her otherwise.

If he argued with her, all he would do was embarrass himself.

Ty cleared his throat. "You seem perceptive, Ms. Barruk. I won't say that you're right about everything, but I'm not going to try and tell you you're completely wrong, either. It's true that I'm new to investigations. I'm more of a fighter by trade. I'm not here to deceive you with a bunch of smooth talk. Everything I ask is in full honesty."

Once again, she raised her eyebrows. "That's a good answer. How curious... Here we are, in a place where an individual can *be anything*, and still, some people try to pretend. They attempt to pass themselves off as something they're not. For *not* wasting my time with that," she added and smiled, "you have my thanks. I think you could grow on me, Executioner Katakura."

That, Tyler thought, was good to hear.

Before he could reply, the low hum of the other patrons' conversations fell silent in time with the approach of heavy footsteps. At least two pairs, Ty guessed, maybe more like four. He looked past Daria and across the floor toward the narrow gap next to the front desk, the only point of access to the club from the front entrance.

There were three of them. A nondescript white man with small round spectacles was out in front, a tall black man with a shaven head to the left, and a fat swarthy guy with a scar on his chin to the right. All wore big, long, heavy overcoats. Ty almost laughed as he briefly wondered *if* they were concealing anything.

Over the shoulder of the widest of the trio, he saw the bouncer with intact hands looking toward Daria's table and smirking.

Daria glanced behind her, then casually turned back to Ty as the three began their approach. "Well, it would appear that your smuggling friends have heard about the events of this morning. Word travels fast on this island."

Ty had turned his head toward the woman but kept the trio in his peripheral vision. He wasn't the slightest bit surprised to see them continue past multiple empty tables and make a slow, deliberate beeline toward him.

He pretended to scratch his side and readjust his posture, then slipped his hands beneath the table, where his pistol and wakizashi would be within easier reach.

Ms. Barruk didn't miss his actions or their purpose. She closed her eyes and gave him a slight head shake. "No. Hold for a moment. I might be able to talk us out of this situation. It's better not to cause a scene in public. You *already* caused one when you first came in."

"True," he admitted.

He steadied himself, his mind once more shifting into the state of no-mind, the all-seeing perceptiveness that was free of any judgments save the ones he would need to make automatically to survive.

As the men drew closer, Daria shifted her posture to face out the side of the booth, pretending as though she were noticing them for the first time.

"Oh, hello," she said with a degree of jovial warmth that caught Ty off-guard. "I haven't seen you in too long, Erich. You too, Jon and Sergio. You should come in for a drink more often. How is Mr. Marnes? You do still work for him, don't you?"

They kept advancing a few more steps, not stopping until the bespectacled man at the head of the group had nearly pressed his belt buckle against the table's edge. "Shut the fuck up, Daria," he snapped, his voice far harsher than his mild-mannered appearance would suggest. The accent was faintly German. "Don't stick your oversized nose into this."

He turned to Ty. "You. Get up and come with us, or else. We will not ask you twice. We wish to speak with you, alone."

Ty had been studying them since they'd entered. They weren't, he decided, men to take lightly, but the two in the wings probably weren't experts. The man in front confounded him, though. He looked like an accountant, but after hearing him speak, Ty wondered if Erich might be a former member of the Wehrmacht or Waffen-SS. If so, he might be extremely dangerous.

It was also tough to tell how they were armed. Their coats were big enough that they might have sawed-off shotguns or folded-stock submachine guns rather than pistols alone.

"Well," Ty began, sighing and casting an apologetic look at Daria, "you heard the man. They want to talk to me in private. Why does that sound familiar?" He leaned over slightly as though preparing to scooch out of his seat. In fact, he was only trying to buy time.

Daria's nostrils flared, and her eyes burned with controlled rage. She was probably unused to being spoken to so rudely.

"Hah," she spat. "I highly doubt that wherever you plan to take this man, it will be any more pleasant than this 'or else' you speak of. Do you think it matters to him whether he takes a bullet to the head here or in the back alley? The outcome is the same. That's your purpose, isn't it? You would shoot him so he falls dead across *my* table without so much as an apology to me. I haven't even finished my drink."

With her left hand, she gestured at her glass, which did indeed still contain about half a sip of liquor.

Erich scoffed. "Cockroaches like you have a limited life expectancy in this—"

Daria's right hand was suddenly in view, holding a pistol. She fired. The lens over Erich's left eye shattered and his eye vanished behind it. The man staggered back a step, mouth agape, before he toppled.

A woman, probably the floozy talking to the JFK wannabe, screamed.

The other two men threw aside their coats and reached for their guns. Daria moved the pistol over to Sergio, the fat man, and fired two more shots that struck him in the sternum and right lung as he pulled out his shotgun. Sergio groaned and gurgled, slumping aside.

Meanwhile, Jon, the tall black man, was drawing a pair of revolvers from his hips. He was fast. Daria wouldn't have been able to shoot him before he had his guns up.

Light reflected off steel. Ty drew his wakizashi, whipped it over the table, and slipped the blade into Jon's chest under his ribcage, thrusting upward before twisting the blade and ripping it free. Jon barked out in pain and alarm and tried to bring his six-shooters into play, but the flow of his heart's blood was too fast and strong. His eyes rolled back in his head, and he toppled over into the seat of the next booth down.

Then it was quiet. Ty wiped off his blade on a complimentary napkin before resheathing it. The smoke had mostly dissipated from the barrel of Daria's gun, an old Walther P38.

She looked at Ty and nodded. "It seems we can help each other," she stated.

"Likewise." He slid out of his seat and stood, alert to any further threats. So far, there were none.

Daria joined him. "You will have to give me a ride. We should leave immediately. I was expecting someone to pick me up half an hour from now. My friends will have to make do without me."

"You've got yourself a deal, ma'am," Ty said. "Which way do you want to—"

Ms. Barruk was already gliding across the floor toward the front exit, fishing around in her pockets with her left hand. The pistol stayed in her right.

Ty shrugged and hurried after her. As they passed the front desk, Daria produced a handful of banknotes, a mixture of U.S. and Canadian currency, and tossed them onto the desk.

"There." She didn't break stride. "For the mess and for some proper medical attention for that poor dear's fingers."

Ty saw the bouncers looking at him. The man with the bandaged hand paled in fear, while the other looked annoyed that the trio of smugglers had failed to kill him. He smiled, bowed, and rushed out behind Daria, climbing the stairs toward the surface.

They emerged at street level into the dim, pale light of an increasingly cloudy day, though it still seemed bright compared to the low lamps in the club.

Ty reflected on how strange Atlantica's weather was. The summers were barely warm, but the winters weren't much cooler. The climate bore little resemblance to that of Newfoundland or Nova Scotia, the nearest major landmasses.

It was closer to what people got in places like Seattle or Liverpool. Complete with mist. Lots and lots of mist. A young man back in the valley's labor town was always looking for science news in newspapers and magazines when he could get them. He'd once told Ty that scientists were baffled as to what could be moderating the island's temperatures so much.

Daria stopped and scanned the street. "Where's your car?"

Ty gestured down the road. "That way. It's more of a truck. You'll know it when you see it."

"Lead the way, then." She waited for him to step in front of her, which he did, and they proceeded the short way down the sidewalk toward the empty lot where the armored vehicle waited. "*That* thing? It looks like a military transport."

Ty chuckled. "It's well-armored. Slow to accelerate due to the added weight, but we'll be protected, that's for damn sure."

Daria shook her head. "Who's funding you? Oh, I'm sure you're not supposed to talk about it. Someone very wealthy, of course."

Again, she could figure enough out by herself that Ty saw little point in arguing with her or trying to lie.

When they reached the side of the truck, Ty went around to the passenger's side and opened the door, holding it open.

"Thank you." Daria stepped toward him.

Before she could squeeze past, the air split asunder with the unmistakable *crack* of a gunshot. Before Ty could duck, the bullet struck him in the back.

CHAPTER TWELVE

Pain shot through his torso and left arm. The bullet had hit him in the left shoulder blade. Or, rather, it had struck his armor. Enough of the projectile's energy still transferred into his body for it to hurt, probably to bruise the hell out of him...but the fancy new Atlantican armor saved his life.

He took in everything at once, dismissing the pain and focusing instead on what he needed to know to live through the next few seconds.

Daria had ducked. Ty grabbed her arm and hauled her toward the truck, shouting "Get in!" the instant the thunderclap from the hidden gun had faded away. At the same time, he spun, drawing his pistol and trying to get a bead on where the sniper had fired from.

He didn't have to look for long. A group of men emerged from an alley beside the block of shops above Absentees. One of them, front and center, held an old lever-action carbine, a Henry or Marlin, with a crude scope attached. Now he was preparing to line up another shot.

Ty didn't feel like giving him the opportunity. The rifle was probably chambered for .357 Magnum, a fearsome enough round for an unprotected man but not enough to get through his vest. They'd need a proper, heavy rifle cartridge for that. Still, the man might've been a good enough shot to hit Ty in the head if he was slow.

They were closing the distance, all of them. There were six or seven. The others beside the marksman held submachine guns, pistols, and shotguns. Two of the men raised their weapons and opened fire.

"Move!" Ty barked. Daria was already on the lower step of the truck, about to climb into the passenger's seat. There wouldn't be time for Ty to circle to the other side. He grabbed her legs and heaved against her, pushing her up into the truck. Briefly, his face smashed against her buttocks. "Shit. Sorry!"

Daria exclaimed something in Polish and stumbled into, then over the seat. Ty grabbed the side of the doorframe and hoisted himself up after her as bullets struck the steel around him, *pinging*, *whizzing*, and ricocheting off into the air, one or two leaving sparks where they struck.

One of Daria's feet kicked Ty in the shoulder, mere inches from where the bullet had impacted, and he winced as he tried to haul the armor-plated door shut with his other arm. The steel rasped as the portal slammed closed right in time to deflect another volley of lead.

Ty twisted around. "We need to—what the hell?"

Daria was still trying to get herself oriented, and his face had nearly smashed into her chest. She put a hand on his head and pushed, giving herself the leverage to scooch backward from him.

"Sorry," he said again. "That one was your fault, though."

She awkwardly pulled her leg up and over as she rolled toward the driver's seat. "Yes, yes. Come on."

Ty crawled forward, intending to get into the driver's seat himself and allow Daria to reposition herself once they were both secure. Halfway there, his shoulder stabbed him with pain, and he faltered, his face landing right on Daria's foot as she was trying to pull her leg back.

"Oh," she remarked, "you're into *that*, are you? You wouldn't be the first."

Blushing and gritting his teeth, Ty got into a regular sitting position on the passenger's side. "You should probably let me—wait. Fuck!"

Peering out the side window, he saw the half-dozen thugs dispersing and running toward a cluster of three big, heavy pickup trucks. None of them were in the same league as the massive armored Executioner's vehicle, but they were still nothing to be taken lightly. Their engines growled and revved as the men piled into them, two or three each.

"Jesus!" Ty exclaimed. "They look like they're going to try ramming us. I don't think *one* of them could do much good against this damn thing, but if all three hit us at once, different story. Hit the gas, woman! You drive a truck before?"

Daria snorted. "Of course. But not this one. Just a moment, please."

Ty saw a couple of the smugglers leaning out of their windows with their guns. "We don't *have* a moment, Daria. Here." He reached into his pocket and tossed her the keys, praying that she could drive worth a damn. If so, it might be for the best since trying to finagle himself behind the wheel with her crawling around would eat up precious time. Not to mention, her driving meant that he could shoot.

As Daria started the engine, he climbed over the seat and into the back compartment, where he dug his AR-10 rifle out from its hiding place. He briefly considered returning to the passenger's seat, but instead, his eyes fixed on the hatch in the rear. Blasting at them from there would be easier than trying to lean out the side window.

Daria's voice announced, "Aha, yes, I have it. Here we go."

Gunshots crackled again, a bullet *pinging* low on the truck's frame, meaning that the thugs were probably shooting for the tires. Ty was halfway back to the rear hatch when Daria stomped on the gas.

"Whoa!" he exclaimed, pitching forward and hurling himself aside against the truck's side as the vehicle rocketed off into the street.

Daria let out a hollering whoop that quickly transformed into a crazy laugh. "Ha, ha! This is the biggest one yet!"

Struggling toward the back of the truck and trying not to drop his rifle, Ty yelled back, "I'm happy for you. Glad you're enjoying yourself. But I need to stay on my feet, okay? Try not to swerve all over the goddamn island. This truck is solid enough that we shouldn't need a lot of fancy maneuvers to stop them from killing us. Just barrel on ahead and pick up momentum."

He lurched ahead a couple more steps, finding it easier to move now that Daria had *mostly* stabilized her course.

"Yes," she replied, "I know that. That's why I hit the gas so hard. A truck this size would take forever to get moving if I was gentle with it, would it not? Ha, ha!"

The truck moved faster and horns honked. Ty couldn't see what was going on outside yet, but it seemed safe to assume that Daria was granting herself the right-of-way in all situations where she might encounter other cars.

Ty shook his head and kept creeping along the wall. "Yeah," he murmured under his breath, "and why shouldn't she? There aren't any real traffic laws. Unless I feel like enforcing them myself. Right now, I'm kind of busy with other things."

He reached the hatch, unfastened it, and flung it open. It crashed aside and disclosed a patch of air about three feet square. Big enough for him to see out and shoot, but small enough that their pursuers would have trouble hitting it while in motion.

Their vehicles, unlike his, weren't covered with armor.

Ty raised his AR-10 and braced it on the bottom sill of the hatch. "I'm getting tired of these goddamn people." He took a bead and cleared his mind, his right index finger resting gently beside the gun's trigger. Putting it *on* the trigger would be a bad idea since Daria might swerve or hit a bump.

As the Executioner, the deliverer of justice, he wouldn't allow himself to cause any collateral damage. Stray bullets would kill no civilians.

The men chasing them seemed far less concerned about such things. The three trucks were gaining on them, slowly but surely. Two out in front hogged most of the road so cars coming in the opposite direction had to pull over and straddle the crude sidewalk or take abrupt turns down side streets, their drivers madly honking or shouting curses. The third truck hung close behind the others, unable to contribute much but ready to jump into the fight when and if needed.

Unfortunately, the guy with the scoped carbine was in one of the pickups in front. He leaned out the passenger's window, the pale sunlight glinting off the lens of his scope as he fixed on Ty.

Then Daria turned. Ty felt like his stomach flew off to the side while the rest of him remained in place, although his legs wobbled and his rifle bobbed off-target. "Goddammit," he grunted.

A shot rang out. The rifleman had popped off a round right as the truck veered left. Ty briefly saw the wall of a building a little farther off, occupying much the same space they would have if Daria hadn't turned, and a ring of dust appeared around a sudden hole in the concrete.

Ty shouted, "Daria. Stay on course for a minute. I need to shoot a couple of these pricks, or they're going to run us down and pick us off."

She was still laughing like a madwoman, or perhaps more like a college girl whose boyfriend had given her the wheel of his convertible for the first time. He wasn't sure she'd heard him.

"I wonder if she knows as many nasty remarks in Polish as I can think of in Japanese right about now," he snarled and re-braced his rifle as the first of the pickups came around the corner behind them.

This time, since they needed a moment to adjust after swerving onto the perpendicular street, Ty had the advantage. Some idiot in a sports car was about to try and weave in behind the armored truck. Then the driver noticed all the guns pointed in both directions and hastily decelerated, pulling over onto the shoulder and letting the convoy pass.

Ty exhaled and didn't breathe back in. He noted both the guy with the scoped carbine and the driver of the same vehicle. Then he squeezed off two shots in rapid succession. The gun reports echoed down the corridor of the streets and off the walls of the half-completed buildings.

The first bullet caught the rifleman in the forehead. He flung up his arms, the lever-action weapon flying from his grasp to clatter onto the asphalt, and slumped half-in and half-out of the truck, the upper half of his body hanging from the window.

The other shot, less precise, caught the driver in the shoulder. Ty had been aiming for his heart, but it did the trick, anyway.

The truck swerved, then veered, looping around backward right as the second of the three trucks accelerated to join the first. Two men were hanging out and preparing to open fire, one from the passenger's seat, the other from the bed in the rear. Both of them screamed.

The first vehicle looped around uncontrollably as the driver lost the use of his arm, staggered by pain, and smashed head-on into the second.

Ty grinned in animal satisfaction at the *crunching* of metal, the explosion of the first truck's engine, and the way the men leaning out to shoot him went flying head over heels through the air like scattered bowling pins. One struck the concrete walk beside the road, leaving a long red skid mark, while the other fell directly beneath the wheels of a speeding car coming down the opposite lane.

As for the second driver, Ty couldn't be sure, but he doubted the man was going to have a good rest of the day no matter what.

The third truck was still coming. He'd half-hoped that its occupants, seeing how things had gone for their buddies, would've peeled off in the opposite direction and thought about getting into a different line of work. But, no.

The driver accelerated, weaving around the wreckage of the first two vehicles and running over pieces of debris, forcing a construction truck off the road in his pursuit. The civilian vehicle bumbled into a lot and crashed against a parked car, spilling sand from its bed as it went.

Ty grimaced. The chase had already done more damage than he would've liked. It was on the smugglers' heads, not his.

Daria had stopped cackling, at least. Ty shouted, "We have one more truck to deal with. Keep it steady."

She sang out something in her native tongue, so Ty ignored her and raised his rifle again.

This time, though, his enemies were both quicker on the draw and less concerned with accuracy. A shotgun boomed, peppering the protective frame around the armored truck's rear wheels with buckshot, and the guy in the passenger's seat opened up with a submachine gun.

Ty ducked. They seemed to be trying to simply harass him with a superior volume of firepower and likely didn't expect to hit much, but he wasn't about to offer them the chance to take him out so easily, anyway. They would run out of ammo quickly enough. The guy with the submachine gun was spraying away, and his volley went quiet after a couple of seconds.

"Right," Ty muttered. He shouldered his rifle and prepared to spring back up to return the favor.

Then Daria slammed on the brakes.

Ty's heart jumped into his throat while his body was driven against the truck's rear door, his face pressing against the surface while he barely managed to retain hold of his AR-10 in his right hand. That lasted only for a second because something crashed into the back of the truck and sent him rolling in one direction and the gun in another.

Metal shrieked and rumbled. Steam hissed. Men screamed briefly, then mostly fell silent.

Ty rolled over and sat up, gasping. The impact of the collision had knocked the wind out of his lungs and rattled his bones. "What the hell do you think you're doing?" he croaked. "Goddammit. You practically killed *us* along with the rest of those assholes."

He looked toward the front of the vehicle. Daria had clambered down from her seat and was heading out into the road. Since it was too late to stop her, Ty shook his head and fumed in silence, found his rifle, and crawled up to the hatch to watch and provide cover.

The entire front of the third pickup had pathetically crumpled from its sudden encounter with the back of the Executioner's truck. Then it had skidded back ten or twelve feet before stopping slightly askew across the road.

From what Ty could see, other motorists had figured out what was going on and were wisely avoiding this stretch of street. Pedestrians, too, had opted not to press their luck. For the moment, they were alone near the edge of the city.

He glanced straight down. His truck looked fine, aside from some scratched paint.

"Well, there's a plus," he remarked.

Daria came around the rear, her pistol drawn, and advanced on the ruined pickup. A man in the bed, who had somehow avoided being tossed out into the street by the crash, was still conscious although stunned and clutching his weapon. Daria raised her gun and shot him twice. He fell over and lay flat in the truck's bed without another sound.

Then she put another round into the guy in the passenger's seat, who appeared to be dead anyway. Just to be safe, Ty guessed.

He shook his head. "Christ. I'm the new face of justice, and here I am participating in shit that would horrify Al Capone. If there were cops, they'd probably be right to arrest us."

If Daria heard him, she gave no indication. She moved toward the driver, probably to check on him or haul him out. He was twitching and moaning, still alive but clearly in bad shape. Ty wasn't so sure the man was going to make it. Still, human resilience in the face of injury was a strange and sometimes amazing thing. He watched closely, his rifle at the ready in case anything happened.

She reached the side of the car and opened the driver's side door. It had buckled well past the point at which the lock would've continued working. It squeaked and fell halfway off its hinges, one corner dragging on the fresh black asphalt.

The driver's arm fell and dangled, fortunately still attached to his shoulder. Daria looked him over, nodded, and bent over to seize him around the waist and pull him free of the vehicle. He budged, but only slightly. He probably weighed close to a hundred pounds more than she did, and despite her wiry strength and the benefits of their recent battle-rush, it was going to take her a minute to get him out.

Ty fidgeted. Seeing a woman struggle with a physical task bothered him when he was readily able to help. But he didn't think it would be wise to abandon the truck. There was always an off chance that further accomplices of the smugglers might be waiting for the opportunity to steal the huge, armored vehicle as compensation for their trouble.

His eyes wandered across the windshield of the devastated pickup truck. The driver's side window was almost completely gone. On the passenger's side, the glass was still intact but covered with spiderweb cracks that made it difficult to see through.

One thing he *could* see was movement. The passenger wasn't dead. And he had something in his hand.

Ty aimed his rifle through the hatch, using the lower rim as support. "Daria! Don't move," he shouted, then fired once.

The rest of the windshield shattered into pieces as the bullet punched through and took it apart along the preexisting cracks, and behind it, blood sprayed and blossomed. The man in the other seat squawked and slumped over, his head hitting the dashboard.

He didn't move again. Still, Ty kept watch on him.

Daria had frozen, as he'd told her to. After the passage of six or seven heartbeats, though, she poked her head up. "I think everything is all right now," she quipped. "Thank you. Some dead men don't stay dead, do they?"

"No," Ty agreed, "not always. This time, he will." His well-aimed shot had gone through the man's lower throat and possibly his spine.

Muttering to herself and wiping some blood spray from her face, Daria got back to work. The driver was still in no condition to fight back, barely conscious. He offered no resistance besides that of his weight. At last, Daria heaved him free of the vehicle. She nearly fell over with him topping onto her, but after wobbling, she shoved him sideways to redirect his momentum and lowered him onto his back on the ground.

Ty winced. The man was coming to again, probably due to pain since the wreck had badly messed up his legs. At least one broken bone in there somewhere, he guessed, along with some serious abrasions.

"Uuugghhh," the attacker groaned, blinking and shuddering. "Whuh..."

Daria had her pistol back out, and she held it over the smuggler, keeping him pinned down. She looked over her shoulder toward Ty. "Do you have some way to restrain him? Tie him up or something."

Ty balked, flabbergasted. Not because her request was strange, but because it was obvious. A hot flush of shame, mingled with anger at himself, rose through his neck and face. How could he have been so stupid as to charge into a job like this without stopping to consider how he might restrain prisoners?

"Guess I'm a little too used to not *taking* prisoners by this point," he mumbled. Then, looking at Daria, he raised his voice. "I'll check the back of the truck. Um, now that I think of it, there might've been some handcuffs or at least a length of chain back there."

He vaguely recalled having seen something of the sort earlier. Next time he would do a more careful inventory of his gear before he started any mission—that he had failed to do so this time indicated he was getting sloppy as a soldier, in addition to being a greenhorn as a cop.

A quick search of the broad rear compartment confirmed that there was a length of chain. It had a manacle at one end, while the other end was attached to the vehicle's floor. Perfect.

Then he rifled through a couple of boxes in the corners. There were a pair of first aid kits, which was good, and also four pairs of handcuffs. He blew out his breath in relief, directing it straight up so the wind puffed his increasingly shaggy black hair out of his face.

Ty rushed outside, handcuffs in hand. Neither Daria nor her captive had moved. "Okay," he pronounced, "we're in business. There's also a way to shackle him to the truck itself. He's in bad shape, though. Not that I exactly like the guy, but let's be careful. If we're taking him in alive to begin with, we might as well do it right."

"Very well," Daria agreed.

Looking the driver over, Ty refurbished his assessment of the man's injuries. One of his legs was definitely broken, fractured midway down the calf. The other leg seemed mostly fine.

It also looked like he'd tried to brace himself to avoid hitting the dashboard when the truck had crashed. As a result, he'd shattered both of his wrists on impact. The flesh above his hands was swelling and turning dark. He probably had a concussion, to boot.

Ty knelt and clamped the handcuffs over the man's purplish wrists. He snapped awake, gasping and gritting his teeth in pain, but then his eyes rolled sideways, and he sank back into half-consciousness.

Together, Ty and Daria lifted the man into the back of the armored truck, seating him propped against the wall in the corner and fastening the manacle to the ankle of his good leg.

"All right," Ty said, "I'll drive us out of here. We're gonna have to hope that my employers send someone to clean the rest of this mess out of the street; I'll radio them in a minute and ask about it. Otherwise, there will be hell to pay when all the businessmen realize how much traffic we probably obstructed and how many workers we scared off."

Daria waved that off. "Do what you must. I'll deal with him."

Ty grimaced. "What do you mean? What should we do with him, anyway?"

The woman stood, finally holstering her P38. "Get some answers. I would say that we earned them, wouldn't you?"

CHAPTER THIRTEEN

"Hey!" the prisoner shouted from the back. "Watch it! Fuckin' bastards drive like maniacs. I need a doctor, you know. This shit's in the Geneva Convention."

Ty stared straight ahead as he drove. They were outside of the main city area, and the roads were back to mostly being dirt tracks or gravel. He didn't envy the handcuffed guy, but he wasn't about to bend over backward to make him comfortable, either.

"Yeah," he shouted, without looking back. "We're gonna get you patched up while we ask some questions, and then you'll get to go to the hospital. But don't piss us off. Remember, my friend. There's no law on Atlantica. So far."

The man broke into a series of curses and grunts, most of which the truck's rumblings masked. It made it easier to ignore him for the time being.

Daria, sitting on the passenger's side, gestured ahead of them down the road. "Keep going past this street," she instructed Ty. "It's the next one. Turn left onto that. My house is easy to find from there. Just keep us on this side of the docks."

"Right." Ty's stomach had been twisting itself into knots ever since they'd left the scene of their last crash. It was difficult to put a finger on what exactly was bothering him so much. The post-combat shakes were part of it. So was the uncertainty about what lay ahead and how his village would fare, as well as the little town of the fisherfolk.

There was something else, too. It finally articulated itself in his head.

"Daria," he began, keeping his voice low enough that their prisoner would have trouble hearing. "I agree that we need information. But there are things I'm *not* willing to do to get it. Do you understand what I mean by that? I'm here to make Atlantica a better place to live. If I have to kill to achieve that, so be it. But..."

Daria stared at him, running the nails of her right hand over her palm and thumb. "Ah. Of course. I will say that it's better to *talk* first. If that doesn't work, we will see what we will see."

He shrugged. "Yeah." Their turn came up, and he took it slowly, veering left toward a lower slope that descended to the sea.

Off to their right was the broad expanse of docks that served as Atlantica's major shipping hub, adjacent to the city but not part of it. It bustled with activity as boats came and went and men and women loaded and unloaded cargo or caroused in cheap pubs and brothels. Alongside them, families labored to make an honest living. Somehow, it seemed like exactly the sort of place Daria would want to live near.

They passed a stand of small huts and shanties, where dirty-faced, barefoot children watched their truck in amazement. Ty wondered if their parents were anywhere nearby to see.

He sighed. "Maybe we should've gotten in touch with your friend who was going to pick you up from the club," he suggested. "This truck isn't exactly inconspicuous. A lot of people will know that we've been here."

"So?" Daria challenged him. "You're the Executioner, are you not? Your business is legal, and everyone is supposed to respect your authority. Or something like that."

After a moment of silence, Tyler smiled. "Of course. Is that your place?"

"Yes." She stretched and made ready to get up as the truck slowed while approaching her home.

Daria Barruk lived in a small home, humble enough by most people's standards but somewhat larger, nicer, and more expertly constructed than the slums of the island's common laborer class. The property was about a quarter of an acre, surrounded by a fence of cheap lumber with an iron gate in front.

Next to the house lay a garage. Though even bigger than the domicile, it wouldn't be large enough for the armored truck, so Ty stopped outside the gate.

He nodded toward the house. "Nice place. Not where I would've expected a smuggler to live if I'm honest."

Daria laughed and brushed away her hair, tucking the most undisciplined part of it behind her ear. "These days, I'm not so much an actual smuggler. I'm more of...how should I put it...an advisor. A smuggling consultant. But I don't think I could live downtown. Every once in a while, I start to get feisty, and I need a little saltwater to cool me down."

The sea was only a hundred yards or so from the edge of her property. Ty wondered if in the years to come, the docks might expand, and someone would try to buy Daria's plot of land to construct more shipping facilities on it. He thought about asking her what she would do in such a scenario but decided against it.

Instead, he inquired, "Did you smuggle stuff before you came to Atlantica? Or is it the line of work you stumbled into when you came here? It seems like I've met a lot of people who ended up doing things on the island that they never thought they'd end up doing back home."

He was an exception to that tendency. On Atlantica, he'd done much the same sorts of things that had occupied much of his life for the last fourteen years. Fighting. Running and hiding, getting in trouble. Sleeping on straw or bare ground, often in the cold.

Wondering when, at last, someone would get in the lucky shot that finally sent him to his ancestors.

Daria's answer snapped him out of his ruminations. "Yes, I began smuggling as a girl. Over twenty years ago. Maybe twenty-five. When I was about fifteen, I believe. It's difficult to remember exactly."

The truck was idling. Ty wondered why they'd chosen to sit and have this conversation now when they had a prisoner to interrogate, but he supposed neither of them was much looking forward to it. He turned the keys in the ignition, killing the engine, and pulled them out.

"Why," he asked, squinting, though his tone was gentle, "why would you have begun a life of crime when you were that young? Where were your parents, and what did they have to say about it?"

Daria's expression had been a tad morose but had still held her usual undercurrent of wry humor and good cheer. Now... Her face went flat, blank of any particular emotion. Ty steeled himself for what came next. He'd probably made a mistake by asking.

She exhaled slowly. "My mother and father died in 1940. After that, they weren't around to tell me what to do. I had to choose my path in life without them or their feelings involved. I had...many options, most of them not very appealing. I chose the one that seemed best—smuggling people out of Gdańsk.

"If you don't know of that city, it's a port on the northern coast of Poland. Many ships went to and from it, and I helped those who wished to leave. It kept me alive. I don't regret it."

Ty nodded. He felt as though she were deliberately avoiding telling him the whole story, but he could guess at some of it, given what was going on in Europe at the time.

Daria clapped once, coming back to the present. "Let's get this man in the back into my garage so I can ask him a few questions. Shall we?"

"Yes." Ty pushed the door open with his foot and hopped down. Daria circled to the back of the truck from the opposite side, and when they opened the rear door, the man they'd hand-cuffed still sat there, looking miserable and half-delirious. His wounds were probably paining him badly by now. Ty nearly felt sorry for him. Had the man not tried to kill him and Daria less than an hour earlier, he might've insisted on taking him straight to the emergency room.

Ty studied the man in more detail. Tall, heavyset, around thirty years old, with a broad jowly chin and patchy red hair. His accent had sounded Bostonian when he'd spoken before. Ty marveled at the sheer variety of humans who'd drifted onto Atlantica. Most criminal organizations were fairly homogeneous, but the smuggler's ring they'd run afoul of seemed a motley brew of different nationalities.

"Right." He put his hands on his hips. "You. Can you walk?"

The red-haired man coughed. "My leg's broken, you prick. Maybe you two can carry me. Pretty sure I weigh more than both of you combined, though."

Daria pointed out, "We carried you before. Favor your good leg while we get you down from there. Don't try anything or I'll shoot you in the head. You're lucky we left you alive this long."

"Yeah," the man grunted, "I thank my lucky stars, that's for sure."

Ignoring his bullshit, Ty climbed up and unfastened the manacle around the guy's leg, then helped him down with Daria's aid. He supported the man under the shoulder as he hopped forward while Daria watched over him with her pistol drawn.

As she went to open the gate, Ty noticed something odd for the first time. He hadn't seen it in the club's dim lighting, and they'd been too distracted afterward for him to pay much attention to such things, either.

On Daria's forearm, half-visible under her sleeve, was a tattooed string of numbers in faded ink.

Ty kept his mouth shut. If she wanted to talk about it, she would. Otherwise, he wouldn't ask.

Their captive groaned with the effort of moving, and Ty thought about joining him since supporting half of the man's bulk even for the short walk to the garage was no easy task. Daria opened the side door, and they hobbled in, with her closing and locking it behind her.

She flicked on a light. The space within was surprisingly clean. Then again, Ty thought, the building was unlikely to be more than two years old at most. Everything on Atlantica was new except the land itself. Plus, a proper, closed garage wouldn't accumulate as much dirt as would the barely functional shanties of the itinerant workers.

A folding chair sat near one of the walls, and Ty helped the red-haired man over to it, depositing him on the seat and pulling his arms over the back.

"Watch it!" the Bostonian snapped. "Christ, you broke both my fuckin' wrists!"

Ty retorted, "No, that happened in the crash. If you cooperate, we'll get the cuffs off and you to a doctor. First, you need to talk."

Daria put a hand on Ty's arm. "Let me handle most of this. I'm familiar with much of his organization, and I know his boss." She turned to the heavyset Bostonian. "Isn't that right? Mr. Marnes."

The captive didn't say anything. Ty wondered where his loyalties lay and how strong they might be, if he would resist every effort to get info out of him, or if he would roll over quickly for the sake of having his injuries treated.

He coughed again. "Can I get some aspirin and a glass of water? That'd make it a lot easier to talk."

Daria smiled. "Of course. Mr. Katakura, please watch him."

He agreed. While Daria went into the house to fetch the pills and water, he asked the man's name. He kept his tone friendly enough. A cop he'd known once said it was better to start out being halfway nice to people but never to forget how dangerous they could be.

And so, Ty's hand rested on the hilt of his wakizashi the whole time.

The man stated, "Ben." He squirmed, probably due to the handcuffs chafing against his swollen wrists.

"Ben, I'm Tyler Katakura, Executioner of Atlantica. You probably haven't heard of me. If you live long enough, you'll hear about me again. Believe it."

The man grunted.

Daria came back and dropped two aspirin into a glass of water. "We won't take your handcuffs off yet, of course." The man didn't protest, and she poured the water, along with the pills, slowly into his mouth. Then she set the glass aside. "Now, then. Let us begin."

Ty watched and waited. He wanted to do more, but for the time being, it made sense to trust Daria's more extensive knowledge of the Atlantican criminal underground. "His name's Ben," he remarked.

Daria nodded and brushed back her hair. "Ben. Mr. Marnes isn't usually like this. He's lost a great many men in one day, all while being much hastier than normal. Someone else hasn't replaced him, have they? If they have, it would only be polite for your organization to tell me as much. Professional courtesy, yes?"

Ben's jaw clenched, but his face otherwise looked resigned. "No, Marnes is still in charge."

"Very well." Daria turned and paced. "For him to act so rashly and create so many messes—terrorizing a fishing village, chasing people through the streets, and sending someone like Erich into a place that's supposed to be a safe refuge—he must be under a great deal of pressure. Or there must be something he wants very badly. Has your organization been doing things *it's not supposed to*, by chance? Taking certain big risks, in the hope of a big reward?"

Listening intently to Daria's voice and watching their

captive's face, Ty realized that something was going on here that he didn't know about. An elusive secret that was either common knowledge, or perhaps simply *assumed*, in the world of smugglers, while remaining hidden from the rest of the populace.

Ben shook his head vaguely. "I don't know. They're moving something valuable. That's all they told me. I do what the boss orders."

"Of course you do," Daria snapped back, her eyes flashing. "Maybe you should ask questions about what the boss tells you to do, so you aren't suddenly surprised when it turns out that something is very wrong. In any event, 'something valuable.' No rumors? No gossip from your friends? No one talks about these things at all? I find that hard to believe."

Ben asserted that there was "the usual bullshit" amongst the men but otherwise tried to dodge out of having to say much more than strictly necessary. Ty suspected that the man truly wasn't informed as to everything Mr. Marnes was up to. It wouldn't make sense for a crime boss to reveal everything to his low-level thugs, who might end up in situations much like the current one.

Still, he wasn't telling the whole truth. Even Ty could determine that much.

Daria and Ben continued their back-and-forth exchanges for a couple more minutes, with her trying to tease more information out of the man and him wasting her time in the hope that she would get annoyed or discouraged and give up.

Finally, she crossed her arms over her chest and, in a voice abruptly louder and harsher than it had been, barked, "Are you really stupid enough to think that transporting crystals off the island is a good idea? That no one will find out and trace them back to you?"

Ty blinked. It took a moment for his mind to register what she meant—Atlanticore, the same mysterious substance that powered his truck and the most valuable of the island's treasures. As well as its best-guarded secret.

Ben sighed. "It's a rumor, okay? Like I said before. Some of the guys thought that's what it was. I never opened the crates to look. I don't do that shit. It doesn't pay to go sticking my nose where it don't belong. What *does* pay, though, is doing what they say and not fucking up. The money on this was too good to pass up. It ain't hard to figure out when you look at it that way."

He smirked as though he'd checkmated her in chess.

Daria tilted back her head and put a palm over her face, practically groaning. "You can't spend money when you are dead, *glupek.*" Watching her reminded Ty of a governess explaining something exceedingly basic to a naughty child for the tenth time.

Ben scoffed, "You can if you get paid *upfront.*"

By now, it was coming together. Ty stood frozen in amazement, wondering if the Bostonian had been this dumb *before* the concussion.

Daria removed her hand from her cheek. She leaned forward, eyes sharpening, and peered into his face. "Upfront? You mean someone on the island is paying you to smuggle it off to a contact who arranged for it in advance. You aren't merely taking it to market, but to a specific buyer or middleman."

Ben blinked, his smug jowly face suddenly going pale. He knew he'd said too much. Daria wasn't about to let him get away with it. She had the advantage and would press it as hard as she could.

"Uhh," Ben stammered, "I guess that makes sense, but I couldn't say for sure if—"

"No, no," Daria cut him off, "I'm perfectly well aware that you cannot say *anything* for sure. Except when you do so accidentally. Well done."

As the man flushed with embarrassment, Ty came up closer

beside Ms. Barruk. "What's this all about? Why can't Atlanticore be taken off the island? Is it a TINA thing?"

Daria chortled drily. "Oh, it's several different things. There are the legal ramifications, of course. Legal according to the laws of other nations, as there is no law here. But we're surrounded by the laws of the rest of the world. Anything that leaves our shores must pass muster with other countries' governments. That's not the only thing, though."

Ty suspected as much. Smugglers, by definition, didn't give a shit about laws.

"It is said, though not quite *confirmed*," she went on, "that the energy crystals will not allow anyone to take them too far away."

Ty froze in place, dumbfounded. He'd expected her to reveal something about the dynamics of the criminal class or some arcane element of corruption among the Atlantican rich. Instead, with a perfectly straight face, she'd said what sounded like the beginning of a ghost story.

"*What?*"

Daria's mouth twisted in amusement at his reaction. "The crystals seem to become unstable when they leave the island. Supposedly. Take them too far out to sea, and they become dangerous, and finally, they explode." She made an expanding motion with her hands. "Just like a bomb."

Ty's mind raced, thinking back to what the fisherfolk had told him that morning.

"And," Daria continued, "like I said, it hasn't been confirmed, officially, that this is true. But as with many things, the official confirmation comes later. People always know about it before then."

Ty noticed that Ben was watching and listening to them. Since Daria had made no effort to speak to Ty in private, he figured she intended the man to overhear everything they said. That raised the question of how much of what she was saying was genuine and how much might be an act to intimidate Ben into further cooperation.

"Wait," Ty started, "you're telling me you've seen this or heard it from a reliable source?"

Daria nodded. "I wouldn't have believed the gossip if I hadn't witnessed the evidence. And by 'witnessed the evidence,' I mean 'almost died.'"

She laughed. "A crew I was working with not too long ago became greedy, and greed made them stupid. They tried to smuggle *one* crystal off the island. Only one. The accursed thing detonated at sea, killing half the crewmen and breaking the boat in two.

"Fortunately, I'd arranged for a smaller skiff to follow us, out of sight—I never trusted those bastards, so it was a precaution I took in case they tried anything foolish. If the skiff hadn't come to investigate, I would've drowned. The water was too cold to swim in."

She hugged her arms around her body. If the anecdote was an act, Daria was a hell of an actress. Ty maintained his belief that she'd intended for Ben to overhear, but he was pretty damn sure she was telling the truth.

Ben piped up. "Yeah? You seem really sure about that. Exploding crystals. Buncha crap. I think you're making it up to scare us. I ain't convinced, and neither are my employers. You can't trust cheap fishing boats run by cheap fishermen. That's all. That's why we're done using those lowlifes to transport expensive goods."

Ty and Daria turned back toward him in unison. Daria commented, "Oh? Interesting."

"Yeah," Ben went on, his tone defiant, as though he expected to outsmart them momentarily. "Next time, we're gonna smuggle the stuff on one of the transport barges. Those ones they use to ferry workers back to the mainland. Those are high-quality and the people who own them and sail them ain't total dipshits.

Besides, nobody would sabotage or booby-trap one of *those* things."

Ty looked at Daria. Her jaw had fallen open, and her eyes were wide. He felt as though his blood had turned to ice, but then something else replaced it. A kind of electric current spurred him to action.

An image formed in his mind of his people back in the village —the boys who followed him around, the older woman who doted on him, and even the ones he barely knew—at the bottom of the sea.

He spun toward the smuggler and took two heavy steps to his side. "Where are the crystals?" he asked.

Ben started to hem and haw, but Ty had no interest in letting him play dumb. He pulled his wakizashi, the air *swishing* as the blade appeared in his hand before the man's face, the dull light in the garage making the razor edge glow.

"I want you to listen to me very carefully." Ty looked the man directly in the eye, and he was deadly calm. "You're going to tell me where I can find these crystals. If you do not, you're going to find out what *seppuku* feels like. Do you know what that is?"

The red-haired smuggler swallowed his spit. "No," he admitted, but Ty suspected he could guess the general nature of it.

Nonetheless, Ty explained. "Seppuku is the traditional, ritual-istic method of suicide for the warriors among my people. Some-times used more as a form of execution, but one that allowed the condemned man to retain his honor even in the face of failure. You've failed your employer, Mr. Marnes. Submitting to seppuku would ward off the shame. I'm going to give you a choice."

He took a step back but kept the sword held in front of the man's face. "First, the disgraced man inserts the tip of the blade into the side of his belly. Here." He tapped himself above the hip. "Then he slowly, *slowly* draws it across his stomach, split-ting himself open and spilling his guts. If he's a man of exem-plary courage and fortitude, he might also make a second cut, vertically, from under his sternum down through the first gash."

Ty used his hand to draw another line from his middle down to his upper groin. "Then, if he's still alive and not paralyzed by pain, he cuts his own throat. That's the *traditional* method."

Ben appeared to have turned to stone.

"There is also," Ty added, "the more merciful and arguably degraded technique used in later years. In that one, the man only makes the first cut or as much of it as he can. As soon as he begins to falter or is about to cry out, to spare him the humiliation of not being able to stand the agony, his *second* will step in. The second is the one who stands over him with a long sword and severs his neck at the appropriate moment."

Ty made a show of looking around the bare garage. "There's no one here, though, who is qualified for that job. I would have to cut your belly with my knife," he pulled out the shorter tanto dagger, "and have Daria wield my sword. But she has no idea how to use it. She might fail to cut through your neck properly, and I would have to go through the whole thing. The old-fashioned way."

He slid the tanto back into its sheath on his leg. The wakizashi stayed between himself and the captive.

"So," Ty concluded, "what will it be?" He didn't blink.

Ben looked down at the floor at the same time that a shuddering sigh escaped him, the sound of a man's nerve cracking. "Uh," he moaned, "yeah. I get it. The crystals. Someone harvested them from this mine shaft, in, um, Development Sector Twelve. Shit. Mr. Marnes has them slated to go on the transport tonight. Before the evening barge leaves at nightfall. I just remembered that."

Ty's head snapped toward the window. Outside, the day's light was fading. The sun would be down soon.

He looked at Daria. "We need to go. Now."

As he stormed toward the door, Ben protested, "Hey! I still need a doctor."

Daria, following Ty, called, "Yes, yes, I will send someone to take you to the hospital. At least you won't need to be treated for disembowelment."

She shut the garage door and locked it. "Let me use your radio when we're back in the truck. I don't want that man in my house for longer than need be. My friend who was going to pick me up can deal with him."

"Yeah." Ty was distracted. There was only one thing on his mind.

As they climbed back into the armored vehicle, Daria looked at him sidelong and queried, "Would you have followed through with your threat if he hadn't told us where to look?"

Ty started the engine. "Don't ask me that."

CHAPTER FOURTEEN

Ty drove in relative silence at first, waiting for Daria to finish making her radio call. He tried to navigate the shoddy dockside roads at the fastest speeds he could wring from the armored truck without crashing it or sideswiping the shanties, the trees, or the other cars that occasionally rolled by.

Daria wasn't merely delivering a message, meanwhile. She had an entire conversation.

"No, no, no," she proclaimed, using the loudest voice that could still be considered a form of conversational speech rather than shouting. "He goes to the hospital first. *Then* you inform Mr. Marnes. We don't owe him an explanation for where his man is when he sent these fools after us to begin with."

She followed up her orders in English with a lengthy string of statements in Polish, interspersed with other sentences in either German or Yiddish. Ty wasn't quite sure which. Occasionally she paused, and the voice of the person on the other end came through. It was a man, and whoever he was, he seemed to stick to Polish rather than lapsing in and out of three or more tongues.

Finally, Daria said, "Goodbye," and switched off the radio. Then she flipped it back on. "You wanted to call your employers, yes? My people need things explained to them with great care, sometimes. Pardon me."

Ty grabbed the microphone and slowed the truck for a minute while he adjusted the dial to find Eleanor's frequency.

"It's Katakura. Ms. Cervantes, come in. Are you there? It's urgent. Over."

Daria, leaning back in her seat, turned to look at him, with one eyebrow arched. "Ms. Cervantes? I might have heard of her. Not much. But the name seems familiar."

Ty waved, hoping Daria would get the message that he didn't want her to interrupt him. She didn't say anything else.

About four seconds later, the radio crackled, and a woman's voice came through. "Hello, Mr. Katakura, it's Eleanor. How can I help you? Over."

There was no time to waste on pleasantries or formalities. "The transport barge that leaves every evening right around nightfall, from the west end of the harbor. Is it still docked? We *must* stop it from sailing tonight. This is major. Lives are at stake. If that thing has sailed, it's never sailing back. Over."

Eleanor caught on to the situation fast enough. "No, I don't believe it's left, but I can have someone make a call. How far away are you from it? It won't be dark out for another fifteen or twenty minutes, I believe. Over."

Out of the corner of his eye, Ty saw Daria making a face, and he feared she might attempt some sarcastic remark, so he held up his hand, palm toward her. "Okay, good. We're almost there. Have someone check anyway, and contact the captain, harbormaster, or anyone else you can get hold of, and tell them that they are *not* to sail until I've been able to inspect the ship. Again, people will die if that ship hits the ocean. Over."

"Yes. Stay on the line for a moment, please."

Ty could faintly hear her passing on his requests and instructions to someone else nearby. Then she spoke into her microphone again. "My assistant is making a call as we speak.

"Now, then, what on Earth happened earlier? I, like everyone else in the city, heard something about a shootout at Absentees, followed by a chase, another shootout, and a multi-car pileup across half of the town. We have some people cleaning up. But we think that whatever problem you encountered could've been solved in a cleaner, quieter fashion. Over."

"No," Tyler barked, "it couldn't have. A smuggling ring, led by some guy named, uh, Marnes, has been trying to kill me all day. They're the ones who were bullying the fisherfolk. We did what we had to do to survive while minimizing collateral damage. Over."

Eleanor responded with a short, scornful laugh. "You have an interesting definition of 'minimizing,' Mr. Katakura. Much of the city will be talking about that little incident for a week. I understand that there exists a primal male impulse to buck authority, to defy restrictions. Your role is to be the authority. And to be a role model. Do you recall what I said about hammers and nails? There are surely better ways to resolve these things than open warfare in the streets."

Ty gripped the steering wheel hard enough that he might have damaged weaker materials. He didn't have time for this bullshit.

"I'll explain the details later," he promised. "I need to know something else, and it's related to all of this. The smugglers, the 'open warfare,' and the ship sailing tonight. Who claimed Development Sector Twelve? I'd be damn surprised if someone hasn't, and the claim was probably recent. Over."

"Ah, allow me to check. Excuse me a moment. Over." The line went quiet as Eleanor opened a drawer, and by the sound of it, began flipping through papers or folders.

With her assistant busy making the phone call, she had to handle such petty tasks herself. The idea was faintly amusing. Then again, based on what he'd seen of her, Eleanor was more than capable of handling dirty work when she had to.

The truck rumbled away from the water, following a broad

arc around the wharves and associated businesses and shanties. The transport barge departed from the westmost dock. Ty estimated that they would be there in two or three minutes. He hoped they wouldn't be too late.

There was no more direct sunlight in the sky, only the orange glow of dusk. Whether or not night had fallen was essentially subjective.

Eleanor cleared her throat. "Mr. Katakura?"

"Yes. Over." He bit his tongue, resisting the urge to snap at her to get on with it.

She informed him that the current claimant of the sector in question was none other than Mr. Lucas Montrosse.

"Twelve was unclaimed as of about three weeks ago if I'm reading the report correctly," said Eleanor. "It seems that Mr. Montrosse selected it as a site for 'potential storage facilities' and that nothing else of value was there. So, essentially raw land that he staked out for investment and development."

Another tremor of anger. Ty had already been in two fights to the death today, but he felt like he was itching for another.

"Unclaimed and storage my ass," he yelled into the microphone, loud enough to create a feedback screech. He imagined Ms. Cervantes wincing on the other end. "Lucas cleared out all the workers who had homes there because he found some goddamn Atlanticore deposits under the ground. Now he's trying to ship the crystals off the island."

He cleared his throat, making a sound like the threatening growl of a dog, and then remembered to add, "Over."

Eleanor stammered for a second. Daria had tensed, but Ty couldn't say if she'd reacted to his radio conversation or simply prepared herself for whatever awaited them at the dock.

Once she composed herself, Eleanor protested, "No, that's not possible. Why would Mr. Montrosse be stupid enough to try and export Atlanticore? With TINA still in effect, he would risk all kinds of retribution from the mainland governments. Which, in turn, would cause severe blowback from the other Executives. It makes no sense. Over."

For a second, Ty nearly believed her. Her logic would have been sound...but she was missing at least one important piece of information.

"TINA be damned," he shot back. "There are ways around it, aren't there? The smugglers don't give a crap about it. The crystals explode when taken off the island. Nobody knows why, but it happens. I have an eyewitness to the fact. The Marnes group is putting those same crystals on the goddamn transport barge. Okay? Over."

Eleanor fell quiet. Then, "Yes, I see. Get there as soon as possible. My assistant, ah, is making the call as we speak. I don't believe she's gotten through yet, but she's still on the line, and I instructed her to keep calling until someone answers. Over."

"Yeah. Good. Out."

He reached out and switched off the radio, then exhaled, the sound of it long and ragged, like a wind coming over the mountains.

Daria gestured ahead. "We're here. I hope you saved some of your strength. I think we'll need to run instead of walk."

Ty snorted. "I spent that whole chase crouching in the back of the truck. I haven't even broken a sweat since this morning."

A cluster of roughly ten people, all of whom looked blatantly, shamelessly, hopelessly drunk, gathered to watch as the massive steel-plated truck lumbered into the crude mud-and-gravel lot. The driver of the armored vehicle came in too fast and had to brake too hard. The truck skidded, coming dangerously close to swiping or crushing a flatbed truck and a couple of pushcarts parked at the lot's far end.

A red-nosed man in overalls, arm-in-arm with a prostitute

wearing a short skirt and carrying a tattered handbag, raised his brown glass bottle. There was hardly anything left in it. "Whoa, hey! What's that thing? A fuckin' tank? Ha, ha. We at war with Canada now? Or Iceland?"

A couple of his buddies, along with their temporary girl-friends, laughed. Still, they all gave the huge vehicle a wide berth. Everyone wondered who or what would emerge from it.

Once the truck stopped, its doors flew open, and out jumped an unlikely pair. From the driver's side, an Asian man, Japanese or Chinese or something, with choppy, shaggy black hair and wearing a suit of expensive-looking body armor. A Colt 1911 lay against his hip in a military holster, and he also wore what looked like a samurai sword at his other side.

The red-nosed man stared. "What the hell?"

In tandem with the Asian man, a woman with wavy dark hair who was probably Jewish or Italian appeared from the passen-ger's side. Her dress and overall demeanor were about as normal and unremarkable as any Atlantican woman's could be. She had a wild glint in her eye, though, and she too wore a pistol at her side.

The prostitute with the tattered handbag remarked, "You know, I think I seen her before. Around the docks. Don't she work for one of the shipping companies?"

"I don't know," someone else mumbled.

Once the pair's boots hit the ground, they both sprinted across the lot, toward the docks—and the group of drunks.

"Hey!" the Japanese guy called. "Did the barge leave yet? The transport?" He didn't slow down, let alone stop to talk. He expected them to answer while he bolted past. The woman with him was only a few steps behind.

The man in the overalls shrugged. "I dunno. What barge? They're all barges, ain't they? Shit. Hey, where do you think you're—"

The Asian guy and the wavy-haired woman both stomped

right through the group, who'd chosen to occupy the most direct route between the parking lot and the docks proper. Half the revelers tottered or fell to their knees or rumps in the dirt.

Scowling, the red-nosed man looked after them. He'd stumbled against a tree stump. The hooker he'd been locking arms with had drifted off to be scooped up by one of his friends.

"Son of a bitch," he grumbled.

Ty and Daria paid them no heed. They'd hit the ground running and couldn't afford to stop until they knew what had happened. Both had noticed as soon as they'd emerged into the fresh salty air that even the orange glow from behind the horizon was all but gone. Full darkness was creeping over both sea and land.

Ty slowed. He couldn't remember which dock number the transport barge usually anchored at. It had been months since he'd been there and stepped off the boat and into his new life.

As Daria came up beside him, he admitted as much. "You lead the way. I'll follow."

"Yes, yes." She motioned him along. "You can run faster than I can, but I'll do my best."

She was a few years older than him and not as tall, but she was nonetheless in good shape and was able to consistently move at a full run or fast jog as Ty stayed by her side. He wanted to sprint, to keep sprinting until he found the barge. Images of people, dozens of them like his friends and neighbors back in the valley, kept filtering through his head.

He trusted his legs, and he'd decided that he also trusted Daria. The only thing left to trust was luck.

They wove between rows and columns of people, carts piled with supplies being pulled or pushed by both people and pack animals, and cars honking and buzzing along through the thickly choked lanes and lots.

"This way." Daria waved. "I don't see a barge, but let us have a look. It doesn't always dock in the same place. Whichever is closest and available."

That failed to surprise Ty much. Without any true authorities to ensure consistency, docks would operate on a first-come, first-served basis, or the wealthier shipowners would grease the palm of the harbormasters with bribes to ensure they got the best spots to anchor. Or hire thugs to bully competitors out of the way.

The docks were long platforms of unadorned wood, supported by wooden columns that ran up high enough to support a crude roof. Generators arranged at various intervals provided electricity for stage lights that provided some illumination.

Ty could feel his heart sinking. No ship was in sight that could, by any stretch of the imagination, be called a transport barge. He hesitated, uncertain whether to keep looking or to try and track down the authorities, someone who might be able to send a telegram to the captain and tell him to turn back.

Daria stopped, flinging her arms up in frustration and cursing wildly in Polish. Ty closed his eyes.

"They have gone," Daria raged. "How could we have missed them? There was still daylight."

Ty ran over to a group of halfway-respectable individuals chatting near the corner of the platform, not too far from an office-type building situated back from the water.

"Hey," he called to them. "The transport barge that takes workers back and forth, did it leave already?"

A man with spectacles and a white mustache looked back at him, annoyed at being spoken to with such brusqueness. "Yes. I believe you'll find the harbormaster there if you wish to speak to him." He pointed toward the building.

Ty clamped down on the awful sensation of his hopes plummeting into the abyss, the total helpless rage and sorrow that would consume him if he succumbed and gave up. There was still a chance. He bolted toward the office and heard Daria's boots close behind him.

They flung open the door and charged over the threshold. Within was a waiting room of sorts, along with a desk, behind which lay a private room where the harbormaster probably conducted his business.

Ty went straight to the desk, where a fiftyish woman with a beehive hairdo eyed him with a look of mounting concern.

"The transport barge," he gasped. "It's an emergency. The ship has been sabotaged and will sink unless you recall it immediately. We need a phone, radio, telegraph, anything to get in touch with the captain. When did they leave?"

The woman shrank back, shocked and intimidated by the barrage of demands and questions. "Sir, we can't tell them to halt their entire schedule based on your say-so. What evidence do you have that someone sabotaged the ship? They left about five minutes ago, or less."

Daria stepped up to Ty's side. "I'm known here. Get the harbormaster, *now*. We *must* speak to him."

Sighing, the receptionist stood and pushed into the rear office. Seconds later, a tall, bearded, copper-skinned man appeared. "Daria," he began. "What's this all about?"

Ty repeated his earlier brief report, barely containing his anguish. He wanted to take these people by the shoulders and shake them, or shove them aside and commandeer their communications equipment himself if he had to.

He was in luck. Though the harbormaster's face was tight with skepticism, he agreed to at least patch them through to the barge's captain and let them speak to him.

The receptionist let Ty and Daria past the front desk, and they followed the tall man into his office, where he called up the barge on his radio. "This is Harbormaster Alfonso Saraiva. Do you read? I have two people here saying that there is an emergency, that someone sabotaged the ship, and that you must turn back at once."

The communications guy on the other end fetched the ship's captain, who had a loud, ragged voice and didn't try to hide his total dismissal of Ty's concerns.

"Hogshit," he bellowed. "If anyone had tampered with my ship, I would've been the first to know about it. Who are you? Someone looking for a free ride, eh?"

Clenching his hands, Ty snapped, "No, and it's not the ship, it's the cargo. Someone smuggled extremely dangerous materials onboard. Return to port immediately so we can inspect. I am speaking to you as an Executioner of Atlantica. The Executives have put me in charge of justice and safety throughout the island, and I *order* you to return to port. The lives of every person onboard, including yours, are at stake."

The captain made a wordless blustering sound that somehow reminded Ty of an oversized bird puffing itself up and rustling its feathers.

"Exe-what? Who the hell are you? There isn't anyone on Atlantica with authority to *order* me to do anything except the people who pay me. Which 'executives'? This whole thing smells worse than rotten fish.

"I think you're trying to take me for a ride. Another hired thug, someone's business competitor, looking to sabotage your stupid little rival's cargo before he can trade it, eh? Well, bend over far enough, and you'll see where you can shove it. Don't call me again. Out."

Daria cried, "Wait!" but the radio crackled and fell silent.

Ty collapsed into a chair beside the desk. He couldn't believe this was happening. His whole body felt numb. He tried to think. He tried to find some way for it not to end this way, for him not to have failed so badly in his duties...and on his first day, no less.

He barely noticed when Daria turned and ran out the door. The harbormaster, confused and uncomfortable, pulled the radio away. "Well, that man does know his ship and his crew. If there was something wrong, perhaps he already—"

Outside, an engine started, and water *sloshed*. Ty's eyes snapped up toward the window, and it took a second for his brain to register what had happened.

Daria had commandeered a boat. She was waving to him and shouting something, although he couldn't make out the words.

Blinking, the harbormaster opened the window. "Hey! Does that vessel belong to you?"

Daria ignored him. "Ty! Come on. Looks like we have to catch the damned ship ourselves. And yes, I can drive this thing better than you can drive that truck."

Tyler sprang to his feet, his body launching out the door. He planted his hands on the half-wall next to the reception desk and vaulted over it. The lady with the beehive hair gasped in horror.

Ty hit the ground running. By the time he was outside, Daria had brought the boat right up to the platform's base where the barge should've been.

She was grinning, probably at the prospect of getting sea spray in her face again. Ty might've shared her enthusiasm under other circumstances. Now, all he cared about was haste.

CHAPTER FIFTEEN

A single coherent thought, important to his survival over the next ten seconds, forced its way into the center of Ty's consciousness. Daria was a better sailor than he would've guessed. Maybe even better than her boastfulness would suggest.

She'd brought the boat within about three feet of the dock, and while moving it fast, stopped at exactly the right time to end up directly in front of him. The distance was something most human beings could jump with ease—even those who weren't at the same level of physical fitness as Ty.

He sprinted across the wooden surface, ignoring the stares or comments of flabbergasted onlookers, and leapt the short distance straight into the boat. He landed hard in the center, stumbling toward the side and rocking the vessel amid the waves.

"Hey!" Daria exclaimed, widening her stance next to the outboard motor to brace herself. "Watch out, fool. You could've *stepped* in with the space I gave you. You didn't have to *jump*."

Ty lurched sideways toward the center as a way of stabilizing himself as well as the boat. He waved in a short chopping motion toward the open sea beyond the docks. "Just go. *Go.*"

Daria was already buzzing away from the platform. Someone

was running up behind them, cursing madly and shouting at them to stop, to come back with his boat. Ty couldn't see who he was, nor did he care much at the moment.

The water churned and sloshed beneath them, much of it turning to white, foamy spray as Daria picked up speed. The boat blasted out through the dark waves.

The docks fell away, and with them, the artificial lights and sounds and voices of people. It didn't take long. The smallness, the relative insignificance of the human structures built on land became readily clear as they headed off into the vast, hostile wilderness that was the ocean at night.

"Daria, how long will it take us to reach them?"

She grimaced. "I don't know. We didn't check exactly when they left, and there's no way to be certain how fast they're going. They couldn't have gone far. Five or ten minutes, if we're lucky. I'll go as fast as we can."

Ty gave a slow nod, breathing in through his nostrils and out through his mouth. For now, there was nothing he could do but wait. He examined his surroundings and tried to formulate a plan of attack.

The boat looked like it could comfortably seat about five or six people. So, it would be big enough to maneuver in without the risk of knocking one another overboard while being far smaller than the barge they were chasing and able to weave in and out of tight spaces while, hopefully, not being seen.

Ty glanced at the motor. It was too dark for him to read the labeling and determine what horsepower it was. Still, its size and relative newness suggested a quality model and that Daria could achieve some impressive speed.

He suspected they would need it. She was picking up the pace as they got farther from the docks, pushing the little boat as fast as it could go without capsizing. The water around them turned white, and the craft began to bump along the waves.

Ty went back through his memories of riding the transport

out to Atlantica. It seemed so long ago, but the details were surprisingly fresh. The barges typically held around a hundred, sometimes more like a hundred and fifty people in cramped and primitive conditions. The pilothouse, which held the steering wheel, compass, and navigation system, was at the rear.

It occurred to him that it might not be the same ship or type of vessel as he'd been on. He supposed it might've been the type of barge that was essentially towed through the sea by a smaller boat. However, those were less stable and poorly suited to rougher conditions on the open ocean, so it seemed unlikely even given the relatively short voyage to Nova Scotia.

A couple of minutes later, Daria pointed. "There."

Ty squinted. It was difficult to see much since the night was cloudy and they were well out in the water now, with no artificial light sources nearby. As his eyes adjusted, he made out a broad black silhouette up ahead, hovering atop the water before the horizon. Waves parted before it and left a swirling wake behind.

Daria reduced her speed. The motor, roaring until now so its rough voice drowned out the sounds of the waves and the water sprayed aside from the boat's passage, softened and slowed the tempo of its growls. They continued to gain on the dark bulk of the transport ship but at a less hurried pace.

Ty's first instinct was to yell at her, to demand to know why she was slowing down when everything depended on getting the ship turned back as soon as humanly possible. Instead, he bit his tongue and forced himself to keep quiet. If the barge's crew saw them approaching, they might blow them out of the water to be safe. Then all would be lost.

He had to trust her judgment. So far, Daria had proven that she knew what she was doing and when she took action beyond his immediate comprehension, she had good reasons for it.

She motioned with two fingers and caught his eye. "Tyler," she began, "we don't have much time. The barge is about as far out to sea as the one I was on when the crystal exploded. I'm slowing down to make less noise. When I get close, you must get on quickly and go straight to the cabin. Make them stop, or better yet turn around. I'll wait and support you any way I can."

Ty nodded. He was going mad with impatience, but years of self-discipline kept him reserved for the moment, saving his strength and capacity for frenzied action until the time was right.

Daria sailed in ways that didn't make much sense to him, weaving around and continuously adjusting her speed up or down. He ordered himself to trust her. She was probably keeping them out of sight or keying the engine's noise to the ambient sounds of the water to ensure they remained undetected.

The barge's silhouette grew bigger. At last, they drew close enough for Ty to make out some of the details, partially with the aid of the few dim electric or gas-powered lights onboard. It looked like there was a hanging ladder beside the rear pilothouse area, but its bottom was a few feet above the low ebb of the waterline.

He would have to jump. Leaping would be the easy part. Grabbing and holding on, particularly if the metal was slippery or disintegrating with rust and disuse, would be where the real challenge lay.

Daria picked up speed to power them through the barge's V-shaped wake, the extra noise of the water covering their motor sounds. She saw the ladder, too, and guided them toward it.

Ty stood. He debated leaving his rifle behind for the sake of mobility, but decided against it. He didn't know what sort of opposition might be waiting for him. Instead, he tightened the sling so the gun lay more closely against his shoulder.

"All right," he said. A visual scan of the ship beside and above them didn't reveal anyone looking at them, so they'd probably remained unseen.

Ty drew a deep breath, tasting the salt spray and smelling his nervous sweat, crouched, and sprang off the boat into the air.

He realized at once that he'd jumped too hard. He slammed

into the side of the barge, his hands madly grasping for the ladder as his stomach lurched around within him. His left hand gripped the metal's right bar while his right hand clawed at empty space. He swung aside, being dragged toward the rear of the barge by momentum until his right hand reached up and caught the same bar above the first hand.

Below him, Daria throttled down, falling into the barge's wake to hide nearby and keep watch.

Ty clenched his jaw and began climbing. The barge was a flat and low-lying ship, so it wasn't a long climb, but it was harder than he'd expected thanks to the vessel's rolling forward motion.

Near the top, he took a rapid glance down at the sea, and his heart sank. A massive wave was coming up on them, rolling toward the barge like a mobile dune of blackish-blue, the *hissing* sound of its approach growing to a roar as it loomed closer. Ty reached up, found a vertical bar protruding from the edge of the deck, and seized it. He hoisted himself upward. It was too late to escape the wave. It was already breaking against the front of the barge.

"Goddammit," he grunted and held on for dear life.

The surge of water, rising as high as the deck itself, crashed along the side of the ship and engulfed him. The shock of its chilly wetness and the incredible force of its pull and momentum strained his muscles and nearly dislocated his shoulder, but he held. Then the wave moved past, leaving him gasping and drenched in the brisk and salty evening air. He gave thanks that at least the ocean wasn't too cold at this time of year.

The crystals. Everyone aboard might die at any second, he recalled. He hauled himself over the edge and landed on his feet upon the deck.

His eyes were everywhere at once. He needed to take in all the necessary information while discarding anything superfluous. His focus on the one overriding goal was total.

To his left was the main transport area, where a huge cluster of people huddled together in the center under a crude roof of sheet metal with tarps nailed over top of it to keep out the rain and sea spray. There were a pair of gas lamps at either end, providing low orange light. It was a relatively short voyage, and the barge was intended as a "budget" form of transportation anyway, so passenger comfort wasn't a priority.

Someone, a woman, noticed Ty immediately. She gasped and turned to a man beside her and began yammering away in a language Ty didn't recognize. He had no time to address her concerns.

To his right was the pilothouse. It looked bigger than he'd expected, and it was lit from within, amber light shining out its broad windows. Ty dashed toward it. He patted himself down, making sure that none of his weapons had washed away in the wave—they hadn't—and flung open the door.

Within were three men chatting around the steering wheel. They stopped. All heads turned toward the intruder in unison.

Ty ordered, "Stop this ship. Turn around immediately, or you're all dead."

The biggest of the three men made a barking, sputtering sound. "I'm the captain, friend, not you. This got something to do with that lowlife who called me a little earlier, does it? You one of his accomplices?"

The captain looked almost exactly the way Ty would've expected. Tall, broad-shouldered, thickset but in a way that suggested stolid strength more than sloth or gluttony. An iron-colored beard encompassed the lower half of his round face, and he wore a white cap. All that was missing was a smoking pipe jutting out from his mouth.

"No," Ty responded. "I'm trying to help you. You have dangerous cargo on board that *will* destroy the ship. Turn back *now*." He had no intention of asking again.

The man's eye twitched. "I told you people, I know my goddamn ship, including its cargo. I have a schedule to—"

In one rapid motion, Ty unslung his rifle, twirled it end over end, and brought the flat side of the buttstock directly into the captain's head. The man grunted once and fell over, his hat toppling off and his mouth lolling open as he sank into unconsciousness.

Ty spun the rifle back around, now aiming it at the next closest man, whom he assumed was probably the first mate. "Do as I say." His voice was low, his words precise. The gun's barrel pointed directly at the man's heart. "I'll kill you if that's what it takes to save the lives of everyone else on board. *Take this ship back to the docks.* Now."

There was a split second's hesitation as the man, younger and smaller than the captain, wrapped his mind around what Ty had said. Outside through the window, Ty could see some people amidst the crowd roiling and moving around. They probably wanted to see if everything was all right.

Then the first mate stepped forward, grabbed the wheel, and began turning the barge. The ship veered to the side, making a wide one-hundred-eighty-degree arc through the waves. Ty prayed to whatever divinities might've been willing to listen that the extra couple of hundred feet they went before turning wouldn't be enough to push the crystals past their exploding point.

Nothing happened. The boat was now heading back to Atlantica. For a second, Ty closed his eyes and breathed deeply, savoring his moment of success.

Still, he'd somehow known that it wouldn't be so easy.

The other man in the cabin, crouching near the unconscious skipper, looked up at Ty with wide, pleading eyes.

"Hey, we're willing to do as you say, but we don't know who you are, and we never heard anything about any dangerous materials on board. There will have to be an investigation when we get back, and a lot of people will be mad over this ship not arriving on time. Isn't there some way we can—holy shit, what are those guys *doing?*"

Ty, acting on a mixture of instinct and reflex, hit the floor and crawled sideways toward the door. Half a second after he'd dropped, a heavy wrench, spinning sidelong end over end, crashed through the cabin's front window and sent glass fragments spraying in all directions.

The first mate barely dodged the flying tool and cried out in alarm. Ty shouted at him, "Keep sailing! Keep us moving back to the docks! I'll take care of this."

From his crouching position beside the door, Ty leaned out the opening and took a bead on what lay beyond, his rifle in a low ready position. Whoever had thrown the wrench probably didn't have a gun. It *might* have been an accident. Possibly.

The first thing he saw was half a dozen men storming out of the crowd, directly toward the pilothouse. And him. They looked nothing like average workers who wanted to figure out what was wrong. They had a specific purpose in mind. As though someone had ensured that they would be present on this particular voyage and instructed them to intervene if there were any complications.

"You!" bellowed the man out in front. "What gives? We paid to go to the mainland. You're gonna come in pointing a rifle and make us go back? Who put you in charge, huh?" He slipped a box cutter out of his jacket with his right hand. With his left, he picked up a heavy coil of rope.

Behind him, the others had armed themselves as well. Ty didn't see any guns. Sharpened screwdrivers, hammers, chains, stuff like that. Things that would be easier to explain away if someone searched them but still perfectly capable of maiming anyone they needed to harm.

If they could get close enough.

Ty snarled, "You're not the ones in *any* position to threaten me. I'm turning the ship back to save your lives along with everyone else on this damn boat. I'm guessing the smugglers hired you pricks to make sure their illegal cargo makes it to the mainland, didn't they? Well, don't think I won't shoot every last one of you. Like I told these guys," he gestured with his head back into the cabin, without taking his eyes off the group, "if I have to kill a few to save the rest, I will."

They hesitated. If Ty hadn't felt the motion of air behind his head, they wouldn't have needed to do anything else.

Ty jerked his upper body aside as the ax blade *swished*, falling through the space where his skull had been an instant earlier. He brought up the butt of his rifle, striking the haft of the fire ax below the head and knocking it aside. The dark, wiry man holding it stumbled as he tried to retain his grip.

The sailor behind Ty in the cabin, the one tending to the captain, cried, "What the hell are they doing? Who are these people?"

Ty raised his rifle and fired. The axman screamed and stumbled aside, dropping his weapon so it clattered to the deck. The bullet had pierced his right arm and entered his chest from the side. He crumpled, already half dead.

"Smugglers," Ty explained. "They've been giving me trouble *all fucking day*." Eyes blazing and teeth grinding, he sprang to his feet.

The rest of them were charging the bridge. The brief window of opportunity they'd had while their friend snuck up on Ty from behind the cabin was more than enough for them to press the attack. Three were coming for the cabin's door. The others headed for the shattered window.

Ty threw his rifle back over his shoulder, once again tightening the sling. When he'd shot the axman a second ago, the bullet could've gone nowhere except into open air and out to sea if it penetrated through the target. The other thugs had innocents behind them.

Not to mention there was a chance of a round piercing the

ship's hull, potentially endangering the whole craft by causing it to take on water. Plus, he didn't know where the Atlanticore crystals were. Accidentally shooting one of *those* would be even worse.

His 1911 ought to work if he was careful. The lower velocity and less aerodynamic shape of the .45 ACP round usually stayed inside the person unlucky enough to get shot with it.

Frightened civilians were unpredictable, too. They sometimes tended to jump into the line of fire. With the dim lights making barely a dent in the oceanic darkness...

Ty scrambled back into the cabin. The first mate continued to steer, his trembling hands locked around the wheel and thick beads of sweat pouring down his forehead. He had a couple of superficial cuts from the broken glass, one on the chin and another on the arm.

"Keep doing what you're doing." Ty found the wrench amid the debris. When he picked it up and turned back, the first of the thugs was clambering into the cabin over the jagged edges of the broken window.

Ty hurled the wrench. It struck the man on the crown of his head. He let out a loud "Oof!" and stumbled, cutting his leg on the glass, and fell backward out of the cabin. Behind him, two others advanced.

The captain was starting to come to. Ty looked at the younger man tending him and barked, "Keep him out of the action." The captain might've been good to have on his side in a fight, but the man might well assume the smugglers' hired minions were merely "concerned citizens" and take their side against him.

Ty drew his pistol, which gave pause to the pair of thugs about to try the window. Then he dashed out the door. The guy with the box cutter was there, ready to strike. With his free hand, Ty caught the man's wrist, twisting his arm aside and slamming him into the railing along the edge of the deck. Then he pistol-whipped him in the face, grabbed him by the belt, and heaved him overboard. The thug screamed briefly before striking the water below.

One of the smugglers shouted, "You! Go around back o' the cabin. Get him that way!"

Ty backed up. The other four men advanced toward him, their pace deliberate and inexorable, while the fifth scrambled to head him off from behind.

Then he turned and sprinted around the back of the cabin. The fifth man, armed with a foot-and-a-half length of lead pipe, froze in place as it dawned on him that Ty had so easily outmaneuvered him.

Ty shot him in the face. He instantly dropped as though someone had tied his feet to the back of a car and stomped on the gas. Curses erupted from the other side of the pilothouse.

Continuing forward, Ty swung around the corner of the small structure and caught the other four men as they clustered near the front of the cabin. They were the only thing in the line of fire.

Raising the pistol again, Ty fired another five shots in a rapid burst, allowing the muzzle to travel around in a slight arc as he pulled the trigger to pepper the whole group with lead. Shrieks and groans arose as two men detached themselves from the sides of the human mass, scampering away, while the two in the center crumpled against the deck or railing. One of them twitched enough that he might still have been alive, but he was out of the fight.

Only two thugs remained. If Ty could deal with them one at a time, he would have a far better chance. He'd reloaded his pistol on the trip here, making sure to chamber the extra round, so he had two more left in his magazine. He considered loading a fresh one, but his enemies didn't give him the time.

Having split up, they kept an eye on one another, each taking cover to advance and keeping Ty unsure of which might attack first. He backed away onto the small open area behind the cabin as the two approached from opposite sides.

Daria's skiff reappeared at the corner of his vision. He looked down and saw her piloting the little boat closer to the barge, no longer concerned about detection. With her free hand, she was motioning toward him and looking at his face, trying to get his attention.

Their eyes locked. Then she pointed backward and shouted something, although he couldn't make out her words over the noise of the engines combined with the endless sloshing of the sea.

His gaze followed her hand to the waters behind the barge. He saw it at once. Another boat was approaching, and it was moving fast.

Ty snapped his attention back to what was ahead of him—the pair of the smugglers' hired kneecap men who remained on their feet. They were circling to flank him from either side, and the guy with the rope was starting to twirl it like a lasso minus the loop.

The other man, who only held a crude knife that looked like he'd made it from a sharpened ruler with cloth wrapped around the handle, was twitchy and terrified. His employer had probably never briefed him on the prospect that a single man could defeat four of his coworkers so quickly.

As if daring Ty to get it over with, he spat, "You gonna shoot us? You think you're a big fuckin' man for having a gun when all we got is—"

Since the man had the ship's cabin to his back, whose walls would have likely intercepted a stray bullet, Ty raised his pistol and put his last two rounds in the man's chest. He fell over after the second slug took him in the ribs, the *crack* of the gun's report fading to disclose his scream of rage and pain, and he turned halfway over before seizing up and going still.

The other man bellowed a war cry and threw the heavy rope

at his opponent. Ty had expected the move, but he'd figured the thug would aim for his head. Instead, he threw the rope laterally toward his legs. Its thick coils battered his shins as he tried to dodge to the side, and he faltered.

His hand went toward the sword at his side as the man charged him.

Everything seemed to move at a tiny fraction of normal speed, and all that happened revealed itself to Ty's mind at a bizarrely casual pace.

Off to his side and down below, Daria was yelling something else as the other boat approached. His hand wrapped around the grip of his wakizashi. The last of the smuggling ring's enforcers bore down upon him, swinging a short but heavy hammer toward his temple.

Two sounds echoed through the salt-spray air at once. One was the swish of the sword clearing its scabbard.

The other was the crackling of gunshots behind him—automatic fire, definitely not Daria's pistol. The boat tailing them had to be a shadow escort belonging to the smugglers, and its crew had stopped playing nice. Greed and desperation had overcome their better judgment.

What Ty didn't know was whether they'd opened fire on him or Daria. There was no time to think.

The man with the hammer crashed into him, the crude weapon a foot from his head, at the same instant that Ty ducked and rolled, lashing out with the wakizashi. He came out of his roll facing his foe. He couldn't tell if he'd wounded him yet.

The thug threw the hammer. Ty hopped aside, and it passed him, striking the back of the cabin with a loud *thud*. Behind them, the shadow ship fired another volley of automatic gunfire, but it sounded like Daria was shooting back with her P38.

In a last-ditch effort, probably knowing it was hopeless, the last of the enforcers tried to tackle the Executioner. Ty calculated the man's trajectory and stepped aside, transforming the movement into a diagonal slash with his sword.

The man squawked and collapsed to his knees. Ty saw that he'd put a light cut in the man's calf with his rolling strike earlier. Now, he'd also split open his shoulder and upper pectoral. Bleeding and moaning, the thug gave up and did nothing but clutch a bloody hand against his wound.

Leaving him, Ty turned and peered out at the ocean. The smaller boat trailing them had turned on a spotlight and was aiming it at Daria's craft. They were gaining on her and the barge. Once they got close enough, neither she nor Ty would stand much of a chance.

Unless...

He stepped around in front of the wounded man. "Look up at me," he stated.

The thug looked up. He was relatively young, maybe twenty-five, with big brown eyes. For a second, Ty hoped he would make it.

"You're not dead yet," he pointed out. "Stop the bleeding, and you can survive this. But I need you to help me and do as I say."

An idea had forced its way into his mind, something crazy enough that it might turn the tide in his and Daria's favor.

The man gasped, "What? What do you want?"

Someone on the shadow ship interrupted them, shouting into a megaphone with what was probably a French-Canadian accent. "Turn this ship back around. You must go to the mainland, or we'll open fire. We will board if you do not comply. We will punish anyone who doesn't do as we say."

Ty saw a flicker of hope in the eyes of the man before him. "They won't have the chance to rescue you," he snapped. "Either you tell me what I want to know, or you're dead."

He paused, letting the statement sink in before he asked his question. "Where are the crystals?"

CHAPTER SIXTEEN

The young man winced in pain as the adrenaline faded and the horror of his injuries became harder to ignore. He looked like he was going to try and stall for time. He hesitated, and his eyes flicked off beyond the deck toward the approaching ship filled with his coworkers.

Ty leaned in closer and brought the edge of his wakizashi closer to the man's throat. "I will *not* ask a third time. The crystals. Don't pretend you don't know what I mean."

The thug squeezed his eyes shut. "They're below deck," he groaned. "The hatch is over there between the cabin and the main deck. They're toward the front, in some boxes with, uhh, fake girls' clothes or something? Under a blue tarp. You gotta help me, man. Get me out of the cold, okay?"

There wasn't much time, but Ty hauled him to his feet, ignoring his yelp of pain, and marched him toward the cabin, leaving him in the doorway. "You," he said to the third of the three sailors, "tend to this man's wounds, but if he tries anything, *kill him.*"

Then he sprinted past the bridge, toward the edge of the main deck where the passengers still huddled in fear. The smugglers on the boat fired up their megaphone again and repeated their orders from earlier. The sound was louder since they were now adjacent to the barge's rear corner. Ty hoped that Daria knew what she was doing and had sailed clear of them.

He also prayed that she was still somewhere nearby. He needed her, or his plan was doomed—and with it, everyone onboard.

He spotted the hatch leading below deck. Noting its location, he then rushed to the side of the deck. His passage to the railing brought him close to the crowd of civilians. Most had inched toward the front of the boat to be as far as possible from the unexpected battle.

A few people gasped. Ty raised his voice. "I'm not here to hurt you. Everyone stay calm." He wasn't used to speaking to big groups of people like this unless it was under familiar circumstances as with his community back in the valley.

No one reacted. They watched him with bulging, wary eyes but left him to his business. He suspected most were simply hoping he would ignore them and that this would all be over soon.

Given their numbers, they could've crushed him if enough of them had put their minds to it. Bitterly, he reflected that they might also have stopped the smugglers' henchmen and saved him and themselves precious time. But they probably had no idea what was really going on.

Ty reached the edge of the deck, keeping low to make himself a less tempting target for the shadow boat. He saw Daria's skiff almost directly below him.

"Daria! Can you hear me?" he bellowed. His voice was getting hoarse.

She looked up. "Yes. Come down from there. We have to—"

A burst of submachine gunfire from the other ship drowned her out. She ducked, and Ty did likewise. A few bullets sparked off the barge's hull or drew up columns of disturbed water, but none found their mark. Passengers screamed and cried behind them.

Ty yelled, "I have a plan. Stay close and wait for me. Just a minute, okay?"

"What?" She stared at him as though he'd taken his clothes off and begun to dance naked with an upturned bucket over his head. She broke into a stream of colorful-sounding Polish or perhaps Yiddish ranting and profanity.

Ty dashed back toward the hatch and flung it open. He stopped himself before he descended, though. The barge's interior was pitch black.

He ground his teeth together. "Goddammit. Nothing is ever simple, is it?" At least they were still sailing in the correct direction. The smugglers wouldn't be able to do as much damage as their precious cargo would.

Which, at the moment, was the whole point.

Ty retrieved one of the oil lamps from the deck, then returned to the hatch and climbed into the ship's depths. He moved at a fast trot, holding the lamp out in front of him to ensure he didn't stumble over any of the cargo and looked for a pile of stuff covered by a blue tarp.

Annoyingly, two loads met that description midway through, but the wounded man had said they'd stored the crystals at the front of the hold. Ty kept going. Outside, he heard another volley of gunshots. This time, it sounded like semiautomatic pistol fire, which might have been Daria trying to ward off the smugglers.

Ahead of him, the end of the storage hold was in sight. No blue tarps. He leaned left and right, sweeping the lamp around and trying not to panic or drive his fist through the nearest box in frustration before a flash of azure revealed itself. It was off to the right, half-hidden behind a pile of crates and wooden pallets.

Ty rushed over, set down the lamp, and grasped the edge of the tarp, yanking it off before he bothered to inspect the pile of stuff that lay beneath. Three big, heavy cardboard boxes set within an open plastic container reminiscent of wooden milk crates rested there. He dug his fingers into the top of the nearest box and ripped away the cardboard.

He recalled the injured man's bizarre description—that they'd hidden the crystals within a mass of "fake girls' clothes." *It made no sense,* he thought. Why would a volatile power source be shipped surrounded by something as potentially flammable as clothing? Putting them in cardboard boxes, too, seemed moronic.

Then it all made sense. The material beneath the box's lid was pink and fluffy. He stared at it blankly for half a second. "Asbestos. Got it. The people who packed it to begin with were smart enough, even if the guys they hired to protect their shipment were dumb as posts."

He grabbed two handfuls of the asbestos coating and ripped it away. It came off in fluffy, fibrous streams and chunks, which he tossed aside. There was no time to do things gently. He needed to be damn sure he had the right box before he ventured back above deck.

Ty tore away another layer, then stopped. His jaw fell open.

Raw Atlanticore, he saw now, was different from the refined crystal that powered his truck. It was somehow both darker and brighter. Darker in that bits of earth, stone, and base metals clung to it, pocking the crystals with blackish patches that also reflected the blue glow up and out where they contained metal or smooth rock.

Brighter in that the Atlanticore itself pulsated and *crackled* with raw, incredible power. It was stunning to think that such a miraculous substance, dangerous enough that it could function as a bomb with no extra measure taken to detonate it, had been crammed into run-of-the-mill containers like this. Then lugged into a damp, dirty space alongside all the other cheap supplies and contraband the ship seemed to contain.

Ty grabbed the edges of the box and hauled it up. It was heavy, more so than he'd expected, and he grunted as he struggled to lift it to chest height. He had to settle, instead, for lugging it forward against his thighs, halfway bent over and stumbling with each step.

It was taking too long. Gunfire had started up outside again, now in the form of careful single shots. The smugglers were probably trying to pick Daria off before they stormed the barge itself. Women, children, and older men up above gasped or screamed.

Ty got a few yards farther. The box started to slip from his grasp. He lowered it, allowing it to strike the floor more gently than if he'd allowed it to drop, and resisted the urge to roar into the space or kick the nearest stationary object in his anger.

Instead, he looked back into the top of the box. He'd left the lamp behind, but the cerulean glow of the crystals themselves still offered him some illumination.

If Atlanticore was as volatile and deadly as Daria had led him to believe—if a single crystal had been enough to sink the ship that she'd been on before—he didn't need a whole crate's worth. A handful ought to suffice.

The problem, therefore, was getting his hands around the stuff without frying himself to a crisp or wrecking the whole boat.

"Okay," he breathed, "the asbestos must contain the heat and power, right? Otherwise, all this shit would be up in flames." He mentally cursed himself for removing so much of the coating.

Still, there was enough. He tore off more of it from around the edges. Then, keeping it between his hands and the Atlanticore like a crude oven mitt used to grab a hot pan, he took hold of the topmost crystal, whose multifaceted spiky surface offered a couple of decent places to hold onto.

As he tried to dislodge it, though, it got caught on the others. The faint humming sound of the crystals grew stronger, and blue-white sparks flew up as they rubbed against one another.

Ty froze, waiting to ensure there would be no explosion, no

sudden surge of electricity. Then he used his left hand, still coated in asbestos, to move aside another of the jagged stones, freeing the one on top. As he pulled it free, he noted with a certain grim satisfaction that he'd chosen probably the biggest one in the entire shipment.

It was about the size of a volleyball, give or take due to its irregular surface. Larger than the one under the hood of his truck. He wondered how big the one on Daria's former ship had been.

Someone opened the hatch and called down, "Hey! What's going on down there? We don't want trouble. You're scaring the women and kids!"

Annoyed, Tyler shot back, "The trouble is coming from those sons of bitches on the ship following us. Not the skiff, the other one. They're smugglers, and they don't care if every last one of you people ends up dead. Help me, and you might make it."

The man made a series of vague huffing sounds as Ty jogged across the rest of the cargo hold, cradling the big glowing crystal, his primary focus on not dropping it or touching its bare surface.

As he started to climb the steps back to the deck, he saw an older, thick-waisted, bald man staring down at him. "What's that? Who are you, anyway?"

"I'm the Executioner," Ty said. "Those guys were trying to smuggle Atlanticore. You'll all be fine, but only if we can stop them. Clear me a path, will you?"

The man continued to grumble, but his face disappeared from the hatch. Then Ty heard his voice shouting, "Okay, make way. Everyone stay out of this man's way!"

It was better than nothing. Ty clambered up to the deck, his eyes quickly readjusting to the night sky after the blackness of the hold, and immediately jogged toward the cabin. He had to trust that Daria had kept herself alive this long.

Once he was close enough to the cabin to be heard, Ty called through the broken window to the first mate. "Hey. Keep going, and pick up speed. Only for a few minutes. We have to get ahead of the ship that's following us. This is important. Don't fuck with me."

The first mate's mouth opened and closed, but he nodded. His hand reached for a lever. Ty didn't know much about ships, but he was pretty sure the engine could run faster than it currently was. The extra expenditure of gas wouldn't matter much with them already being halfway back to Atlantica.

Ty could see the smugglers' shadow boat advancing along the side of the barge. Then the bigger ship's speed gradually increased, causing the smugglers to fall back into the wake. They passed through the dim light coming from the cabin, and Ty saw that there were at least five or six of the bastards, armed to the teeth with shotguns and submachine guns.

They couldn't be allowed to board. Even if Tyler and Daria could take them on in a fight, there would be bullets flying everywhere and a hundred or more civilians nearby. And if a dozen innocents died in the crossfire...

He ran toward the front of the ship, watching his footing as he continued to hold the crystal in front of him. "Someone get me a line!" he called. "Find a line!"

By now, some passengers had grasped that important stuff was going on and Ty was on their side. The older man who'd come to the hatch, along with a tough-looking woman and two young men, hopped to the task. They pushed out of the crowd and looked around.

Ty realized that the two young men were members of the barge's crew. When the fighting had started, they'd sought safety amid the general cluster of passengers, but now that they understood Ty didn't mean them harm, they were back in action.

He went to the edge of the deck. Daria was below and slightly ahead of his position. She'd gunned the motor once she saw the barge speeding up.

Ty was amazed that she hadn't fallen behind yet. She was

slowly drifting back, though. Unless they got a line to her and the skiff, the bigger ship would leave her at the mercy of the smugglers.

They made eye contact. Ty motioned for her to wait a moment. He set the crystal carefully down against a post, still using the haphazard mass of asbestos to shield it.

To the passengers, he said, "No one touch this. It's dangerous and will kill you. I'll need it in a minute. Where are those lines?"

One of the sailors replied, "Got 'em! You want us to throw 'em to that lady down there?"

"Yeah." Ty ran over to help.

Daria figured out what was going on quickly enough. The first line missed, but the second, chucked by the more athletic-looking of the two young sailors, found its mark. Daria caught it and attached it to her skiff. Once that was secured, they threw her the other as well.

Ty leaned over the edge. "Get the skiff as close to us as you can. I'll need to climb down."

"Why?" she called. Shaking her head, she and the sailors worked together to draw the skiff as near the barge's side as possible without the smaller vessel scraping against it and tearing apart.

Then, looking extremely perturbed, Daria left the skiff and started climbing the lines. There was another ladder nearby, and once she was within arm's reach, she caught it and hauled herself up. Ty stood directly overhead and took her arm as she neared the top, helping her clear the deck.

She snapped, "I cannot believe you made me do that. What's your plan? Did you take one of the Atlanticore crystals *out*? What are you thinking?"

Ty waved. "After the way you drove earlier today, you're in no position to—"

Then the smugglers opened fire again. They were gaining on the barge. The first mate was starting to slow, and the shadow ship had increased its speed. Bullets and pellets *dinged* off the barge's hull or splashed into the surrounding waters.

Ty drew a deep breath. He unhooked his weapons and left them on the deck. He picked up the asbestos-coated crystal, held it against himself with one hand, and used his other arm to take a firm hold of the railing. Then he swung his leg over the edge and found the first rung of the ladder.

Daria's eyes bulged in horror. "Now what? Don't drop that! My God, you're madder than I am."

A couple of other people, picking up on her alarm, gibbered and asked what the hell their mysterious protector was up to.

Ty ignored them. His focus had turned entirely to the task of descending the ladder, then waiting for the right moment to get into the skiff.

He assessed the situation around him. The smugglers' boat was gaining again but probably far enough away for safety. He looked up and yelled, "Tell the first mate to slow way down. You're going to need to pick me up in a minute."

One sailor rushed off to deliver the message while Daria threw up her hands and looked away.

Ty inhaled. If he could maintain his hold on the crystal *just right* and get the timing down, it would work. If he couldn't, the jagged piece of Atlanticore would probably end up in the ocean anyway, where it would be less likely to do any harm.

He waited until the bobbing craft beneath him lined up perfectly with his likely trajectory. Then he jumped.

It wasn't a long fall, but the residual motion of the barge accelerated him in the air and made it seem longer than it was. He landed on his feet near the front of the little boat and instantly tucked his head and shoulder into a roll, using both hands to retain his hold on the crystal while the skiff bobbed and churned beneath him.

He came out of the roll on his knees, and the crystal clutched in a trembling double grip.

"Okay," he gasped. "Jesus. I didn't think that would work."

He placed the crystal into a nook near the front of the skiff on the floor. There was a tacklebox nearby, which he used to brace it in place, still protected by the tufts of asbestos. Then he went to the lines and unhooked them, to gasps of horror from the people above.

The boat fell back in the water, and its rear corner banged against the barge's hull, nearly knocking Ty off his feet. He scrambled back to the outboard motor and started it, haphazardly taking the craft away from the larger ship and turning it.

Once it pointed toward the smugglers' boat, he increased the speed. The men onboard noticed him and one of them aimed a submachine gun at him.

"Try it," Ty snarled. "You assholes haven't hit much of anything so far, have you?" He locked the steering lever in place, still at max speed, and as one of the thugs opened fire, he jumped over the edge and felt the Atlantic close over his head.

The water was bracing but not frigid. Ty kicked his boots off. The Executives could afford to replace them. He surfaced for air amid a hail of gunfire that wildly peppered the waves around him, drawing up spraying gouts from the sea.

He swam toward the barge as it slowed. It didn't *look* like it was moving much at all, but his gut sank at the realization that it would far outpace his ability to swim unless they came to a complete stop, and soon.

He glanced back over his shoulder. The men on board the shadow boat were shouting incoherently, seemingly unable to decide whether to focus on killing Ty or pursuing the barge. They chose the latter, he guessed, since they stopped shooting and accelerated.

They paid no attention to the skiff, which was still jetting straight toward them.

Ty focused again on swimming for a few more seconds. He

got no closer to the barge, but he did, at least, get farther from the skiff. Again he looked back.

The smugglers suddenly realized that he'd weaponized the little boat against them. The ship slowed and tried to turn, but it was too late. The skiff crashed into their hull.

In the spotlight's glow, Ty saw sparkling blue objects—the big crystal had fractured into several smaller ones—flying through the air in an azure cascade.

"God*dammit*," he rasped. He'd failed to do anything except deprive the smugglers of part of their precious cargo, making them angrier than they already were by sending the crystals into the deep. Atlanticore wasn't unstable enough to be used as an impromptu explosive, after all.

However, as some of the fragments struck the ship itself and others hit the water, the blast came.

A deep atonal boom resounded as though the earth below the waves had split open. At the same time, there was a blinding flash of blue-white light. In the split second before he could see nothing at all, Ty glimpsed an explosion, coming mostly from *below* the ship, launching the vessel skyward with such force that it tore into three flaming pieces. Men and debris flew dozens of feet into the air.

Then Ty himself was picked up and hurled as surely as if a giant invisible hand had seized him.

"Shit!" he cried, water rushing around him. His head spun, his stomach seemed to have left him behind, and dark shapes whirled around him as he rocketed toward the barge. His ears rang from the blast's terrible volume. Trying to go limp before the impact came, he crashed back into the sea next to the transport.

His whole body went into shock at the impact. Instantly he wondered if he might be dead or if he'd broken half the bones in his body. Everything went numb. Then a second later he felt his hands grasping as people shouted above him.

Daria's voice said, "Grab the rope, idiot!"

He caught the length of cord they had dangled overboard for him and held on tight as seven or eight people hauled him up and out of the ocean. The numbness in his body was giving way to a powerful stinging in his back and chest. He wasn't dead or paralyzed, but he'd be amazed if all his ribs were intact.

The pain increased as he crawled over the railing and landed on the deck, dizzy and faintly nauseous. The ship's crew and passengers stared at him in amazement.

Daria, on the other hand, looked as though she wasn't sure whether to smack him across the face or burst out laughing and embrace him. Instead, she shook her head.

"Mr. Katakura," she proclaimed, "I'm not certain you understand what this word 'executioner' means or how your position works. It would seem you're supposed to kill *others* if you must. Not get *yourself* killed."

She hugged him. He winced, his breath hissing between his teeth as her hands found the damaged spots on his back. Definitely at least two broken ribs, he decided.

"Sorry," he grunted. "It's only my first day on the job."

CHAPTER SEVENTEEN

The mission had succeeded, so Ty no longer had much reason to remain conscious. Sometime in the middle of the voyage back, relatively brief though it was, he passed out.

After that, his memory began to fail him, things becoming spotty and indefinite as he woke back up in a haze of pain and exhaustion, only to slip back into sleep or delirium. It was strange. He wasn't *that* badly injured and didn't think he'd contracted any illness, either. It angered him that he was having so much trouble keeping himself aware of his surroundings.

It was the stress, he realized, during a fleeting moment of lucidity. He'd spent the entire day fighting, running, worrying, and struggling desperately to save dozens of innocent lives. Even during the war, he'd rarely engaged in such an intense period of prolonged and aggressive activity.

He was faintly aware, now and again, of the different phases of his journey following the barge incident.

They were back at the docks. People crowded around, and the harbormaster demanded answers as Daria dragged Ty away. A couple of men in suits appeared to reassure everyone that all was well. Ty's pulse had quickened in alarm until he realized that the suits were employees of the Executives come to vouch for him and provide cover for his actions.

Then he passed out again. He seemed to be riding in a vehicle. Daria was probably driving his armored truck with himself as a passenger, although he didn't know where she was heading. It was still dark.

Next, he opened his eyes and saw red curtains, flowering plants, marble, and mahogany, all lit with brilliant golden lights. They were inside a building—clearly, a fancy one. Someone in a tuxedo was standing nearby, and Daria's voice spoke to another person sitting behind a desk.

Finally, he woke for a moment in a comfortable, modern bed, with springs and a proper mattress—the first he'd slept in since he'd left America, he was pretty sure. Months and months ago. There also seemed to be bandages around his chest and back. He felt no pain, though, and feeling warmer and cozier than he had in a long, long time, he fell back asleep.

Then, in the morning, he woke up and stayed up.

"Uhh," he groaned, rubbing his eyes and sitting up in the bed. "Okay. Yeah." Birds were chirping outside his window, where there seemed to be a tree. "I get it. You feel like singing to celebrate whatever the hell birds celebrate. Now give it a rest, will you?"

He looked around. Dim yellow sunlight partially lit the room. He didn't know much about the minutiae of rich people's lifestyles, but he could tell at once that the place in which Daria had lodged him was high-end, fancy, and expensive.

The walls were richly papered and seemed to have an inlay of gold thread, and there was a curtain of rich crimson velvet that would encircle his bed if pulled out. The furniture was all beautifully finished wood, mostly mahogany and oak, and set with fine vases with real flowers arranged in them.

There was also a relatively compact television set along the far wall, with a strange-looking antenna atop it. Ty idly wondered how good a signal they got out here and whether Atlanticans could watch the same shows as Americans, or if they'd have to settle for the minimal broadcasting coming out of eastern Canada. The distance wasn't too much different in either case.

He furthermore discovered that his bathroom was tiled with marble, the sink fixtures being of what looked like nickel or maybe silver. Plus, there was a coffee pot on a table against the far wall with everything he would need to brew his own.

Shaking his head at the sumptuousness of it all, Ty started a batch of coffee, then noticed a folded piece of paper on the night-stand beside his bed. He picked it up and unfolded it, disclosing a handwritten note.

Mr. Executioner,

You're lucky. I called in a few favors. Your room is on the third floor at the Crystal Skies Hotel in the center of the city. It's a new place, but the rich folk seem to like it. I feel you've earned a stay there.

I also know a doctor, a good man whom you might say works for me. He looked at you and bandaged your wounds. You have three broken ribs and substantial internal bruising, but nothing that seems to require a hospital stay. However, he suggested that you get an X-ray to be sure, particularly if there are any further problems.

Enjoy your vacation. I'm sure you'll be back to work soon. We'll see each other again before long.

Sincerely,

Daria

Ty chuckled. "Well, that was nice of her. I'm curious how the Executives feel about all this, though. Hope they don't think I went AWOL. Then again, there was probably enough commotion and gossip that I'm sure they can find me if they need me."

His mind wandered. He speculated about what had happened to everyone else on the ship. The passengers had all survived unless something terrible occurred while he was out of it. He doubted it. He'd achieved his main objective. Still, there were questions about the aftermath of the whole mess that wanted answering.

Ty set the note back on the nightstand, leaving it there half-folded. He got up and headed into the bathroom to relieve and freshen himself and take a long, hot shower. His circumstances had forced him to stick to sporadic, mostly cold showers or the occasional bath when it came to washing himself since he'd come to the island, the same way he'd had to make do with cots, sleeping blankets, or bare ground to sleep on.

He wasn't sure if he was supposed to unwrap his wounds, but he did so anyway. The skin had broken in two places. One area was beside his sternum, and another on his back a little behind his left armpit and not far from the shoulder blade. Otherwise, the flesh was an ugly mottled purple around his broken bones. The pain was dull, but it sharpened when he breathed too deeply.

While he luxuriated in the shower stall under the stream of warm water and hot steam, scrubbing himself clean and thoroughly washing his too-long hair, his mind turned to the subject of Daria and how she'd pulled this off.

The hotel wasn't a cheap one. Having access to a personal doctor, whom she could persuade and probably pay to treat her friends or associates, couldn't have been inexpensive, either.

Her modest way of dressing and her lower-middle-class house, Ty decided, was a front designed to deflect attention. People would look at her or see her walking into her home and assume she was a small fry. In fact, she had to have a substantial amount of money. Not to the same extent as the Executives. Whether it was the result of her past smuggling or her current "consulting" work, her position in Atlantican society wasn't so humble as she made it seem.

She'd done a lot for him—more than she'd needed to. He would have to thank her when he could.

As he stepped out of the shower and dried himself off, another thought occurred to him. Daria was, technically, a criminal. She had some moral and ethical standards, but much of what she did was against the law. Or, rather, *would* be against the law in most countries that weren't Atlantica.

He frowned. If the time ever came when her way of making a living conflicted with his new career, he wouldn't look forward to it.

Ty put the wrapping back around his chest, wincing a bit at the pain as he tightened it. He took a couple of aspirin and poured himself a glass of merlot from a bottle someone had left near the door. Wine wasn't his specialty. He knew very little about it beyond the bare basics that most people had heard of. It was from somewhere in France, with the year listed as 1949. It had a complex flavor, strange at first but pleasant and satisfying as it mellowed out.

"Nice," he murmured. "Must be the good shit. Probably not top of the line, but definitely not cheap hooch. I'll have to thank whoever left it."

He reclined, relaxing in his bed and watching television. After an hour, it occurred to him that he should probably check in with Eleanor. However, he didn't have access to his radio. He found the room's built-in phone and called the front desk.

"Hello," the concierge began in a reedy voice. "What can I do for you, Mr. Katakura?"

Ty was impressed that the man knew his name and even pronounced it more or less correctly. Westerners tended to overemphasize one or two syllables relative to others, as though they were speaking Spanish or Latin. Japanese was practically metronomic in its lack of accentuation. He had trouble with the "R" sound, but that was forgivable.

Clearing his throat, Ty said, "I need to get in touch with Ms. Eleanor Cervantes. Has she stopped in, or called, or do you have a way of contacting her?"

The concierge hemmed and hawed for a second before

responding, "Err, no, I'm afraid not. However, if you expect her, I can take a message and pass it on to her."

That ought to do. "Yeah. If she calls or stops by, you have my permission to send her up to see me. She's my contact with my employers, and I'll need to talk to her sometime before I check out."

"Very good, sir. If there's time, I can also see if she's listed in the phone book and call her on your behalf."

Ty was impressed. "Yes, that would be great. Thanks." He hung up. Never before had he stayed in a place with such a fine level of customer service that the employees were willing to go out of their way to help him.

He sank back onto his bed, suddenly wishing he'd asked about meals while he was on the phone. An hour later, when the rumbling of his stomach grew too strong to ignore, he called again and ordered a nice chicken dinner, hoping that Daria's tab would cover it. Apparently, it would, since half an hour later someone knocked and handed him a trayful of beautiful, steaming food.

While he sat and ate, the phone rang again.

"Hello?" His mouth was full, and he swallowed.

The same man said, "Mr. Katakura, we received a call from Ms. Cervantes. She says that she will allow you to rest and recover for now and to stay where you are, but that she will arrive to speak with you around noon tomorrow."

Ty wasn't sure if he was annoyed or relieved. He probably *could* use more time to unwind, but he was already beginning to feel oddly useless, doing nothing but hanging around a luxury room and watching television. "Okay, that sounds good. Thanks again."

As the day wore on, he relaxed, ignoring the pain of his wounds, but growing ever more bored. When the sun sank, he began pacing around his room, stretching to the best of his ability and performing combat drills with the empty scabbards of his sword and dagger. They wouldn't slice anything if he accidentally swung too close to any furnishings.

The exercise helped tire him out. Along with a couple more glasses of the nice French merlot. He passed out around 10:45 p.m.

He slept for a long time, although it was a fitful and erratic slumber, during which he kept jarring himself awake with sudden grasping motions, coated in the cold sweat of nightmares. Images of violence, people he'd known, awful days that now lay in the distant past. All kept trying to intrude upon his unconscious mind.

When he awoke for good, it was a little after seven in the morning. The birds were once again chirping madly from the branches of the tree outside his window.

"Don't you guys ever give it a rest?" he grumbled. He made himself a coffee with the available pot and sat in bed, slowly coming to, and wondered what Eleanor would have to say.

He did little for the rest of the morning. At last, at 11:56, the phone rang.

"Hi," Ty opened, "Katakura here."

The person on the other end was someone different from yesterday, a husky female voice. "Mr. Katakura. Ms. Cervantes is here to see you, and my notes tell me that you gave permission for us to send her up. If you have no objections, she'll be at your door momentarily."

"Sure," he replied. "Tell her to come on up." He was glad she wasn't late, as he was growing impatient. Then again, she'd always impressed him as the punctual sort.

The knock on his door came at noon sharp. Ty peered through the peephole to confirm it was her and opened up. "Hello, Ms. Cervantes. What's all that stuff?"

Eleanor had dressed formally again, in a dark blue business dress with a matching jacket, and this time wearing high heels instead of boots. She also had a pushcart piled with gift-wrapped packages.

She smiled. "Oh, these are simply tokens of appreciation from the Executives. That's one of the things we must discuss. I hope you're feeling better. I heard that you sustained injuries on your mission."

Ty closed the door behind her as she wheeled in the cart. "Yeah, I broke three ribs. Not much fun; I don't recommend it. It could've been a lot worse. We were lucky. So was everyone else, except the smugglers."

Eleanor left the cart in the center of the room and looked around for a place to sit. Ty offered her a chair from the room's desk, then sat on the end of the bed. He moved too fast, though, and his jaw reflexively clenched as pain shot through his back.

His guest noticed. "Please be careful, Mr. Katakura. We don't require your *immediate* return to service, so it would be best if you rested and recovered as best you could. On that note, the Executives, myself, and my other coworkers would all like to congratulate you on a job well done. They provided these gifts as an expression of their gratitude."

He nodded. "Don't mention it. I'm out of the loop, though. Could you tell me what all happened? I don't remember much. After I blew up the smugglers' boat, it all gets kind of hazy until I woke up in this room yesterday morning."

Eleanor smiled again and smoothed out her dress. "Of course. First of all, I imagine you'll be pleased to know that no one was killed or seriously hurt, barring the guilty parties. You won't suffer any consequences for dealing with them, of course. Part of your role as Executioner is dispatching such people when they become a problem."

Ty's eyes drifted over the care packages on the cart. Some had names written on them, and he noticed that the largest and gaudiest of them all had a small card hanging from it that read *Lucas Montrosse.*

"Yeah," he said. "The guilty parties. I don't think I've ever killed that many people in one day before. Not that the rest of the island is liable to miss them much, though. I hope this sends a message to the bastards about what happens when they try to push regular people around."

He thought back to "his" town, the labor shanty in the valley beyond the first of the foothills outside the city. Danny and Mrs. Bertolli and all the others.

"Eleanor," he asked, cutting her off as she was about to say something. "How's the village? The one I was protecting. You put that Scottish guy in charge of watching over them. Has anything happened?"

Eleanor reached into her jacket. "Indeed, the message has been sent. Loud and clear, as you say. I'll have more to tell you about that in a moment." She withdrew her hand, and what looked like a folded newspaper appeared.

Ty squinted. If Atlantica had a paper, he hadn't heard of it yet.

"But first," Cervantes went on, "yes, your town is doing very well. There have been no untoward incidents. Senior Officer MacLeod informed me earlier this morning—right before I came to speak with you, in fact—that everything has been quiet. He doesn't know if the mere presence of him and his men is the cause, or if it's simply the case that no one has wished to cause trouble to begin with."

Ty shrugged. "Either way, that's good to hear. I'll want to check in myself before long. Yes, first tell me the rest of the story. You were about to say something a minute ago when I interrupted. My apologies."

Eleanor unfolded the paper. "Quite all right. The Executives, not long ago, funded the creation of the *Atlantican Herald*, the island's first news publication. One of the Executives is from the United Kingdom and would've preferred a different name. The British call this island *Avalonia*, for some reason.

"Everyone else prefers *Atlantica*, so the name has stuck for the paper as well as the country itself. I brought you this morning's edition. The front-page story is related to your recent exploits."

She showed him. The headline read,

One Hundred Twelve Souls Rescued, Over $4 Million in Property Saved.

Beneath that, a subtitle described how the newly created office of the Executioner was, so far, a success.

Ty blinked. Part of him was touched, even flattered. The idea of becoming some kind of heroic celebrity had never occurred to him. Yet he couldn't help noticing that the paper framed the whole exploit in terms of money and "success." From what he knew of the Executives, it didn't much surprise him.

"Well," he commented, "that's good."

Eleanor nodded and set the paper on the edge of the bed. "It's yours to keep if you would like to read the rest. It relays to the public how the island's new keeper of the peace not only rooted out and defeated a violent smuggling ring but also saved a great many innocent people in the process. The writer begins to wax poetic, but it's for the best. They wanted readers to understand that the days of lawlessness are over."

Ty poured himself another glass of wine. He offered one to Eleanor, who held up a hand and shook her head.

"Thank you," she said, "but I have other things to do today and ought to remain sober."

He nodded and took a swig. "If lawlessness is coming to an end, won't we need actual *laws*? I suppose they're working on that, too. A governing body. Elected officials. All that stuff. For now, at least they have me." He stared out the window at the way the sunlight played off the leaves of the nearby tree.

Eleanor laughed and straightened her hair. "Yes." He was unsure if she was affirming that the Executives were laying the ground-work for a real government or if she simply agreed that he would do for now. "They've also started a radio news channel, which has been discussing the same things. You're getting a great deal of good press. The feedback suggests that the idea of the Executioner being out there, protecting the common welfare, seems to appeal to people."

"It should," Ty agreed. "So long as I uphold the spirit of the office and serve justice."

Something dark in his tone seemed to disturb Ms. Cervantes. She cleared her throat and was about to comment when, again, Ty spoke first.

"So, what do I do about Lucas Montrosse?" He turned his face to her and stared with a flat, cold, empty gaze, neutral and patient.

Eleanor turned her eyes away, frowning now, and adjusted each item of her clothing in an awkward sequence. "We can discuss that later. The other Executives have already begun considering it. In the meantime, there are other, more pressing things that we need you to look into. Once again, innocents may be at stake. As well as the economy of the entire island."

Ty allowed himself to blink once. "Oh. I see."

He waited as Ms. Cervantes elaborated upon the broad outline of his next official assignment. In the rural area northeast of the city, where agriculture had begun to flourish, there was a farming collective where a handful of people had begun to disappear without explanation. The instability created by these incidents, she explained, was affecting food production and driving up prices. Food shortages could become a problem for all of Atlantica.

Ty scratched his head and tossed it, flipping the hair away from his eyes. "Noted. But the current case isn't closed yet. Everything that happened two days ago was a direct result of Lucas' schemes in Development Sector Twelve. You confirmed as much yourself, Eleanor. My role is to deal out justice. Isn't that right?"

Tension rippled through her, and her hands balled into fists.

For a second, he thought she would explode on him, but she choked off her remarks at the last instant.

He noticed something, though, which articulated itself in his mind as Eleanor steadied herself and thought about her words before she spoke. Her anger wasn't from loyalty, affection, or pride but from *fear.*

"Tyler Katakura," she stated, growing calm again, although her tone and demeanor were icy. "Allow me to give you another piece of advice. Will you listen? For your benefit?"

He kept his poker face on. "Yes, I will."

She gave a sharp nod. "Good. Last time I offered advice, you didn't take it. You didn't *need* it, in truth, but you do need to hear what I'm about to say now."

Eleanor stood, and something about the way she held herself made it clear how nervous she was.

"Be careful. You risk going beyond what you can do. Mr. Montrosse has had his hand slapped by the other Executives. His standing has diminished. His reputation is tarnished.

"Do you see? It's not as though they've done nothing. But you must understand that the Executives are your benefactors, as well as mine. If you...attack or move against one of their own—and less than a week after you began to serve in your new position— you would *not* find them as supportive and enthusiastic as they've been thus far."

That, Tyler thought, *was a lot of words to say that the Executives didn't consider themselves subject to the same de facto laws they'd hired him to enforce.*

Ms. Cervantes went on. "These are extremely powerful and dangerous people, Mr. Katakura. They aren't without *some* scruples. But we can only play the parts that they allow us to play. To go further than that is to invite destruction. Do good where you are able. And no more than that."

She stood in silence, watching him and waiting for his

answer. From within her jacket, she produced another item; a folder, likely a dossier on his next assignment.

Ty sat, sipping his wine. His eyes were unfocused and his mind distant. He waved at the table. "The information you have on the farming community, the disappearances," he remarked. "Leave it on the table there, please. Then you may excuse yourself. And thanks."

CHAPTER EIGHTEEN

The next night, Ty was pretty well sloshed on his new hoard of alcoholic beverages when Daria visited him.

"What?" he said into the phone. "Why the hell is she here at *this* hour? I thought she only drank during the *daytime*. Whatever, send her up, yeah."

The concierge today was once again the man with the reedy voice, the same individual who had run the desk on Ty's first day at the hotel. "Very good, sir. Let me know if you need anything else."

"Right." Ty's voice came out slurred. He was probably embarrassing himself, but at the moment, he didn't particularly care. "Thanks, buddy." He hung up.

He leaned back in the desk chair, which he'd dragged into the middle of the room and braced against the foot of his bed. In his right hand was a nice crystal tumbler, currently about a quarter full with golden bourbon. Originally, it had been three-quarters of the way to the brim.

His thoughts, which had grown as sludgy as his speech, drifted over the subject of Daria and how she would get up here. Would she take the stairs? Or the elevator? Ty wasn't sure the hotel *had* an elevator, but then he couldn't imagine why a place as swanky as the Crystal Skies wouldn't.

He blew air upward from beneath his lower lip. The gust knocked his forelock aside, so the hair swayed and came to rest beside his eye.

"Damn," he quipped to the empty room, "I need a haircut. Should have told Jeeves down there to send me up a barber. I bet they can do that. Rich people hotels. You can have anything you want. Just have to pay for it, is all."

Yesterday afternoon, after Eleanor had made her departure, Ty had sat, quietly staring at the wall and doing nothing whatsoever for a good hour. The brooding mood that had set in hadn't yet departed, even thirty hours later.

Lacking anything better to do while he healed, he'd dug into the care packages sent by the various Executives. The one exception, of course, being the ostentatious gift—whatever it was—from Mr. Montrosse. That one Ty had set aside and not touched.

As for the others, they'd contained a motley assortment of nice, albeit decadent, things. Mostly food and drink. Also some cologne, cigars, ammunition, and a few books and magazines.

The best of the gifts, though, was a new pair of boots. They exactly replicated the ones he'd kicked off while swimming and which now lay somewhere at the bottom of the Atlantic Ocean. Exactly replicated, that was, in terms of their overall appearance, functionality, and comfort. They were newer, pristine, and made of finer materials by a reputable manufacturer.

The second-best gift was all the booze.

It had been two or three years since Tyler had drunk much. He occasionally partook of the moonshine that the valley town produced or had a beer here and there when he could find one. Still, it had been a long, long time since he'd fallen so far off the wagon. With the bounty before him, it was hard not to.

There were four more bottles of wine in addition to the merlot that had been in his room previously. He'd made a mental note to ask Daria if she'd provided that or if it were compliments of the hotel. He'd finished off the merlot yesterday and had also demolished an entire bottle of cabernet sauvignon.

There were two bottles of top-notch whiskey—the bourbon, which Ty had largely drained, and another of Irish blended. He'd always liked whiskey. It was dangerous stuff, but good. Truly one of the great inventions of Western civilization.

Additionally, there was a bottle of deceptively colorless Polish vodka. It was the highest-proof liquor he could recall seeing, at least as far as formal production liquors went. Some moonshines were stronger. That stuff, he decided, should be saved for a special occasion. If he needed to get *really* drunk.

He'd tempered the alcohol somewhat with the food. Just as he'd not drunk so much in years, neither had he eaten so well. Other gifts had included caviar with crackers, fine chocolates, expensive cheeses, various canned meats, and state-of-the-art packaged snack foods from America. He'd polished off around half of it so far on top of the excellent formal meals he ordered via room service.

He hoped he wouldn't put on weight. The idea of growing fat repulsed him, largely because it would hamper his speed and agility in a fight. Then again, he'd known men, boxers and the like, who swore that having a certain amount of body fat was tantamount to possessing an extra layer of body armor at all times. Not enough to stop a bullet or a sword, but enough to lessen the hurt of a fist, club, or knife, perhaps.

Ty chuckled. "No. It's better not to get hit at all in the first place."

Someone knocked on the door. The sharp and yet strangely cautious-seeming rapping sound was different from the way the hotel employees knocked. Or Eleanor.

"Tyler," a familiar voice called, muffled through the wood, "it's Daria. Are you awake?"

He got up from his chair, swaying a bit, and set his tumbler down on one of the side tables. "Yeah. I'm coming. Just a moment, please."

When he reached the door and looked through the peephole, he was less than shocked to see that Daria was attired much the same way she had been three days ago. She hadn't bothered to "dress up" for her visit to the hotel.

She didn't have anything else with her. Though he presumed as fact that her P38 was concealed somewhere on her person.

Ty unlocked the door and swung it open. "Hi. Nice of you to stop by. I'm drunk. Please consider that your warning."

Daria looked him over, arching an eyebrow. "Yes, you are. I can tell quite easily. What have you been drinking? I wouldn't mind a drink myself." She stepped in, swinging her jacket off her shoulders.

Ty took it from her and placed it on a hanger beside the door. "Bourbon and wine, mostly. There's plenty to spare. The Executives were feeling generous after I saved so much of their...property."

The Polish woman strode in another step or two and removed her boots. "That was kind of them. Oh, thank you for hanging up my jacket. I'm used to doing such things myself. It's a nice gesture. Did they give you any vodka?"

Snickering, Ty went over to the gift cart and found the bottle of clear liquid. "Yes, ma'am. Have a look. This might be a little too potent for me. You people from Eastern Europe, though... I hear you drink this shit like water." He held it up for her to examine.

She glanced over the label. "Yes, this will do. Even I won't need more than, we will say, two glasses. You may save the rest for yourself. But I appreciate your willingness to share."

Ty felt dizzy abruptly and sat on the foot of his bed. "Sorry," he muttered. "I'll trust you to pour your glass. I'm not feeling so good. Oh, hey, that reminds me. Did you leave the bottle of merlot my first night here? That was good stuff."

Daria shook her head. "That was the hotel's doing. Though I do have a few bottles of emergency wine in my cellar."

She cracked open the vodka and filled an extra tumbler a little less than halfway. Sniffing it, she took a long sip, pausing to exhale the fumes. "Ahh. Yes, I needed that."

"Well," said Ty, "I'm glad *someone* did. Do you have your gun? I don't know if I could shoot so well. Right now. I'd feel safer if somebody in the room could hit what they're aiming at. You're pretty good at that, from what I could see."

Daria pulled up a small portion of her blouse, revealing the pistol tucked into the waistband of her long skirt. "Of course."

Ty nodded, then brought a hand to his head to steady it. "Uhh. Good. Hey, I wanted to ask—and forgive me if this is a rude question, you can ignore it if you want—but why do you use *that* gun? I would've thought you'd never want to see one of those things again."

She was quiet for a moment. "You've guessed my past, then. Yes. The German P38 is a good enough pistol. I had to use one several times when I was younger, so I'm familiar with it. Perhaps I could upgrade to something else if I wanted. I keep it as a memento. It's useful not to forget certain things, even things which aren't pleasant."

Daria pulled up Ty's desk chair and seated herself on it, swirling the vodka in her glass. "I came to check on you," she added. "You weren't as badly hurt as we feared. But you were exhausted. Plus, enough people know what you did that you're now...how shall I put this...a famous man, but also a *marked* man."

With his brain slowed down, Ty struggled to decide whether to try and respond to both of the things Ms. Barruk had said or disregard the first and only discuss the second. It occurred to him that he hadn't picked his glass of bourbon back up before stumbling onto his bed. It was probably for the best.

"I understand," he began. "About the, ah, memento thing. I

won't ask you any more about it. Everyone has things in their past. I certainly do as well. I'm fine. Mostly. I've had broken ribs before. They aren't much fun, but I'll survive. If the smugglers want revenge, they should think about what happened a little harder."

He didn't know how big the smuggling ring was, but he and Daria had killed many of their men and probably ruined them for a decade. They might have to fold up their entire operation on Atlantica. If what few of them remained were forced to retreat to Boston, or Montreal, or Belfast, or wherever they were based, so much the better.

Daria took another sip of vodka. "It's good to know that you're so confident. But, since you asked me a difficult question, it's only fair that I can do the same. What's bothering you? You don't strike me as the type of man who becomes drunk very often. You're trying to drink your way out of something, I think, and it's not the pain of your broken bones."

He grimaced and tried to clear his mind. Like most anyone else, he found it too easy to spill his thoughts out in a foolish, undisciplined flood when inebriated. People who did that often regretted it later.

He trusted Daria. In the short time they'd known one another, they'd worked together and saved one another's lives. Still, there were still things about her that were mysterious to him. Plus, he had no desire to involve her in problems that were none of her business.

Problems that might get her killed.

"I don't know," he replied, half-lying. "I'm not sure how I feel or how I'm *supposed* to feel. We saved all those people. Great, wonderful. Now I wonder if anything will change.

"Me being appointed Executioner is supposed to signal this great and glorious shift in the way things work on Atlantica. No more of this stuff where whoever has the money and power does whatever they want, and the little guys have to suck up and deal with it. But... I have my doubts. What happened a few days ago could easily happen again."

Daria was looking over his cartload of goodies, but he could tell she was listening, regardless. "May I have one of those chocolates?"

Blinking, Ty flapped a hand. "Yeah, knock yourself out."

She smiled and plucked one from a tray, eating it slowly while her mind appeared to wander. "You may be right," she opined, washing the chocolate down with liquor. "It is difficult to change things *much*. If you wish to make a big change, there will always be resistance, for better or for worse. What about that man you mentioned? Development Sector Twelve. Where the crystals came from."

Ty scowled at the floor. Even if he'd made up his mind to keep Daria out of it, she probably would've managed to figure things out for herself regardless.

"I raised the issue," he admitted. "Eleanor Cervantes—my contact, the woman I talked to on the radio—she came over yesterday, and we spoke about it. I asked her about Montrosse, and she brushed me off. She—they, the Executives—want me to investigate some disappearances in a farming village. I haven't looked at it yet. The folder."

He felt foolish, stammering away, and began to wish he'd ceased his drinking with the second bottle of wine, saving the bourbon for another day.

Daria found the folder in question. She picked it up and flipped through it, not reading everything thoroughly but skimming over it to apprise herself of the main details.

"This looks important," she observed. "Food prices have been highly unstable lately. For you to move on to this case would be a good thing. It could benefit everyone on the island, and perhaps some others on the mainland, too."

Ty clenched his hands, surprised at the level of anger that suddenly swelled up from deep within his core.

"Goddammit, not you too. You're telling me I should ignore Lucas? He's responsible for this entire mess! Eleanor says the other Execs slapped him on the wrist for it, but that's all. For God's sake, *at best* he was careless, stupid, and greedy and his fuck-up almost got a lot of people killed. At best.

"Maybe he knew what would happen. Maybe he wanted to cover his tracks and get rid of the witnesses who knew that Sector Twelve had an Atlanticore vein. If that's the fucking case, he's guilty of the attempted murder of over a hundred innocent people."

He had, briefly, gotten lost in his head as he ranted away. As his eyes refocused on his guest, he saw that Daria was looking straight at him with a sharp, steady gaze. It was the same steely glare he'd noticed in the club when they'd first met. Now it was more intense.

"No. I didn't say that." She tossed back her glass, draining it, and set it down hard on the nearest table. "When people such as this man, Lucas, are caught in the act of grave and terrible crimes, the *worst thing you can do* is ignore them.

"Grift and fraud give way to assassinations and tyranny to keep up the lies, to cover for the lies. Cruelty becomes the normal way of doing things, and mere bullies become tyrants. With no one to recognize their crimes, and without punishment, evil becomes a way of life."

Ty sat up straighter. He wasn't sure what he'd expected Daria to say, but somehow, it wasn't this.

She moved closer to him and rolled back her sleeve, exposing the tattooed number. "Do you know what this is, Mr. Katakura?"

He responded with a single nod. "Yes, I do. I noticed it before, but I figured you wouldn't want to talk about it."

Daria waved a hand sharply. "When the wicked are allowed to get away with these things, when no one bothers to serve justice, it sends the message that they can get away with it. Others will hear of what happened, and those who seek to come to Atlantica to become bullies, tyrants, bandits, and liars will know that there is no one here to stop them."

She poured herself another half glass of vodka, downed it in a single gulp, and slammed the tumbler down on the table. "So evil builds upon evil, and the blood in the gutters gets ignored because that's simply the way it is, no? No one cares because no one can imagine an alternative. So Atlantica, with all its potential, becomes the worst place on Earth instead."

Her tone was bitter enough that Ty almost flinched. She sat and lit a clove cigarette with a silver lighter she produced from her pocket, crossing her legs and looking out the window.

Ty rubbed his eyes. "You would've figured that we would learn. We, meaning, y'know, people. Maybe we could begin anew here. Atlantica, everyone's fresh start. I guess not. It seems like we didn't only bring our dreams to the new world. We brought our nightmares, too."

Daria made a small throaty sound of acknowledgment and puffed on her clove.

Ty got up, found his mostly empty glass of bourbon, and finished it off, setting the empty tumbler down next to Daria's. His mind began wandering places he didn't wish it to go.

He remembered the day his father had come home from the war. He returned not to the house they'd had originally but to the tenement where Ty and his mother had been shuffled to after the camps let them go. His father had been a strong, proud man, not ostentatiously so, but stoic and unfaltering.

The war hadn't broken him, despite being middle-aged. What broke him was the way the people in power had shrugged, whistled, and strolled away from what they'd done to his family. And others like him. They'd tried to sweep it all under the rug while telling him to smile for the camera with the medals he'd won fighting in the 442nd. Then they sent him off to rebuild his life from scratch. Everything he had achieved before then was gone.

Tyler considered another drink but decided against it. He was drunk enough as it was. The sooner he could sober up, the better. He had a glass of water instead.

"I think," he began, "that I'm going to put an end to one of those nightmares. Slaying the demons, or however you want to put it. But I have to admit...I'm not sure I can do it alone."

Daria turned to look at him. "When slaying demons, I hear that it's helpful to have someone with you who has been through hell." She snuffed out what remained of her cigarette.

Ty flexed his hands and stretched his arms. "Know anyone with time to kill?" he asked. His smile was grim.

"I might," said Daria. "What did you have in mind, may I ask?"

CHAPTER NINETEEN

The truck hit a bad bump, causing Ty to buck in his seat and his armored vest to press directly against the injured portion of his back. He made a hissing sound, sucking in air between gritted teeth. He had taken a couple of painkillers before they'd set out, but the damn things didn't seem to be working too well yet.

Daria glanced over at him, arching an eyebrow. "Are you all right, Mr. Executioner?"

"Yeah, I'm fine." He focused on the road. "Starting to wonder if we should've brought a regular old car, instead. Sure, we'd have a lot less protection, and it wouldn't be as intimidating, but at least we would be able to sneak up on the villa a little easier. You could barely hide this thing by driving it into a valley behind a mountain, and even then the people in the next valley over would probably hear it clanking and grinding along."

She sighed. "Yes, that's why we should work on a cover story or spend more time scouting the area ahead of ourselves to find the best approach. Did they not teach you things like this in the Army?"

They were rumbling down one of the dirt roads behind the

city, rarely used except when supply trucks or VIPs needed a shortcut through the hills.

Ty coughed. "They did, but they also taught me the importance of getting shit done, double-time. If Lucas figures out that we're coming for him, he probably has sixteen different ways to flee the city, and maybe the entire island, without anyone to stop him. Not to mention, they're going to notice pretty soon that I'm not investigating the farming community as they said."

Daria flapped a hand dismissively. "Days. That would take days, not hours. If Montrosse isn't home now, he'll likely arrive at night. We can spare the time to make sure we do this *right*. Charging in without a plan won't profit us much."

He thought it over. "I suppose you're right. I drank a little too much yesterday, and I'm still not feeling the best. You might say I'm overly enthusiastic to start cracking skulls again. I get like that when I'm in a bad mood."

"Hah!" she scoffed. "I believe it. I've seen you fight. When we come close to the villa's grounds, pull off somewhere out of sight. You can stay with the vehicle, and I'll go ahead on foot. On one condition, that is—you won't peek into my crate while I'm away. Deal?"

Ty scowled but had to agree. "Deal. If you don't come back, though, I'm driving this thing through the front of the house and figuring out the rest later."

She brushed a greying lock of hair behind her ear. "That's fair enough."

When they'd met that morning in the foothills north of the city, Daria had a crate, inside which was a burlap sack, and inside *that* was...something. She refused to tell him until the moment was right.

His immediate suspicion, fueled by his experiences on the barge, was that she'd come by a stray stash of Atlanticore crystals and planned to use them as weapons. When he hoisted the crate into the armored truck, the weight and balance, and the metallic *clanking*, didn't seem much like a load of crystals. He figured it was a few spare guns or something like that, which would serve them better than the crystals.

Based on the map he'd reviewed earlier and his memory of the trip there, the Montrosse estate was only about another half mile down the road. He'd have to pull over momentarily. But he decided to wait and trust Daria's judgment rather than kick her out of the truck to do her thing prematurely.

"You know," he mused, "it's crazy, really. Biting the hand that feeds you. Lucas was the one who gave me the job. He was the spokesman for all the Executives. Still. I wouldn't be where I am now if it wasn't for him. He said I was supposed to enforce justice. He was full of shit the whole time. He wanted me to enforce justice in ways that would benefit him and ignore it when it didn't."

Daria nodded. "That's my impression, as well. Slow down. I should get out soon."

Ty took his foot off the gas but didn't brake yet. The truck had enough forward momentum that it would continue to roll for a couple of hundred feet.

He added, "Putting it that way—biting the hand that feeds, that old expression—puts it into perspective. Am I their pet? Or their attack dog, to be fair. Yeah. That wasn't how I interpreted the arrangement."

"Of course you didn't," Ms. Barruk agreed. "People often have different views. In any event, coming to Atlantica only to be someone else's trained animal...it seems like a wasted opportunity. As we agreed, he cannot get away with what he's done."

There was no reason to discuss it further. They'd both made up their minds.

Ty pulled the truck off the road, hiding it to the best of his ability in a low-lying area surrounded by trees, shrubs, and a small ridge. Then Daria got out, promising to be back in an hour or less.

Although he worried, Ty let her go. He brooded and sipped coffee from a flask. He'd drunk enough water and taken enough aspirin last night that his hangover wasn't *too* bad, but it was bad enough.

Daria surprised him by returning less than twenty minutes later.

"Tyler," she reported. "There's good news. Construction right next to the villa's grounds, and I found a ravine that we can drive up in. We should be able to observe the front of the house, and the construction vehicles will make enough noise for us to approach without being heard."

She hopped in, grinning, and her enthusiasm was infectious.

Ty nodded. "Good. Well done. Glad I brought you along." He started the engine and followed her directions toward the ravine.

Soon, the truck sat parked in a broad ditch. The ground around it was high enough to hide the lower half of the vehicle while still giving them a clear line of sight to the villa, and with some surrounding foliage that was a dark enough green to blend reasonably well with the truck's slate hue. It was a cloudy, dim day, as well.

Ty took out his binoculars and observed the estate from afar. He remembered most of the layout details. More concerning was who was present, plus where, when, and how much muscle Lucas had to guard the place. What he saw wasn't encouraging. Especially combined with Daria's report.

"I saw four men patrolling the grounds. All with armor and rifles. Additionally, there were two cars with dark windows. More guards, maybe, in those, and even if they were empty, I'm sure they've trained to pile in if they must and chase any troublemakers."

Ty grunted. He could see three of the men and one of the cars so far. He knew Lucas had more lackeys than the ones visible. There were probably a couple inside the house and others on standby somewhere in the city or the hills.

When he'd visited before, they'd seemed like professionals—former military, former police, mercenaries. Their gear was as good as his. Directly taking them on wouldn't be as easy as the low-rent thugs he'd dealt with earlier in the week.

They sat, watched, and waited. There was no activity to speak of within the house, no indication that Lucas Montrosse himself was present. Earlier, Ty had radioed Eleanor, asking if the Executives could answer questions about the farm case. Her vague replies suggested that the Execs were busy, which meant that Lucas might've been doing things in the city.

Daria asked, "What sort of organization does the office of Executioner have, anyway?"

"Not much," Ty admitted. "There's no system beyond the radio, and what I hear from Eleanor Cervantes. That's it." He tapped the device in question. If Eleanor tried to call him, the plan was to ignore it. She probably thought he was still in bed back at the hotel.

Ms. Barruk shook her head. "You're supposed to watch over this whole island, and that's all you have? You'll need much more help than that. Other people, more lines of communication, contacts. It's too bad you couldn't ask for those before we did *this*. They might not be so accommodating afterward."

"Yeah," Ty mumbled. He wondered if there might be a way to deputize Daria. Already, she was practically his partner.

The day wore on. As the sun sank behind the horizon, the magic hour darker than usual under the overcast skies, two vehicles appeared on the road and pulled into the estate grounds. A limousine and another black sedan, presumably a guard escort.

Daria pointed. "There. That must be him."

"I see it." Ty raised his binoculars again, breathed deeply, and observed.

The limo stopped about halfway between the patio and the mansion's front door. Out of it stepped Lucas Montrosse, once again dressed in a white suit. Three women were with him. Two were young floozies, obviously drunk by how they reeled and stumbled and laughed constantly; a pale blonde and a darker-complected girl with short black hair. Another was a brunette in a short dress, whom he couldn't get a good look at.

Before Lucas or his entourage could go anywhere, the sedan pulled up alongside them and disclosed four more armed and armored men. Two of them joined the four already patrolling the grounds, and two stayed by Lucas's side. As they approached the villa proper, two more men came out the front door and took up positions beside it.

"Damn," Ty grumbled. "That's ten guys so far, and only the ones we can see. Might be more inside or hidden nearby. They're not going to be pushovers. Soldier types.

"If there's one consolation, they could probably find work elsewhere easily enough. We might be able to get away with wounding them and scaring them off instead of them fighting to the death like the desperate schmucks who worked for the smuggling ring. Who knows. Maybe they figure that turning tail and running would fuck up their reputation. In which case, we have a war on our hands."

As the front doors closed behind Lucas and the women, full darkness settled in. The night was quiet.

"Well," Daria said, "it's a good thing that I have something to help even the odds a little. Have a look." There was something oddly playful in her tone that made Ty nervous but also curious. Daria was full of surprises.

She reached back into the burlap sack within the mysterious crate. Again Ty found himself wondering if she'd somehow acquired a chunk of Atlanticore, but the object she withdrew from the bag couldn't be mistaken for a crystal under any circumstances whatsoever.

It was a gun. A *big* gun.

Ty scrunched up his face as he stared at it. "What the hell is that thing? A 10-gauge shotgun? Grenade launcher?" It had a wooden stock, like a traditional rifle's, but its barrel was enormously broad and made for something far larger than a rifle cartridge. It had blued metal parts, a pistol grip, and a cylinder that looked like an oversized suppressor fitted to the end of the barrel.

"Not exactly," Daria explained. "It's a Federal Riot Gun. FRG. It's for firing non-lethal ammunition, like baton rounds—large rubber projectiles, for knocking people over—and used to manage unruly crowds. Also..."

Ty was about to protest that rubber bullets, even if they were the approximate size of caulk canisters, wouldn't be much help to them against Lucas's heavily armored paramilitary goon squad. Daria had more to show him.

She threw back another section of burlap. "...something better still. Something they wouldn't expect." She picked up one of the projectiles. It was a metal can with military codes or serial numbers stamped on the side in white lettering. There were seven or eight of them in total.

"Tear gas," Ty concluded. "Nice. Damn nice." His face split into a sudden wolfish grin. "I haven't seen anyone with gas masks. Too bad for them."

Daria quipped, "No one except us. I have two of those, as well. We can breathe comfortably and walk right through them. Maybe we'll be lucky and won't have to fire a single shot."

Ty shrugged. "I wouldn't get *that* optimistic. But it will give us an edge. We can probably take half of Lucas' guys out of the fight before the other half can get their rifles into play. Where'd you get that beauty, anyway?"

She looked up at him, cock-eyed and with a half-smirk, as though she wasn't sure whether to laugh at him or sigh and ignore the question.

"Oh," Ty muttered, annoyed with himself. "Right. You're what's known as a smuggler. Excuse me, a smuggling *consultant.*"

She laughed. "Exactly. If the tear gas doesn't do the trick, I have something else as well. You might find this interesting."

He knew she had her pistol—not that it would be much use against heavy armor—so he couldn't wait to see what else she'd turned up.

Daria produced the last item in the bag. It, too, was a type of gun he'd never seen before.

"What in God's name is that thing?" he inquired.

It looked like a massively oversized black pistol. A long magazine protruded from the grip, which was in the approximate center of the firearm rather than toward the back. It had an unusually designed bolt rather than a slide. Both the front and back sights looked like a pair of Mickey Mouse ears.

Daria held it up and unfolded a metal stock. "Uzi submachine gun, nine-millimeter. Named after Uziel Gal, who designed it. A friend in Israel sent it to me not long ago. I wasn't sure if I would need it, but it would appear that I do. Conveniently enough, it takes the same ammunition as my P38."

"I see," said Ty. "If it fires pistol ammo, it might not get through the guards' armor, but it will still sting like a bitch, and maybe you can pepper their legs or something. Heck of a lot better than a handgun, anyway."

She pouted. "Next time, I'll ask for a rifle. As you say, it looks scary and the sound of automatic fire 'means business,' as Americans say, no?"

Ty chuckled. "Yes, yes it does. Just make sure you know what you're doing. I wouldn't be surprised if you've fired a submachine gun before."

"I have," she insisted. "By now, I would think you'd be well aware that I'm capable of handling myself in a fight." She wasn't mad at him, exactly, but there was a prickly undertone to her words.

He recalled how quickly she'd taken out two of the three men who'd come for him in the club. She might've dropped the third, too, if Ty hadn't stabbed him first. "Oh, I am. Don't you worry. I think you should let me handle that FRG thing, though. I used tear gas once or twice back in Korea. Different delivery method, but I have a pretty good idea of how to make the most of it."

"Very well," Daria conceded. Then she smiled in a way that was borderline disturbing. "But since you'll be handling it, whoever will have the honor of driving this great beautiful beast of a truck?"

Ty leaned back in his seat and groaned, realizing he'd walked straight into a trap. He recalled their flight away from Absentees through the city.

"Someone," he suggested, "who only drives like a complete maniac when it's smart to do so."

Warner coughed and sniffled. The humidity on Atlantica was getting to him. He looked forward to finishing his year-long contract with Mr. Montrosse—only two more months! Then he could get the hell off this fucking weirdo island with its chaotic jumble of peoples, its strange weather, and its creepy misty jungles that looked like they belonged in Africa or something instead of on a chunk of land off the coast of goddamn Canada.

He reminded himself to save money, to not waste his pay on drinking, gambling, and hookers. If he had enough left over at the end of the year, he might be able to afford to go back home to California and relax for a few months. Otherwise, he might have to take another job in Algeria or some fucking place, although at least there it was dry.

Having circled the grounds again, he went through the rote motion of raising his walkie-talkie receiver to his mouth and reporting in. "This is Blue Four. All clear. Over."

Mr. Fesal, the villa's head of security, responded, "Good, Blue Four. Continue your patrol. Out."

Algeria, Warner thought. Montrosse was some French Algerian guy, Warner was pretty sure, and he'd brought one or two men with him from the old country. Weirdos, all of them. Still, they could put in a good word for him when he moved on. Although if he went to North Africa, Warner realized he'd probably end up working for the French. His father had hated the French. He decided he didn't care that much.

He glanced around, shouldered his rifle, and strolled away from the front drive, continuing to watch the tree line around the estate grounds.

The rhythmic sound of debris *crunching* came from somewhere nearby. A vehicle was approaching. Warner scanned the area but couldn't see any headlights in the darkness. He could've sworn the construction trucks had wrapped up business after nightfall. Maybe one or two of them had lingered to finish something.

Then a huge black silhouette, something tall and broad and blocky like a semi-truck or a military vehicle, barreled out from between the trees and into the area about ten feet to Warner's left.

"Holy shit!" he sputtered. He unslung his rifle and ran toward the vehicle. "Halt!" He knew they couldn't hear him; the truck was too noisy. The other guys had undoubtedly noticed it too, so it was pointless to try and call in the breach. He aimed his gun and fired three rounds at the truck's wheels.

The shots crackled and sparked off the metal casing that protected the rear wheels. "Dammit," he cursed. One of the other guards was running up toward him, probably McDowell. He pulled the receiver off his belt. "Blue Four. Unauthorized vehicle, intent unknown. Armored car. We're going to need heavier—"

Then a hatch on the back of the truck opened, and a man leaned out, holding what looked like a shotgun or a grenade launcher. He fired, and an object trailing a line of smoke or gas shot out with a *thunking* sound.

Warner's eyes bulged. He ran and dove aside, rolling into the brush beside the trees and staying on his belly, trying to crawl away. He knew tear gas when he saw it.

McDowell, who was new and stupid, wasn't fast enough. He screamed and bawled as the gas got into his nose, mouth, ears, and eyes. He dropped his rifle and curled up in a ball on the ground.

Then, as Warner watched and tried to figure out what the hell to do next, the armored truck changed course and drove right toward one of the black cars positioned near the side exit from the mansion. Nobody was inside. It was left sitting there at all times, ready to go in case of an emergency.

The truck plowed straight into the car, crumpling it like a cardboard box driven against someone's knee. Beneath the screeching of tortured metal, Warner could faintly hear a woman laughing her head off.

"Jesus." He contemplated turning and running away. However, that would void his contract.

Inhaling sharply, he hitched up his rifle and plunged toward the vehicle, trying to weave around the cloud of tear gas. The guy leaning out the back hatch fired another canister. This one struck empty ground, but the cloud it created blocked Warner and another guy off from a direct line of attack toward the truck. The bastards were smart.

His receiver crackled. "This is Fesal. Disable the truck by any means necessary. Terminate the people within it if they resist. Over!"

"Yeah," Warner grunted. "Sure thing, pal."

Back in the truck, Ty found that Daria's cackling was already starting to distract him.

"Keep it down up there," he shouted. "I'm trying to *aim* here."

Daria was wheeling the vehicle in a broad loop, giving him a clear shot at the cluster of men who'd positioned themselves near the front entrance to the house. They'd all opened fire, but most of their shots *dinged* off the truck's armored body. Still, he would have to deal with them quickly before they noticed him and concentrated their barrage accordingly.

The truck bounced and swayed, and Ty had to tighten almost every muscle in his body, drawing a burning sensation from his back, to brace himself against the hatch. The heavy FRG tried to fall from his hands as he reloaded another canister. The nice thing about gas bombs, though, was that you didn't need to aim too precisely.

Ty pulled the trigger. The projectile soared out and shattered apart a statue on Montrosse's front porch, then clattered onto the pavement, spewing out hissing gas. The four guards realized what had happened and tried to run or dive for cover, but it looked like most or all of them had nonetheless taken a nice healthy whiff of the fumes.

Pulling his head back inside the vehicle, Ty yelled, "Take out their other cars. We need to crush every last one of them. Including the limo."

"Of course!" Daria snapped back at once. Her chortles rose again, becoming another maniacal peal of laughter as she hit the gas and knocked the limousine ten feet into the air. The impact crushed its whole front driver's side, and it toppled end over end toward the patio, rolling across the marble and sending a stray guard running for dear life to escape it.

Ty reloaded the riot gun and returned to the hatch. They were off to a good start, but there was more to do. He fired all the remaining canisters but one, either targeting the guards directly or using the tear gas to interfere with their movements and block them off.

Meanwhile, Daria tore around the property, annihilated the two remaining cars. The last one, a sedan on the opposite side of the villa, had an occupant. He stupidly remained inside, firing vainly at them with a rifle or submachine gun until the last instant.

When he jumped free, Daria swerved. The corner of the truck struck him and sent him flying while the truck sideswiped the car and busted it into a mass of twisted metal and shattered glass. The man she'd run down didn't get back up.

Finally, they went straight for the mansion itself. The guards, the three of them still able to fight, had regrouped and were taking potshots at the wheels or the hatch. Ty pointed his AR-10 out the hatch and blind-fired a three-round burst to send the mercs looking for cover or otherwise interrupt their counterattack.

They stopped firing, if only for a second or two. It was enough time for Ty to pop out of the hatch with the FRG and blast the final canister through one of the first-floor windows, flooding much of the mansion itself with gas and sending another of the nearby guards into convulsions of agony.

By now, the cloud of hazardous fumes was growing thick all across the property, giving it the appearance of land in the grip of a forest fire—or, Ty thought, somewhat resembling the mists that covered Atlantica's forests. He put on his gas mask. He'd left it off until now for the sake of being able to aim from a moving vehicle.

It was time to begin the ground assault.

Daria braked as the truck crashed up the steps of the porch, grinding to a halt about six feet from the front doors themselves. She had her mask on as well, and taking up her Uzi and charging the bolt, she hopped down.

Ty climbed out of the hatch, quickly checking for his rifle, pistol, and blades, and jumped to the earth.

Instantly, a guard appeared, his AR-10 ready to fire, but he hesitated for a half-second, either because he wasn't sure whether to target Ty or Daria first or because the residual tear gas was starting to afflict him. The delay was all the time Ty needed.

He fired one round at the man's center of mass. Although he'd shot to kill, the bullet struck the hanging magazine of the guard's gun, knocking it from his grasp and sending him off-balance.

Then Daria jumped around from the front of the truck and opened fire, her strange Israeli gun chugging and spewing fire as she peppered the man with 9mm rounds. Two took him in the legs, and he cried out as another three or four hit him in the chest, failing to penetrate his armor but knocking him back.

Ty advanced on the injured man, stepping on his wrist as he tried to draw his sidearm. "I'll take that," Ty said through his mask and picked up the gun. A Smith .357 Magnum. Ty tucked it into the back of his waistband while he held onto his rifle with his other hand.

He looked around. "There was one more," he said.

The air crackled and thundered as the last door guard opened up on them from behind a shrub near the shattered front window. Ty dropped to his belly, and Daria did likewise. He saw the muzzle flash moving wildly around. The gas was dissipating some, but there was still enough of it that the poor bastard had to be succumbing by now. He was firing blindly.

Stray bullets could kill as surely as deliberately aimed ones, though. Ty hitched up his gun and pumped three rounds into the man's silhouette around the chest and neck. He squawked and collapsed against the wall.

Ty sprang to his feet. "All right. We're going in. Stay close behind me."

Within the house, screams and angry shouts had begun to echo. Feet stomped down stairs and hallways.

"Of course." Daria's voice sounded uncanny through her mask. "You're the one with the armor."

CHAPTER TWENTY

Ty's initial estimate was another four men within the mansion. Maybe more. And he suspected they were Lucas's best, not merely his security detail, but his bodyguards.

The house's lobby looked vastly different with a wispy haze of tear gas wafting through it, shattered glass and broken furniture everywhere, and a handful of bullet holes through one of the walls and one of the couches. Fluff was scattered on the floor from the ravaged cushion.

Ty stomped directly down the center of the room, trusting his armor and his mask, following the literal red carpet toward the stairs—he somehow suspected that Lucas had taken refuge on the second floor.

Behind him, Daria advanced in a crouch, using him for cover at first and ducking behind the violated couch as men stomped down the dual flights of stairs to engage them.

While the gas was growing thinner, not only dissipating with time but starting to clear out courtesy of an evening breeze from the west, there was still enough of it that their enemies, lacking respirators, would be at a disadvantage.

Ty saw the first two men coming down from either direction.

He figured they would shoot at him first; Daria, mostly hidden, would be able to take potshots at them while he offered a distraction.

His mind was well-adjusted to the situation at hand. The state of no-mind, the focus so intense it was paradoxically relaxed. Beneath it, rage simmered, fueled by the memory of the one hundred and twelve souls who had nearly gone to the bottom of the sea as a write-off on Lucas Montrosse's accounting books.

Ty's rifle sprang up to meet the first of the guards, firing two shots that took the man in the face and shoulder right as he pulled the trigger. His rifle sprayed lead haphazardly as he fell, two of the rounds tearing up the floor a foot from Ty's legs and the others blasting sawdust and plaster from the walls and ceiling.

Behind him and off to his right, he heard Daria open fire with her Uzi. The second guard, advancing down the other staircase, stopped for a moment and held himself firm as the first of the rounds ricocheted off his vest and helmet. Then one of the bullets took him in the knee. He yelped and stumbled, rolling down the stairs and losing his grip on his rifle. Ty was about to finish him off when the doors in front of him, seemingly leading to the ground-floor dining room, burst open.

A man with a heavy mustache, bloodshot eyes, and a red fez cap snarled as he appeared, aiming a pump shotgun. Ty dove to the side, tucking his rifle beneath him as he rolled clear, while the man's gun boomed and sprayed buckshot through the lobby. Too quickly for Ty's liking, he tracked his target and fired again.

Ty had managed to duck behind a chair. The shotgun blast tore it apart, annihilating the cushions and shattering the wood, which slowed the pellets. Two struck him in the chest with half or less of their muzzle velocity intact. They felt like someone throwing a couple of stones at him. He ignored them and blind-fired a single shot around the edge of the chair. Up above, he heard another guard coming down the stairs.

A burst of Uzi fire followed by a groan suggested that Daria had finished off the man she'd injured a moment ago. She turned her gun toward the guy with the fez, but only two shots rang out before the gun clicked dry. Cursing in Polish, she ducked back behind the couch as the man aimed his shotgun at her.

Ty jumped up. He charged straight toward the shotgunner, who, rather than trying to pivot his weapon, thrust the butt at Ty's face.

Ty dropped to his knees, letting his AR-10 fall, and drew his wakizashi as the shotgun's stock passed through the air above his head. The blade entered the fez-wearing man's side above the hip, penetrating deeply into his lower chest. Then Ty ripped it free out the front of the man's torso.

Fesal's face went pale in anguish and disbelief. Gutted, he fell to his knees, then to the floor, his fez toppling off his head to roll along the carpet.

Daria shouted, "There's one more!" A metallic *clicking* suggested that she'd loaded a fresh magazine into her submachine gun.

Ty knew. He dashed forward through the open door to the dining area, scanning it for hidden foes as the next and perhaps last guard on the staircase fired at him. Three bullets struck the door and floor he'd vacated.

He froze in the short hallway. If he wasn't mistaken, the man was directly opposite him, on the other side of two layers of wall, about ten feet above him on the staircase. He recalled that the AR-10 fired a heavy and powerful round, about on par with his old Garand, which he'd once used to kill a man by shooting through both sides of a car.

Ty raised the rifle and fired in full auto, emptying the rest of his magazine. As the din of the gun faded, he heard the sounds of a body rolling down the steps. He ducked out of the first-floor interior doorway and saw the guard tumble to the floor before him, with two holes through his chest and another through his pelvis. He wasn't moving.

For a moment, the house was silent. Then Daria exclaimed, "Aha! I see you." She sprayed bullets at the banister on the second floor. Someone shot back, but the erratic nature of his return fire made Ty think that he'd gotten a face full of the leftover tear gas. Daria fired again, emptying her second magazine, and the entire railing above the staircase to the right collapsed in a mass of wood chunks.

Ty charged up the steps, holding out a hand to signal Daria to hold her fire. It looked like her second volley had blasted the gun from the man's hands and wounded him, to boot. Getting closer, he saw that the gunfire had ravaged the last guard's arm.

"Don't shoot," he pleaded. His face was red, and his nose was running. "I can't even see. I can barely breathe."

Ty glanced ahead and to both sides. No threats were immediately forthcoming. He grabbed the man's pistol, an old Colt 1903, removed the magazine, then tossed the gun into the debris on the first floor. "Stay there, and don't try anything. Wrap up your arm. Daria! Come on."

Daria dashed across the floor to the opposite staircase. Once she'd climbed it, they advanced together into the second-floor main hallway, leaving the wounded bodyguard behind.

Ty knew it would be safer to kill him. But he didn't like the thought. The man was a hireling, and he'd surrendered. So the Executioner rolled the dice of fate, trusting the poor bastard to keep his end of the bargain and stay out of the rest of the fight.

The second floor, as Ty had remembered it, consisted of a single long hall from which multiple rooms branched off, all of them separated by closed doors. Daria crept up to his left flank, and he turned his head toward her and whispered.

"We go room to room, one at a time. You hear anyone trying to run, tell me. We take Lucas alive."

She nodded. "I suppose the idea is to execute him *later*, then?"

Ty didn't have time for smartass remarks. "Something like that." He regretted that they hadn't been able to check the house for secret exits or emergency stairs and that they lacked extra people to watch the villa grounds in case Lucas tried to slip out from under them.

They kicked open the door to Montrosse's study, finding it empty, then the room across from it, which also held nothing. Daria watched the hallway as Ty battered the next door off its hinges. A cacophony of screams greeted him.

Within were the two young women from the limo, now terrified as well as drunk. The blonde was only wearing a small nightie, and the darker girl had stripped to her panties. Shielding them both was the third woman, who was none other than Eleanor Cervantes. In her short, stylish, and alluring dress, Ty hadn't even recognized her.

Their eyes locked. Then Eleanor's eyes widened. "Behind you!"

Acting purely on reflex, Ty pivoted to the side as someone burst out from a hidden spot behind him and opened fire with a handgun, firing three shots into the space where he'd been.

One of the bullets missed, but another hit the blonde girl in the calf. She sobbed slightly louder than she had been, seemingly only half-conscious of what had happened. The third grazed Eleanor's arm, leaving a long red gash along her bicep.

As Ty spun back, he saw Lucas Montrosse's face, glaring at him with unbelieving hate, and the barrel of his pistol aimed at Ty's heart.

"Stop," Daria commanded.

Everything froze in time—Ty's arms, trying to bring his rifle to bear before Lucas could finish the job. Lucas's hand, about to squeeze the trigger. And Daria's hand, holding her P38 with its barrel against the side of Montrosse's neck. His dark eyes rolled sideways toward her.

As he stopped, Ty slung the AR-10 back over his shoulder and instead rested his hand on the grip of his 1911. "It's over, Mr. Montrosse. You're under arrest."

He let out a dry, raspy chuckle. "Is it?"

Daria moved closer. As she did, Lucas twirled aside with stunning speed, his left hand suddenly producing a knife and slashing it along Daria's wrist. She sputtered an unrecognizable curse and dropped her gun as Lucas dashed for the door.

Had he focused solely on escaping, he would've made it. Daria was in Ty's line of fire, and it took him a split second to draw his pistol.

Montrosse slowed as he reached the door, turning and raising his gun at the people who'd humbled him.

Ty's 1911 appeared in his hand as Daria, bleeding, stumbled aside. He fired once. The .45 slug took Lucas in the gut, drawing a gout of blood across his white suit and knocking him back into the hallway. He collapsed to his knees, face straining with disbelief.

There were still a few thin fumes of tear gas wafting through the mansion, and Lucas inhaled a bit of it. He choked and his eyes reddened and watered. It sounded like he was trying to make some sort of demand, or threat, or bargain. All that came out was a strangled exhortation of pain and anger.

Eleanor had produced a first aid kit from one of the closets within the room and was pulling out bandages and disinfectants to tend to the blonde's and her gunshot wounds, as well as Daria's slashed wrist. Ty assessed that they would be all right for now.

He stepped out into the hallway.

Montrosse was still a mess, clutching his abdominal wound with both hands and fighting against the gas, but he was doing a respectable enough job of remaining defiant. "Who do you think you are?" he rasped. "Another common thug! A burglar, an assassin."

"Lucas," Ty stated, assuming his voice was recognizable

despite the gas mask. "As Executioner of Atlantica, it's my duty to bring you to justice for the crime of attempted mass murder. Your means of covering up your illegal land claim, your plundering of resources, and your usage of me, under pretenses, to eliminate the smugglers who could've turned on and incriminated you after your dealings with them went sour. But I'm not going to kill you here and now, as though this were merely another one of Atlantica's private business feuds."

Lucas's face slowly fell, not only in despair but in confusion. "What? Are you stupid enough to try and take me back to the mainland? Based on crimes against laws that *do not exist?*"

Ty holstered his pistol. "There will be a law. Ultimately, that's why you hired me."

He turned to Eleanor, who was in the process of binding Daria's wound. "Get this man patched up, Ms. Cervantes," he declared. "He'll need to be healthy enough to stand at his sentencing."

Eleanor moved with fast, careful motions across the threshold and into the hall, squeezing a mixture of iodine and peroxide onto a cloth while keeping a length of gauze and medical tape in the crook of her arm. Her wound didn't seem to be bothering her much. Yet.

Ty realized that she was as terrified as the two girls were, but she was doing a better job of hiding or subsuming it. Her skin had gone pallid, she was sweating, and her legs constantly trembled, perhaps to compensate for the surprising control she exerted over the precise motions of her hands and the way she kept herself from crying or asking questions.

He wondered what, exactly, Eleanor's role in all this had been. Was she Lucas's mistress? The madame of his harem? His secretary? Had she simply agreed to meet Lucas for a pleasant night out before returning to her supposed usual duties as a managerial go-between for all of the Executives? Ty pushed such speculations from his mind.

Daria, her hand and wrist now wrapped in gauze, stood watching and shook her head. "We cannot do anything the simple way when you're involved, Mr. Katakura, can we?"

Ty smiled grimly. "You were the one who ranted about the importance of 'sending a message.' You were right. We might not have courts, or laws, or judges, exactly. But we have me, and we have people who are tired of lawlessness, corruption, and senseless thuggery. Now, we've completed our first true assignment."

As Eleanor applied basic first aid to Lucas's wounds, she mumbled, "There isn't anything I can do for this except slow the inevitable, Mr. Katakura. He'll need to go to the hospital if you want him to live for much more than an hour or so."

Lucas, surprisingly, laughed, though the sound broke off into grunts of pain. "Let me guess," he sneered. "An hour is all you need, isn't it?"

Ty nodded. "Yes. Should be enough. Daria, help me get him back to the truck. We're heading into the city."

CHAPTER TWENTY-ONE

Before they'd left, Eleanor had ducked off somewhere for a moment, only to then hurry up to Ty's side as he and Daria were helping Lucas down the stairs toward the truck.

While Daria held their prisoner at the base of the steps, one hand around his arm and her other holding her gun at his back, Eleanor pulled Tyler aside. She had a manila folder stuffed with documents in her hand.

"Here." She looked at the floor instead of his face. "I'm sorry. I didn't have all the information on...on what happened. I suppose I could've looked harder. I could've found out if I'd wanted to. This is what you need. It shows everything. You were right. I..."

A lump seemed to form in her throat, and she turned away, hurrying back up the stairs and leaving the folder in Ty's hands. He said nothing. Sliding the documents into the front of his belt for now, he returned to Lucas's side and continued the tedious process of moving him out of the house.

He didn't particularly care about Mr. Montrosse's well-being at this point. Still, Lucas had to survive a little longer. Long enough to send the message and for Atlantica to hear it loud and clear.

The tear gas was clearing out. The night breeze, aided by all the holes Ty and Daria had put in the house, had swept the last of it away.

As the three emerged through the front doors, the exterior guards greeted them. They were the men who'd survived the Executioner's assault, incapacitated by gas and left to their suffering while Ty and Daria stormed the mansion. They'd assembled in a line, guns held at low ready, all of them looking confused and miserable.

Ty hesitated, removing his hands from Lucas's arm, ready to unsling his rifle and fire if he had to. Again he cursed himself for charging into things without enough backup plans. Or, for that matter, without backup in general.

Another one or two team members could've helped him avoid a standoff like this. He'd assumed that Lucas's hired muscle would flee once it became clear that they were overmatched.

The man in the center cleared his throat. He was only now beginning to recover from the effects of the tear gas. "Mr. Montrosse," he sniffed, "we're at a loss as to what you want us to do next. Someone called and told us to stand down, although we couldn't do much at the time, anyway."

Daria laughed. "Oh, this is rich. Why are you people still here? You had plenty of time to be halfway over the hills by now. Do we need to teach you another lesson?"

Ty looked at her and motioned for her to stand down, shaking his head. It looked like they could talk their way out of the situation...even though the guards had the drop on them.

Montrosse snorted and spat blood on the ground. "You're fired," he croaked. "You all failed in your duties, so anything else would be pointless by now, wouldn't it? I suggest you seek employment elsewhere...with the other Executives. Go straight to them. Perhaps they'll pay you better."

Ty tensed as a tremor of anger went through him. The implication of Montrosse's words didn't take long to sink in. The rich bastard had more or less accepted his defeat but was trying to ensure that he would still get his revenge, even if it came posthumously.

"Shut up, Lucas," he snapped. "Eleanor told me that you lost a lot of respect with the other Executives after the shit you pulled. Don't be surprised if they decide that it's time to toss you under the bus, anyway. As for me...I do my job."

He and Daria walked straight ahead, dragging Lucas between them. The defeated and uncomfortable guards parted to let them pass, then had a low, muttering conversation among themselves, probably deciding what to do next. They'd grasped that Tyler was someone with a real position, with authority, despite coming out of nowhere.

Lucas groaned in pain as they lifted him into the back of the truck, lying him on his back on a blanket and fastening his ankle with the attached fetter. Daria produced a flask of vodka. "Here," she offered.

She glowered at him with blatant dislike but held the flask to his lips. "I hate to see anyone suffer, even a *dupek* like you. I would've finished you off. But this is Mr. Katakura's job, not mine. I am, how do you say, tagging along for the ride."

Montrosse sipped the vodka and settled into a writhing delirium. Daria left him and climbed into the passenger's seat.

Ty took the folder out from his belt and handed it to her as he started the engine. "There's a flashlight on the floor to your right," he explained. "Read that over. Eleanor said it was important. We might have to make use of it very soon."

Daria dug around and found the light, clicking it on. "Yes, of course. Where are we going, exactly? Is there someplace where these 'Executives' all meet?"

Ty sat behind the wheel, saying nothing. He reversed the truck to get it clear of the shattered mansion, then rumbled into the drive leading out toward the city.

"If there's a place where they all get together," he told Daria,

"I've never heard of it, and I don't know where it is. But we're not going to the Executives, anyway. We're taking him to *everyone else*. Middle of town. Wherever there are the most people at this time of night. Do you have any suggestions?"

Daria tilted her head, gawking at him. "You truly are crazy, aren't you? Well, there's always Crystal Square. It's one street over—south—of the hotel you were at.

"Atlantica doesn't have as much nightlife as we want yet, but already the city has some. They want Crystal Square to rival Times Square back in New York. It might have fewer people, but," she laughed sardonically, shaking her head, "I imagine it has even more forms of vice for sale. Anything people want... If it's on the island to begin with, they can buy it."

Ty stared ahead at the road. The buildings were sprouting up around him, the electric lights growing brighter as he passed through the outskirts. "That," he remarked, "might also be something I'll have to deal with. Depending on what it is. We'll see. One thing at a time."

He hadn't spent much time in Atlantica City and couldn't recall having been there after dark. Discounting, of course, his time spent lounging around in his room at the Crystal Skies Hotel. Daria would know better than he would what to expect.

Despite what she'd said, though, the city surprised him. Neon glowed from signs and storefronts, and people crowded along sidewalks and avenues. Half the town was still under construction, but the urban populace had lost no time inhabiting their new home and making the most of it. It seemed that the place never truly slept.

Like any other big city, he speculated. Except without any police. No laws to ruin anyone's fun, only the law of the jungle, as enforced by individuals, or gangs, or syndicates, or Executives.

The idea was romantic. He wondered how many of the people who'd come here had boarded the ship specifically for the promise of a wild new oasis of freedom in a stultifying ordered world... Only to find a land where those with money and power bulldozed aside those who inconvenienced them and got away with it, gloating over their omnipotence and plotting new means to harvest the fat of the land.

Until now.

Daria has spent the last four or five minutes flipping through the folder. "Yes," she commented, "this is juicy stuff. Payoffs to people I know and who happened to be involved with that disaster with the barge. Funds shifted toward Development Sector Twelve. Conveniently vague and bureaucratic language and reams of numbers and charts to obscure what's truly going on here.

"Mr. Montrosse had a plan, it seems, to grow richer still on Atlanticore and systematically eliminate everyone who knew about the vein he'd discovered who might tell the outside world. He didn't want anyone else coming to the island to butt in on his source of income. Hence, trying to kill off the workers who'd lived there *and* the smugglers. People who had contact with the mainland."

Ty nodded. "Noted. I'm not surprised. I bet a lot of others will be. Is this the place?" He gestured toward what lay ahead, beyond the windshield.

"Yes," said Daria.

Four massive lamp posts at the corners of the four streets that opened onto it identified Crystal Square, each of them powered by an Atlanticore stone that flooded the square below with brilliant blue light. It was eerie, in a way, but captivatingly so. The hustle and bustle of humanity in all its drama and squalor milled around and filled the air with a multitude of voices.

Gleaming skyscrapers, some yet incomplete and showing their skeletons of girders and beams, towered above the human mass, blotting out half of the night sky.

Ty found an open space amid the crowd, a section of the broadened street where no cars seemed to drive, and he rolled onto it, parking the massive, armored vehicle in clear view of everyone around. A few of the assembled pedestrians had taken notice.

Then Ty slammed on the truck's horn for good measure, three long, even blasts. He heard the commotion outside grow softer as the populace turned toward him, their conversations and arguments and drunken singing all fading away.

He drew a deep breath and looked at Daria. "Okay. I'm not one for speeches but bear with me. Go around back and open up the truck. I'll get Mr. Montrosse."

She nodded. It was strange that she'd been so accommodating, willing to allow him to do this his way. She was certainly tired, and she'd taken a nasty cut from Lucas's last-ditch effort to escape. It was more than that. Daria wanted to let him take the reins in this, his first true act as Atlantica's enforcer of justice.

He climbed over the seats, wincing as his back screamed in pain. He'd barely noticed it during the battle. The rush of combat did wonders. He'd known men who had taken astoundingly severe injuries without being aware of them until after the fighting had settled.

His flask of coffee still had a little left. He unscrewed the cap and tossed what remained in Lucas's face.

The man roused. He jerked up his head, blinking and moaning. "What? Now what are you planning to do? Is this the hospital?" Some of his fatalistic defiance was gone. The fear was creeping in.

"No." With one hand on his pistol, Ty unshackled Lucas's ankle, then heaved him toward the rear door as Daria opened it. The back of the truck swung open, revealing the city.

A crowd was forming. Teenagers and twentysomethings partying after work, the boys chasing the girls, and the girls enjoying the chase. Folks older than that as well, drunk, relaxed, overemotional, or anything in between.

Sleazy pimps and fences and drug dealers, peddling their

wares; prostitutes and pickpockets as well. Legitimate street vendors selling hot dogs and drinks and shoes and jewelry. Random gawkers, lacking anything better to do.

All had begun to drift toward the intrusive presence of the official vehicle and the strange figures emerging from it.

Lucas cursed as Ty slowly lifted him, only to lower him to the ground, where he collapsed to his knees immediately. In the bright blue light of the four lamps, the white bandages over his stomach went dark with fresh blood as his wound reopened.

"Hey!" a voice shouted. "That guy's hurt!"

Ty grimaced. Lucas's pitiful state meant that the people might misplace their sympathies. It would be up to him to tell them the truth.

Lucas was coming back, so to speak. His awareness of the situation had sharpened. Although he'd taken a wound that was all but guaranteed to be fatal, he might still have some fight in him. The hungry gleam was back in his eyes, and his big frame seemed poised as though for one last act.

Ty raised his hands, looking around, and the throng went silent.

"People of Atlantica," he began, hoping that he would make the necessary impression on them but without being so dramatic that he embarrassed himself. "I am the Executioner. You might've heard about me in the papers or on the radio. I was appointed to protect you and to bring justice to our island after too many years of endless, merciless injustice."

He'd captured their curiosity. If what Eleanor had told him the other night was true, many of the individuals he saw watching him now had been gossiping about his exploits ever since word got out.

"I saved the people on the barge a few nights ago," he went on. "Now, I've caught the man responsible for them being in that predicament to begin with."

Lucas snorted, and a bead of blood appeared on his lower lip before running down his chin. "Responsible? I'm one of this city's greatest benefactors. I was planning to develop Sector Twelve. You think that the actions of those despicable smugglers was—"

Ty backhanded him across the face. He convulsed as his stomach wound bled again. Someone screamed.

Daria handed Ty the folder of documents, then stepped back, her arms folded.

Ty held up the folder. "I have here the proof—which will be photographed and reprinted in the press—of what this man, Lucas Montrosse, has done. He made an illegal claim on Sector Twelve and forced the people who had settled there off the land.

"With no other place to go, they went to the transport barge, intending to return to the mainland. He made a bargain with the same smuggling ring I fought against, which they *thought* would enrich *them*."

The crowd stared. Some of them still looked concerned for Lucas, but they wanted to hear more.

"But," Ty continued, "it was all a ruse. Someone discovered a rich vein of Atlanticore. Montrosse wanted sole access to it. He arranged for the smugglers to ship a few cartloads of crystals off the island—which is against *international* law—on that same barge. *Knowing full well* that Atlanticore is unstable and violently explodes if it gets too far from Atlantica itself.

"The smugglers were blinded by their greed, thinking of how much money they would make peddling the crystals in Canada or America. In fact, Montrosse intended for all of them to die. The secret of Sector Twelve would be his alone to exploit for profit."

Lucas piped up. "This is nonsense! I had no idea of any such thing. Look at the state of me! This man attacked me in my home, killed my employees! I'm badly hurt. Please, someone. I need a doctor!"

Ty wasn't sure how much of Montrosse's sudden sympathy play was genuine. Back at the estate, Lucas had seemed grimly resigned to his fate. Now, with death approaching more swiftly, his will to live had apparently returned. Gut shot though he was, he might still save himself if someone got him to a hospital and into emergency care.

But that would not have been just.

"*No*," Ty boomed, and everyone near him flinched. "You were one of the people who hired me, Lucas. To my face, you told me that I was the law, that I was the hand of justice, that Atlantica would at last become a real nation and realize its potential. And to my face, you lied.

"I took all of that *very* seriously, Lucas. You hired exactly the right man. Exactly right, if you'd meant what you said instead of expecting me to simply clean up the messes you made while leaving you untouched."

Lucas repeated, "Someone call an ambulance. Get this madman away from me!"

Ty smacked him across the face. Some of the audience seemed horrified by the brutality of it all. Nevertheless, he needed to make an impression. Something they would all remember.

"We're building a new nation here," he proclaimed. "In a way, a new world. The other countries don't officially recognize our existence. This island has remained hidden from human knowledge for hundreds, maybe thousands of years. The foundations of a new civilization are what all of us have been working toward.

"As Executioner, it's my job to ensure that those foundations aren't rotten. If I am the hand of justice, I must bring justice even to the people who chose me. Because justice has no biases, it can only be blind, or it isn't real. And with justice, at last, we can have law."

Again, Lucas beseeched the crowd for aid, but nobody intervened. Some of them might've sympathized with his wounded and battered state or been skeptical of Ty's claims, but they were unwilling to challenge the Executioner.

The grim resignation returned. In a way, Ty respected his foe.

Loathsome though he was, Montrosse had maintained *some* dignity in the face of total defeat.

Ty raised the folder again. "These documents will bear me out. So be it, then. I hereby perform my first official execution. Lucas Montrosse, you are charged with fraud, embezzlement, misrepresentation, consorting with known criminals, conspiracy to murder on a vast scale, and resisting arrest. The sentence, to be carried out immediately, is death."

A handful of people in the crowd gasped, but others began to nod and cheer in agreement.

Ty added, "You will have one final say. Your last words?" He stared into Lucas's eyes.

Montrosse met his gaze, and his face was dark with cold malevolence. Again, Ty recalled what he'd said to his surviving guards about seeking employment with the other Executives and the possibility that even in death, Montrosse might have his revenge.

"Katakura," he boomed, wringing the last of his strength from his body to lend malevolent authority to his deep voice, "if you carry out this so-called sentence of justice, you'll regret it. The people who made you will break you.

"No one wants a weapon that they can't wield, that harms themselves as well as their enemies. Only your first week on the job, and you've failed. The Executives—all of us—made a mistake in thinking you were the man for the job. With me or without me, they'll soon *correct* that mistake."

He smiled, and his teeth were bloody.

Ty stood in silence while the audience waited with bated breath. His face was an expressionless mask.

Then, swiftly as a bolt of lightning, his wakizashi flashed from its scabbard and swept through the space occupied by Lucas Montrosse's neck. The man's dark-haired head toppled and rolled into the street. Women screamed, and men cursed. A couple of drunks and hardened criminal types laughed, enjoying the gory spectacle.

Ty turned to face them. "This is an object lesson," he stated, "in what happens when people think that the office of the Executioner—and by extension, justice itself—can be used to their advantage. Let everyone remember what happened here tonight."

He sheathed his sword, and with no further words as the crowd set to clucking and murmuring and roistering about, returned to his seat behind the wheel of the truck, leaving Lucas's body in the square.

Daria hopped into the seat beside him. "Good speech," she quipped.

He gave her a short bow of his head but said nothing as he fired up the engine and drove off, leaving the city behind.

CHAPTER TWENTY-TWO

While the nightlife in the central city had impressed Tyler with its upsurge of vivacity, construction notwithstanding, certain improvements were being made elsewhere on the island as well. When he returned to the labor town in the valley—the closest place he had to a "home" these days—he discovered that the people had begun smoothing out the streets, laying gravel atop the mud, and making a few other improvements. Without the constant threat of clearance teams or other such thuggery, they were free to build a better place to live.

Additionally, they now had an open-air cantina.

Danny and his friends, the southern boy and the girl, appeared from around the corner of a nearby house. "Hi, Mr. Katakura!" they called, waving. "We heard about what you did."

The red-haired boy in particular seemed virtually in awe.

Ty raised a hand in greeting from where he reclined at one of the little tables set up at the cantina. "I did my job." He shrugged. "I'm glad people.. appreciate it. We can talk more about it later. I'm meeting someone shortly."

"Okay." The trio left, but Ty could tell they were curious to hear more. His spirits grew somber again as he wondered if they

231

appreciated how close to death he'd come or the ugliness of having to kill so many other people in the course of his duties. Still, the innocent lives he'd saved far outnumbered the guilty lives he'd taken.

He didn't have long to wait. Daria appeared a moment later, materializing out of the crowd when he least expected it. He hadn't noticed her approach at all.

"Oh, there you are." He motioned her over. "This is new to me. They got halfway to making a proper town of this place while I was gone."

Daria bobbed her head, looking around with bemused appreciation. "It isn't too bad a town already, I would say. I've seen far worse. Do they have vodka?"

They did, and Ty ordered her a drink, insisting on paying for it himself, although the kindly older man who ran the place decided it was on the house instead. Ty's drink, a beer, had come with no charge as well.

"But," the old man reminded him, "I have to stay in business, so no more freebies after today. You're the Executioner. You'll be able to afford it."

Ty couldn't argue. "Agreed. I'm happy to support local businesses."

As Daria settled in, they both sipped their drinks, not bothering to talk too much about what they'd been up to. Each had a fairly good idea of how the other had passed the intervening week.

Seven days had passed since Tyler had executed Lucas Montrosse. After a good night's rest, he'd plunged straight into his next assignment the following morning. The details would be in the paper soon enough.

The farming community in the northeast had its problems, but they proved relatively mundane, albeit disturbingly medieval. Ty vaguely recalled reading something about how, in feudal territories long ago, warlords would sometimes kidnap their neighbors' serfs to increase their workforce. Much the same thing had afflicted the agricultural zone. A rival farm had been stealing workers and forcing them to till their land.

Ty had sorted it out. He'd only had to kill one person. His reputation was already beginning to precede him, so the guilty parties hadn't offered much resistance once he discovered their wrongdoing.

Meanwhile, he hadn't seen Daria. He presumed she had smuggler things to do, and since he had no interest in arresting her, he'd rather not know about it. He told her as much.

She laughed. "It only qualifies as 'smuggling' because of that TINA nonsense," she pointed out. "Otherwise, I would be a legitimate businesswoman, and most of my clients simply merchants. People who ship things that other people need or want."

Ty shrugged. "I don't see any injustice in that. But if you encounter anything truly *wrong*, let me know."

She ran a finger around the rim of her glass. It was little more than half a hollow cylinder, lacking the fine craftsmanship of the tumblers at the hotel, and the vodka was also quite a bit less fine. But it would do.

"I'll keep that in mind, Executioner Katakura. What have you been up to?"

He told her about the farms, pausing sporadically when people from the town strolled by to say hello or congratulate him. Some of them stopped for drinks. Many of the non-disabled adults were at work in the city, so if anything, the village was quieter than usual.

As Ty's account drew to a close, Daria chortled with approval. "Good, good. I'm glad you took care of it. You seem... What is the word that begins with an 'M.' Ah, *melancholy*, yes. Why?"

Ty drained his beer and looked at the empty glass. "I think 'bittersweet' might be a better word. I'm not unhappy, exactly."

He recalled his thoughts from a couple of weeks ago. Not

such a long time, yet he'd practically been a different person then. One who then—as now—had no expectations of a long life.

"I'm happy," he said, "that when I go out, I'll at least have resolved two situations and made this place that much better for it."

Daria frowned. "What do you mean, go out?"

Whether she didn't understand that it was an American expression for death or *did* but was confused as to why he would say that was irrelevant. "I expect that the Executives will send someone after me. Probably sooner rather than later. Might already be out looking for me, watching my movements, and so forth. I've made peace with it. I never expected to live *this* long."

The bartender appeared and set another beer on his table. Ty wasn't sure if the man had overheard. Either way, he thanked him and took a long, deep swig. "I'm *trying* to make peace with it, anyway."

Given a choice, he would prefer to live a little longer. His thirty-third birthday wasn't far away. Still, warriors tended to die in the line of duty.

"Hmm," Daria reflected. "I'm not so sure that the Executives will, or can, get rid of you so easily. They created you, in a way. You're their investment, along with the news apparatus they funded.

"While you were off in the rural farming zone, the radio and the paper interviewed some random people and asked their opinions. Of course, there are always disagreements. But most of the people respect you and are grateful."

Ty frowned, not bothering to voice his skepticism. Certainly, his people in the valley seemed to feel that way. The crowd in Crystal Square had, to a large extent, been fearful rather than admiring. He'd intimidated them more than he'd inspired them.

While he pondered the matter, another visitor appeared. It was Eleanor. She was wearing her boots again.

"Hello, Mr. Katakura." As Ty and Daria looked up at her, her face flushed with momentary discomfort as everyone recalled the circumstances under which they'd last seen her—dressed provocatively, shepherding Lucas's floozies. It passed quickly enough, and her usual professionalism reasserted itself.

Ty bowed his head. "Hello, Ms. Cervantes. Thank you again for handing over the information from Mr. Montrosse's office. How can I help you?"

She pulled out a chair and sat. "Well, I have information on another situation we would like you to resolve."

"Go on," Ty urged her.

She produced a notebook from her jacket and glanced at it before she resumed.

"There have been serious disturbances of late, associated with a particular machine shop that was, er, 'liberated' by a militant union. These people seem to be intent on taking over production facilities across Atlantica by any means necessary.

"The rhetoric sounds familiar, of course. We're concerned that they might be receiving support from the Soviet Union. Despite the standing international policy of non-recognition—TINA, as you've heard it called. It was perhaps inevitable that Atlantica would begin to be drawn into the Cold War before our existence is acknowledged."

Ty chugged his beer. "Hold on. So, this means that the Executives still consider me their golden boy? I'd assumed they would turn on me after what happened with Lucas. He was one of them."

Eleanor closed her eyes and shook her head. "The Executives understand why you made the choices you did. They empowered you to make those sorts of decisions to begin with, and they'd censured Mr. Montrosse shortly before you passed judgment upon him, anyway. They see no conflict in continuing to work with you. There is one thing, however."

Daria had been listening intently. She seemed amused by the

fact that her presence made Eleanor a tad standoffish. "This should be good."

Ms. Cervantes stated, "They would like you to find and recruit other Executioners. Only a fraction of Atlantica is settled thus far, yes, but growth has been rapid and expected to continue. It's a big island. You cannot do everything yourself."

She waited, her face neutral, for Tyler's reaction.

He looked across the table at Daria, raising his eyebrows. "Are you thinking what I'm thinking, Ms. Barruk?"

Daria smiled. "Of course."

THE STORY CONTINUES

The story continues with book two, *Aiming Blind*, coming soon to Amazon and Kindle Unlimited.

Claim your copy today!

AUTHOR NOTES MICHAEL ANDERLE
OCTOBER 26, 2021

First, thank you for not only reading this story, but these author notes in the back as well.

If you are coming 'new' to this Atlantica story, know that you can read this prequel series without needing any of the other Atlantica trilogies.

I'll get to a little about me in a second (which you can skip if you already have read books with me involved) but first...

Coke Floats.

So, I'm in Germany last week and I am seriously missing the food in America. Not that the steak and hamburgers in Frankfurt are bad... Actually, the steak is seriously good and the hamburgers are...*different.*

I've learned that the term "hamburger" is one of the most basic American foods that is different from country to country. I thought that it would be a pretty simple dish that would stay consistent.

I mean, it's hamburger cooked with some salt and pepper and tossed onto a bun. You could add additional condiments and lettuce / tomatoes (what they call salad in Europe) but, I mean, how do you localize those ingredients?

The answer, it turns out, is ridiculously easy.

First, the beef is often not the same and therefore the basic flavor is changed. Now, update the spices for the local pallet and *boosh, baby.* That hamburger works for the local populace. Not so much for me.

I've learned to be very circumspect when I see hamburgers on the menu overseas.

Now, for those who don't know much about me, here is the basic "Who am I section" I add to the beginning of new series ;-)

I wrote my first book *Death Becomes Her* (*The Kurtherian Gambit*) in September/October of 2015 and released it November 2, 2015. I wrote and released the next two books that same month and had three released by the end of November 2015.

So, just under six years ago.

Since then, I've written, collaborated, concepted, and/or created hundreds more in all sorts of genres.

My most successful genre is still my first, Paranormal Sci-Fi, followed quickly by Urban Fantasy. I have multiple pen names I produce under.

Some because I can be a bit crude in my humor at times or raw in my cynicism (Michael Todd). I have one I share with Martha Carr (Judith Berens, and another (not disclosed) that we use as a marketing test pen name.

In general, I just love to tell stories, and with success comes the opportunity to mix two things I love in my life.

Business and stories.

I've wanted to be an entrepreneur since I was a teenager. I was a very *unsuccessful* entrepreneur (I tried many times) until my publishing company LMBPN signed one author in 2015.

Me.

I was the president of the company, and I was the first author published. Funny how it worked out that way.

It was late 2016 before we had additional authors join me for publishing. Now we have a few dozen authors, a few hundred audiobooks by LMBPN published, a few hundred more licensed by six audio companies, and about a thousand titles in our company.

It's been a busy five plus years.

Have a great week or weekend and I look forward to talking with you in the next book!

Ad Aeternitatem,
Michael Anderle

CONNECT WITH THE AUTHOR

Connect with Michael Anderle

Website: http://lmbpn.com

Email List: http://lmbpn.com/email/

Social Media:

https://www.facebook.com/LMBPNPublishing

https://twitter.com/MichaelAnderle

https://www.instagram.com/lmbpn_publishing/

https://www.bookbub.com/authors/michael-anderle

BOOKS BY MICHAEL ANDERLE

Sign up for the LMBPN email list to be notified of new releases and special deals!

https://lmbpn.com/email/

For a complete list of books by Michael Anderle, please visit:

www.lmbpn.com/ma-books/